YOU DON'T HAVE TO DIE IN THE END

"This is a party. Best kind."

I didn't like it, but I understood. The drunk was toying with us and for that he would pay. Time for me to suck it up, soldier. I was with Luda and they were with me. We fought together. Even when it stopped making sense.

The man was back off the ridge, turned toward us, his face obscured by a white fog of breath.

"Hang on, he's getting mouthy." I rolled down the window, while Luda hit "mute" on the stereo.

"You boys get out of that car!" the guy yelled. "There's one of me, and two of you."

Boys.

Luda snorted. They were non-binary and queer, but to most of the people in this town, Luda dressing and acting how they did meant they were sometimes read as a boy. Luda was fine with being assigned female at birth, but felt what their gender meant to them was no one's business but their own. I was cis female and enjoyed his mistake. Better'n being treated in the stereotypical, gender-specific way dictated by our current societal standards.

I was brilliant when drunk.

Luda tapped leather-gloved fingers on the steering wheel, as if they needed time to consider, but the man outside wasn't inclined to wait. Fast as spit he was on us and I was yanked half-way out the window. This didn't sit well in my gut. "Luda," I shouted. "Help me out here!"

My arms weren't working right, otherwise I'd swing at the guy. If Luda didn't pull me back in right now, I was going to get a beating.

Luda hit the gas and in the split second it took for their tires to spin and catch a grip, I stared into a bulldog face with eyes like blue ice. Clear. Definitely not drunk, and a little surprised. Guess I wasn't what he thought, either.

The guy's lips bunched to say something, but I was pulled away, torso flapping and bouncing with every rut and groove.

Two blocks down, Luda stopped, and I emptied my guts.

I looked back, but the man in red was gone.

CHAPTER TWO

Darcy was in a mood. I could tell by the way he slammed a bowl of the boys' Lucky Oh wheat flakes down in front of me. I never ate this crap, not anymore, and he knew it.

"No thanks," I mumbled, wincing.

"What's the matter, Eugenia? Your head hurt?"

The kitchen was too bright and Darcy too loud. Purposefully loud. Mr. High and Mighty wanted to punish me for the night before. My memories were hazy, but I could still see that cowboy's face as if it were right in front of me. In the cereal, floating in the milk. My stomach lurched and I pushed the bowl away. "Just let me drink my coffee, Darc."

"So drink. It's something you're good at."

Right into it then. "I don't need a lecture."

He looked at me with eyes and face way too worn for his age. Only eight years older than me, but he wore them heavy. "I don't want to give one, but someone has to."

"And I got no choice but to listen, that right?"

He was stone still but I could feel him bristle. Wasn't always like this between us.

It's gonna be all right, Genie. That's what he'd said the day Ma left. I could still feel the weight of his hand on my shoulder, how it spread all the way through me like a comfort. That was nearly two and a half years ago, right after my fourteenth birthday. Darcy and Jen took me in, tried to lift my spirits by promising it would be great. I worried I'd be a burden, not that any of us had any choice, but they insisted I'd be a help as Darcy spent a lot of time away driving truck, and their twin boys had more energy than Jennifer could spare.

I felt bad for my nephews with one parent absent more days than not, but they still had it easier than us. If Darc and Jen fought, they were quiet about it. Ma and Pops, they'd fought loud and hard. Each on their own they were fine, but in the same room they were a cat and a dog scrapping in a box, too tough or desperate to know that neither would come out ahead. And then Pops got sick.

So many times I'd find Ma at the kitchen table, drinking tea from a chipped china cup her own Ma had given her before she died. She'd packed it up, boarded up her family farmhouse and moved right into marriage with Pops in Fort St. Luke. The cup had shattered at some point, knocked off of where it should have sat, but Pops glued it back together for her, all but that one chip. I could never tell if she was sad or mad or worried as she tipped that cup to her lips, blew softly, and sipped, the whole while staring at the door of the bedroom she and Pops shared. Tip, blow, sip and stare. Repeat. Then, as if she'd just woke up she would realize I was there, put down her cup and tell me to go out and play.

One time, one terrible, awful time, she held both my hands in hers and said, "We have to live with the choices we make, Eugenia. Remember that." She didn't say what she meant, and I didn't ask. Pops never came out of that bedroom again.

Before me and my brothers came along, they'd only had each other, kin all dead and gone. I wasn't sure if hazy memories of laughter, Ma and Pops holding hands, loving each other and us was real or wishful thinking. Just a dream I had once. Had to be. To think otherwise made it worse. There was only us now, me and my brothers, except we hardly ever heard from Jackson.

Like he was thinking the same thing, Darcy's eyes softened. He poured himself a coffee and sat opposite me. "I'm just worried about you. Me and Jen both are."

"I get it."

"You always say that Genie, but do you believe it?"

"You going TV evangelist on me, Darc?"

"I'm trying to have a serious conversation." He shook his head. "Jen's better with this kind of thing. She took the boys out so we could talk."

An ambush. Super. I spat a sour milk taste into a paper napkin. No amount of toothpaste would scrub away the night before. "Don't worry about it," I mumbled.

He leaned forward, elbows on the table.

"You gotta straighten up, Eugenia. You want to end up like Jackson?"

Our eldest brother, a scrapper, thief and a drunk, always in and out of jail. Also the most content with his life, near as I could tell. "Don't be stupid."

"I'm not the stupid one here, Eugenia."

Glaring at him made my eyes hurt. "Oh, no?" He heard my sarcasm. I intended him to. Words, locked and loaded.

His brow furrowed. "What do you mean by that?"

"Nothing."

"That wasn't nothing. Just say it."

It was like poking a stick at him, but I was sick of his preaching, and just plain sick and ornery. "You go on about how I should straighten up and get on with a good life. Make the most of the opportunities I've been given. But what about you, brother? A wasted education is the very definition of stupid, if you ask me."

"No one did."

"Driving truck is not what you went to school for."

"It's what I like."

"And I like drinking."

Points for me. Bet he didn't think it would go like this, wasn't part of his plan. I took satisfaction in his silence.

"For now," I added, thinking about Jackson and uncomfortable with the parallel I'd just painted. Maybe I was like Jackson, a little. Just not so far gone. "I'm still young, Darc. I don't know what I want."

He cleared his throat. I could almost hear him breathing, slow in and out like he was trying to stay calm. "I suppose you haven't had stellar role models in your life, but at least what I do is honest. Stop changing the subject. This is about you, Eugenia. You gotta know this is no way for a girl to act."

"You seriously see me running around in an apron, baking cookies for the boys?"

He hung his head for a long while before looking back up at me, out the tops of his eyes, like he was embarrassed. "I can see now that how we treated you when you were a kid, me and Jackson ... we shouldn'ta done that. I don't know. You never wanted us to treat you like a girl—"

"You treated me fine—"

"You know what I mean—"

"No, actually, I don't."

He looked at me so serious I got a shiver down my neck. "Is it our fault, Genie?"

"Is what your fault?"

"Are you gay because of how me and Jackson treated you?"

For a second I was so shocked I didn't think I even heard him right. It was like his words travelled slow motion from his mouth to my ears and into my brain, and all I could do was sit there with my mouth hanging open.

Darcy coughed. "Look, it's okay that you are, but you should know that there are some really nice guys out there, not like—"

I recovered. "Wait. It's *okay*?"

"Course it is."

"No, stop. You can't assign fault in one breath and then say it's okay."

He leaned on the table. "Give me a break here, I don't know how to talk about this stuff."

"Stuff?"

"You know what I mean. It's just ..." He took a breath, rubbed his forehead. "I want you to have an easy time of things, Genie, and if you're gay, that's fine, but you won't. Have an easy time, I mean. You know that as well as I do."

I was numb. I couldn't believe my brother would think like this. I mean, Fort St. Luke wasn't Vancouver or Toronto or even Regina for shit's sake, but we weren't a town of uninformed bigots. At least I hadn't thought we were, and for sure not in my own house. Correction: Darcy's house.

Why would he even say this? He was my brother, which meant he loved me, even though that wasn't the vibe between us right this minute. It was like a blood law or something. Maybe he thought talking would make things better for me.

Or for him.

Pretty obvious that what he really meant was that it would be better for everyone if I wasn't who he thought I was.

Something hot sparked deep inside of me.

"I'm not gay, Darcy. And even if I were you don't talk about it like it's something bad or even some kind of choice. What the hell era are you from?"

He furrowed his brow. "But you and Luda—"

"Me and Luda what?"

The clock ticked on the wall one-two-three-four-five-six as Darcy stared hard at me, like he was trying to see inside my brain. I stared right back.

Go ahead, brother, spit out what you really think. My good and responsible brother wasn't the saint everyone thought. It was one thing to judge me, but this I would not tolerate. Luda had been through hell and back in life and had been there for me in ways Darcy would never understand. He would not disrespect them. I wouldn't let that happen. Ever.

He looked away first. "Guess I was mistaken."

I breathed. Hadn't realized I'd stopped. "Guess you were."

"Sorry."

"Luda and me are friends, Darcy. Best friends. I love and accept them for who they are, and they love and accept me. That's it."

"I don't know about these things."

"Do you know it would be none of your business even if I were gay?"

"Jesus, Eugenia, I said I was sorry!" At least he had the decency to blush. "I want you to know I'm not one of those homophobes."

I stared at him. My lip curled over words so bitter they had a taste. "Of course you aren't."

"Just forget I said anything."

"Fine. Right. Let's do that."

He looked at the wall clock like it was time to get gone.

I still felt raw and bristly and wasn't ready to forget anything. I poked at him again. "You got another pick-up, Darc?" I asked all sing-songy. "Someone with a dire need for 200 cases of toilet paper and dill pickles? I just can't get over how much you like driving that truck of yours."

He looked sharp at me. "Genie, you got no business criticizing. You say I wasted my education, but you know there were no office jobs when I got out of school."

"So you said."

"Damn it, driving truck was what there was. It's good honest work, I like it, and I'm grateful for it. You should be too."

"It always comes down to that, doesn't it, brother? How you took in your poor orphan sister and I'd better show I'm grateful."

"That is not what I am saying."

"Your poor baby sis, such a loser even her own mother couldn't stand to be around her."

"Cut it out."

"Why? It's what you think."

"For crying out loud, just stop it! I just don't know why you make things so hard for yourself. I don't know why you get up to the things you do." He huffed a breath, and his voice got soft "I just don't get you, Genie."

"Neither did Ma." The first time I shoplifted I was twelve. Got caught, but it didn't stop me. Learned pretty quick that the cops wouldn't or couldn't do much. Started getting lippy—to the cops, Ma, everyone. "She couldn't handle me. That's the truth of it. No one could."

"That is not why she left."

"How do you know? It's in our blood, Darc. Pops left, Ma left, Jackson's good as gone, and what about you? You're outta here every chance you get."

"Goddamn it, Eugenia, you watch yourself."

"Anything to take you away from this shit town, and your marriage. No dreams come true in this house, right, Darcy?"

His chair clattered behind him as he pushed away from the table.

"You punk-assed kid!" he snapped. "You don't know anything. You don't know anything about Jen and me and what we got."

"Don't I? You may not fight out loud but it's easy to see how happy you are to get out that door."

"Stop it."

"Truth be told, Jen's easier when you're gone. Happy, even."

Before I thought up my next jab, Darcy came at me and hands on my shoulders shoved my back against the wall. I braced myself for more shouting, but nothing came. We stayed frozen like that, his face bunched and red while the clock on the wall went tick, tick, tick.

He let me go.

Without a word he turned, grabbed his coat, and flung the door so hard it banged against the wall. Slowly, it whispered shut.

"That's right," I muttered, shaking, but taking the victory. "Gone again."

CHAPTER THREE

Holy hell it was hot, even for June, had been for days. The long soul-freezing winter of our discontent was folded into memory, and depression over desiccated fields had more than a few farmers stagger out of bars after falling into pitchers of beer, half the price during unhappy hour. Much of the land surrounding Fort St. Luke looked like a scraped knee scabbed over.

I wiped sweat from my neck, tipped my new hat up off my brow, squinted at a few half-hearted wisps of mares' tails against endless blue. Nothing rain-like on the horizon. I loved this hat, natural straw with a faux suede band and studded underbrim. Found it at the Boot Barn and had to have it. So I took it, was glad for it as Luda and I waited behind the pool hall, a two-storey brick walk-up offering little to no shade under the mid-afternoon sun.

Not a bad thing for us, this dry spell, not since my big idea. Dry meant brush fires, which meant jobs were available on fire crews. "It's a chance for us to get the hell out of Fort St. Luke."

"They won't hire us," Luda said.

"Course they will. They need to show gender equality and inspire the next generation."

Luda rolled their eyes, but didn't say no.

It wasn't like we had any reason to stay in Fort St. Luke. School wasn't an issue since I quit before final exams. Besides, we always talked about leaving, how we'd blow this cow town, find our fortune and never look back. Also, I could use the cash.

After my fight with Darcy the morning after that crazy drunk-not-drunk cowboy chase, things had stayed sour between us, so I bunked on Luda's couch whenever he was in town. Living away even part time was expensive, and my last job as grocery store stocker ended when I got caught grazing through bags of coconut chocolate rings.

Before she left, Ma never pushed me to find a job, not even a paper route, even though other kids were delivering flyers, babysitting, mowing lawns, even cleaning dog poop for a buck. Instead, she'd go on about how studying was the way to better things, especially for a girl like me. I asked her what she meant and she said I took after her side of the family, small and wiry.

She meant that without a lipstick-of-the-month club subscription and a whole lot of effort I had no chance at landing a boyfriend so I might as well go the brain route. Did she think brainiacs didn't have boyfriends? Or maybe a different grade of boyfriend, like people were commodities in a department store, and if you were *this*, you shopped *there* for *that*. Brainiac? Aisle seven, just past the band-camp display. Watch your step around the robotics. The woman had no clue. And anyway, why should attracting a boy be a life goal? Just thinking on it made me want to scream.

I could have taken to wearing girly things and putting my hair up just so to fit in, but instead I got ornery. I cut my hair short and kept it that way and never shied from a fight. Maybe I even looked for them. Between me and Luda I'd lost count of the number of noses we'd bloodied.

Maybe my penchant for punching was why Darcy thought I was gay and that Luda and I were together. I mean, we *were* together, just not like that. When I told them what Darcy'd thought they laughed and punched me in the arm, said I wasn't their type.

I had no type and wasn't looking. Every relationship I'd ever seen ended up miserable.

Best friends forever was all I wanted or needed, so why not join a fire crew together? Firefighters got paid pretty good, plus you stayed in a camp and had someone cook for you. Luda thought it would complicate things with the money they got from MCFD, as if honest work was a bad thing. Isn't that what Social Services wanted for its wards?

Luda looked at their watch, got into position in front of the blue Honda.

Something was different with them lately. The only reason I could think of was the drink, which was more than it used to be, but I wasn't about to go all Darcy on them. They were angrier, too, hadn't let go of last winter's knock-the-drunk-off-the-road incident. Didn't help that the cops found them the next day, said someone reported they were driving erratic. Cops couldn't prove nothing but it didn't matter. When Luda got something under their skin, it festered.

There it was: the nod. Luda's signal that I should join them. Girly-girl in the pool hall had given Luda attitude—some glammed up bougie-girl, hair in her eyes, putting on sass for the sake of her friends, all badass for cutting school on a Friday afternoon. Amateur. Took our table like she didn't know we were using it. Shoved Luda and made like she'd accidentally fallen into them, like it was some big joke.

Then she took her finger, ran it soft down the side of Luda's face. I expected them to shove the little bun-bun, tell her where to go, but they just stood there, frozen, mouth open. I don't even think they were breathing. Then glam girl laughed all cruel like and said, "Don't you wish," and spit in their face.

Her friends called her Justine.

Just-ine time to get a beating.

The Luda I knew shoulda come out swinging. But their face was stone, the spittle shining in florescent light. Then they smiled like they knew something and I got goosebumps down to my toes. They spun and walked out, signaled for me to follow, then keyed a giant "FU" on the hood of the only other car in the lot. Had to be Justine's, or one of her friends. Same difference.

Then we waited.

Tick.

Tock.

Justine and friends buffaloed down the back stairs, saw me and Luda waiting on them. They had to know they were screwed. Luda was big and I didn't give up.

"Go ahead, My Little Pony," Luda mocked. "You got us two to one."

No fear on Girly-Girl's porcelain face, but safe bet her plumbing was about to get active.

"I got no argument with you."

"No?" Luda stepped aside so she could see the hood.

Justine's face was deadpan: "Jeez, that's too bad."

She and her friends shuffled sideways along the limestone. Collectively they looked like a pouffe-haired crab, skittering into the heat of this intolerable day.

I looked a question at Luda, ready to fight, but they only frowned and said, "Hmm."

"What the hell did you do to my new car?" came a roar from behind, and I realized it wasn't Luda and me that those girls had skittered away from. It was The Great Kazoo.

Chris Kazinski was an abomination of nature, a giant from the moment he was sprung from the womb. Now in his early 20s, he was big like Bigfoot with meaty slabs for fists you didn't want to see the wrong side of. He was also quiet, always had been. He worked at the library, which meant even his job was hushed. He wasn't quiet now. "I'm gonna kill you!"

Kaz grabbed me with those hands, and I watched the world tip sideways then erupt into white agony as he bowled me across the gravel lot. *Holy crap!* Pain like hot Hades. About fifteen feet from where I'd begun I groaned and pushed myself upright.

Kaz had Luda off the ground, held by their shirt collar against the bricks of the building. Their knees were bent toward their gut while hands flapped and mouth gaped like they'd just been punched. Hard. They were pale as the limestone behind their head, as if all the blood in their face had dropped to fill the hole in their stomach.

Kaz shifted, spat out a surprised, "You're a girl!"

A whistling sound took the place of whatever Luda tried to say back.

I don't remember getting up, never mind walking—or stumbling—but somehow I was behind Kaz, unsure what I might do other than tap him on the shoulder. Okay, there was one thing. I readied to accept the consequences of my idiocy, lifted a shaky leg and kicked the back of his knees.

As the giant fell, adrenaline fired through me. I grabbed Luda, now crumpled to the ground, and dragged them to the Nova. Passenger door open, I yelled for them to give me the keys.

"No … fucking … way."

They never let me drive.

Hand over hand, Luda pulled themself into the driver's seat. I climbed in beside, slammed and locked the door. Luda fumbled the keys, so I snatched them and put them in the ignition. The engine turned, caught. *Thank you, Baby Jesus!* Shaking, Luda put their hands on the wheel.

"Move it, Luda! If we don't go now, we're dead."

A double fisted blow landed on the hood and I stared into the eyes of fury. "Just steer!" I shoved the stick into drive and cranked the wheel to avoid hitting our oppressor. Then I kicked Luda's leg out of the way and slammed my foot hard onto the gas pedal. Roaring, Kaz reached the driver's door as the Nova spit gravel. I stayed heavy on the gas as Luda spun us around the corner and down a back alley.

"Okay," they gasped. "Get over." They took back the gas pedal as I looked behind.

"He's not following."

Luda slowed. Three streets over they stopped, moaned, coughed, then cackled, which morphed into an all-out guffaw. "Holy crap. I think he relocated my liver," they gasped, and then they were laughing so hard tears leaked from their eyes.

Before I could ask what they'd been smoking there was a deafening BANG!

We flew forward then stopped, my face full of dashboard.

Luda moaned.

Rear-ended. We'd been hit.

Gasping in pain, I explored my face with my fingertips. It hurt to touch but I found my teeth and nose in place. "Luda?" Where were they? Ah, there: face up, seat back like they were taking a nap. Except for the groaning. Their seat mechanism must have let go. It did that sometimes. "Kaz," I grunted, as the giant's head filled the open window.

To Luda he said, "Sorry about the punch." And to me, "I called 911."

He didn't wait for my thanks.

Slam of a car door, firing of an engine. He drove past, his front bumper cracked and hanging low. Adding to the damage Luda had done didn't seem a wise choice, but I was hardly in a position to judge.

Next came the sirens and flashing lights. Both help and hassle were never far away.

While paramedics fussed over Luda, I checked out the Nova. It wasn't too bad, all things considered. One more dent wouldn't make much difference, and Luda would heal after a patch-up. They weren't too happy about going to the hospital, but oh well. Kaz's fist might have caused internal damage, but Luda wouldn't fuss. They didn't trust doctors, nor teachers, cops, social workers or anyone else other than me. They'd always trusted me.

"You trying to tell me you skinned your face on that dash?" the cop asked.

"Sure," I said. "You can see the blood."

The cop wasn't overly interested in getting the real story. He hollered "Wheels intact," to his partner, who nodded and relayed the note through his radio.

He knew me, this guy. I recognized his tiny red eyes, his fat, alcoholic nose, and the way he looked at me like I wasn't worth his time. He thought I should clean up and shape up, blah-de-blah, heard it all before. But this time it wasn't me and Luda who were the aggressors. We would have been, given the chance. It just hadn't worked out that way.

With a few ripe words of caution, Luda handed me their keys. They expected me to park it but what they didn't know wouldn't kill them. I'd never understood why they were so fussy about someone else driving a car they abused on a regular basis.

Tough days made me thirsty. With the cops and ambulance gone I adjusted the seat and decided to check the Nova's drivability. For Luda. On the way to the beer store.

Usually Luda pulled for us—their size made them look older—but the counter attendant never truly seemed to care. Today he was more interested in my scraped-up face than my age. I adjusted my hat, lowered my voice. "Trouble in the cattle pens."

"Yeah, right," the guy said, but he handed over the two-four and I was back outside where it was still hot enough to blister a baby's bottom.

Luda was in the hospital and my face hurt like hell. When had this day turned to shit? It had begun with high hopes and decent plans. I replayed the shoving at the pool hall, bougie-girl's spit followed by Luda's uncharacteristic response, Kaz turned Hulk and my skin on the dash.

A tire crunch on gravel made me look. *Well, well.* It was the pouffe-haired crab crew. They were stuffed inside an orange, rusted-out Datsun, and bougie-girl was at the wheel. "Loser!" Justine shouted through the open window, then she flipped me the bird and spewed word-vomit.

This had the texture of something that needed seeing to.

The burn in my veins turned to ice as I placed the beer on the back seat, calmly turned the key. The crab-car fishtailed around the corner, but there was no need to rush. Fort St. Luke wasn't that big.

Down one street, then another. Justine knew I was following and drove sloppy at first, too much gas and spinning back tires on gravel, but as I kept coming her driving settled out, turns got tighter, more controlled.

Finally, three houses from the end of a neat, residential street, the Datsun rolled to a stop. On the lawn there was a pink tricycle knocked on its side.

"The hell is wrong with you?" Justine squeaked as I locked my hand on hers to stop her from rolling up her window.

"You." I smiled as I grabbed a fistful of T-shirt and dragged her halfway through the window. She was slight. I held her with one hand, wound up and smacked her with the other.

Smack. Smack Smack.

Over and over in my head like I was stuck in a time loop all I could see was bougie-girl's spit and the look on Luda's face, bougie-girl's spit and the look on Luda's face, bougie-girl's spit and the look on Luda's face.

I got your back, Luda.

Something strange happened then. There was blood and tears and snot and Justine must have made some noise, but I didn't hear it. I just kept pounding.

Smack. Smack. Smack.

A flutter in the corner of my eye finally drew my attention. It was from the house, a window with a yellow curtain pulled shut as soon as I looked.

Life sounds returned. A blue jay, a car honking, Justine's friends yelling, one voice louder, more desperate than the rest: *You're killing her!*

I lowered my fist, let go of Justine's shirt. She was bloody and whimpering, but definitely breathing.

Wusses.

I retrieved my hat from where it had fallen and brushed away the dust.

CHAPTER FOUR

The cops found me back at the pool hall, said—all frowny-frowny, shame-shame—that I was being arrested for assault. I didn't deny it, nor did I feel shame. Pretty much the opposite. The surge of endorphins from doing right by Luda had me floating in a pink haze, somewhat aided by the beer.

Before going inside the hall, I'd cracked open a tall boy in the parking lot. It was one of those nice moments that find you sometimes. The condensation from the bottle ran onto the back of my hand, turning the blood that had begun to dry there into tiny pink rivulets. Then I had another and hadn't thought to wash. When the cops asked me about it, I told them straight out: Justine deserved what she got.

Another ride to the cop shop for another slap on the wrist. They never kept me long. I'd texted Luda from the back seat to tell them where I'd left their car. With any luck their patch-up would be swift, and we would resume our plans for the day. Or non-plans. Whatever.

At the station, G.I. Cop directed me down a puke-yellow hall to where Irene sat behind a broad counter. "You got more of those black jellybeans, Irene?"

"I saved some just for you."

Irene always talked like she was everyone's favourite granny but looked more like the cool aunt, the one you just knew was out dancing in the clubs after dark. She kept her hair in tight copper curls and wore swaths of lime green over her eyelids. In the glare of the booking room lights I couldn't tell if her lips were pink or purple.

"Stand straight now, honey."

"I know."

I lined up next to the wall, stepped on the painted footmarks. Afterward, Irene gave me a cream to soothe my scrapes, and I scooped a handful of candy from a bowl on the counter.

The last time I was in this place I was falling down drunk and the cell they'd put me in had a drain in the middle of the floor. Today's accommodation was small, with a bench and a stainless-steel toilet. Alone, like always. They can't put someone my age in with adults. Might corrupt me, har-dee-har.

I lay back on the bench, yawned big. Maybe I *was* getting too familiar with these accommodations, but despite what Darcy thought, I had no intention of following the same path as Jackson. Darcy's neither. I was a kid. I was supposed to be irresponsible and free. If I couldn't do it now, when?

My eyes were barely closed before Irene was back. "Your lawyer is here."

The room they put us in had barely enough space to turn around in, but all we had to do was talk. The man taking measure of me was slight and bald headed. His shirt was white cotton with a shiny thread woven through and there was something funny about the collar. It wasn't the kind you could wrap a necktie around.

"Sidney Boyer," the man said.

"Boyer the Lawyer," I deadpanned. The man across from me did not laugh. I coughed.

My Counsel leaned close, indicated for me to do the same. For an uncomfortable few seconds the man peered into my eyes and I fought the impulse to look away. "You under the influence of intoxicants, my dear?"

I wasn't his *dear* nor anyone else's. "That wouldn't be very ladylike."

"Answer the question."

The man had no sense of humour. "No. Maybe. But I wouldn't say I'm drunk."

"After polluting your body, how can you trust your mind to be truthful to you?"

"I don't understand."

"You should explore this idea when you are not under the influence of an intoxicant."

The lawyer stood, and I sat back, confused. "Wait. You're supposed to get me released to my family."

"The only family you have in town right now is a worn-out young woman with two children at her knee. You should be helping her out, not adding to her burdens."

"I don't add anything—"

"That is correct and I suggest you meditate on that while I'm gone."

"But I'm not intoxicated!" It was clear Boyer didn't much care. I muttered, "If I were, they would've put me in the drunk tank."

As Irene shut me back in my cell, I argued. "He can't just leave me! Until I turn eighteen, the law says you gotta treat me like a juvenile."

Irene smiled and waggled a shiny red fingernail at me. "The law also says if you're intoxicated, you can stay."

"But I'm not."

"Of course not, honey. Just sit tight. Your lawyer will be right back."

Sit tight. *Meditate.*

Of all the bull crap, hooey woo-woo. Boyer was probably the type who went on weekend yoga-bear retreats to pound his chest and push a triangle around a witchy-board to cue up a chat with his ancestors. How could people buy into that stuff? The dead could stay that way, far as I was concerned. I never knew any kin who died except for Pops, and he and I weren't talking.

It was true Jennifer was tired, though. She'd been like a sister to me since the day she and Darcy started going out back in high school. When I stopped talking for those three weeks after Pops died, she was the one who held my hand and didn't push while everyone else was losing it. Jen was closer than my true blood and nicer than any one of us.

"Okay, Sunshine," Irene sang. "Your counsel is waiting for you next door."

I rubbed my eyes. "What time is it?"

"Twenty past four."

Must have drifted off. Must have drifted deep as it felt like more than 40 minutes had passed. My tongue tasted like a skunk had taken up residence, but my head was clear. Sure, I was a little buzzy earlier, but not near as much as that hippy lawyer had implied.

Irene handed me a blue, button-up shirt still sporting store tags. I looked at my own shirt, rumpled and smeared with dirt and blood. "You didn't have to do that, Irene."

"I didn't. Your lawyer brought it. Clean yourself up and get your best behaviour ready for the judge." She winked at me.

She left me to put on the shirt. It was clean, fit well, and had the stale scent of store. I called through the cell window. "Irene? I'm ready to go."

My police escort marched me past the booking desk where I scooped another fistful of black jellybeans.

"Someday you're going to choose another colour."

"You think so, Irene?"

"I know so."

The Fort St. Luke Government Building and Law Court was conveniently located right next to the cop shop. The concrete and glass mashup rose like a fortress partially obscured by a willow tree sweeping tendrils of melancholic leaves over a neatly manicured lawn.

My escort marched me up a set of back stairs and through a door with a sign that warned food, drink, and candy would not be tolerated. I sucked what was left of jellybean from my teeth and wished I'd swiped a few more.

To the left there was a single wooden door leading to the sheriff's office. Beside it, a rack of pamphlets and a fire extinguisher. Down the hall to the right there were double doors to the courtroom with a notice asking visitors to leave knives, cameras, and recording devices at reception prior to entering. Hard to believe that some shit for brains would bring a knife to court, but since they'd made a sign, somebody had probably tried.

Instead of marching me into the courtroom, the uniform led me through the sheriff's office and into one of three small rooms. Inside there were four thickly padded chairs at a laminate table surrounded by concrete walls. It also held my lawyer.

I nodded hello. "Boyer."

With a firm hand on my shoulder, the cop indicated I should sit in the chair opposite. I considered thanking him. After all, I would never have figured that out on my own. The man took his leave before I had a chance to get smart.

"Hello, Eugenia," Boyer said. "You do some thinking like I told you?"

"You said I should meditate."

"Did you?"

"Not my thing. Took a nap."

"Sleep well?"

Irritation scratched at me. "Like a baby. Is this a social call, or what?"

"You ever heard that saying about how only the guilty sleep well?"

I rolled my eyes. "Guess I've been guilty my whole life."

"According to this file, that looks almost true."

Boyer scanned several documents, then placed them in an open folder, set it to the side. He clasped his hands together and leaned toward me. "You think you know how this will go?"

"Same as always. I'll say that I understand I broke the law. The judge will say his piece and I'll go home. Speaking of which, what are we doing here? My lawyers usually just meet me in court."

"Thought we should talk."

"I don't want to talk."

"Assault is a serious offence."

"That girl had it coming."

"The court isn't likely to accept your justification."

I shrugged. "So?"

"You may be entitled to more than community service this time around."

"You mean jail? Not for a punch in the head." Closest juvenile detention centre was 500 miles away as the raven flies, and everyone knew it was already too full. "It's not like I killed anyone." An echo of *You're killing her* came to me. But I hadn't. "This is bullshit."

"The young woman you assaulted is concussed, and you are sixteen years old."

"So?" I said again. Sixteen was still juvenile in a court of law, and otherwise just a number. I hated birthdays and mostly ignored them, though Jennifer always made a fuss. This year there'd been a vanilla cake with chocolate icing, and *Happy Birthday* sung by her and the boys. Darcy was gone driving truck, like always, not that I cared. Not anymore. It was like he gave up, or maybe I did. The only good thing about turning sixteen was that I got my driver license. "Sixteen's not eighteen," I said.

Boyer leaned back. "You think you're clever?"

"Not in the way you mean."

"Given the tragic circumstance of your father's death, the courts have been lenient in the past, but have you considered all that is in here?" He tapped the file with his thumb.

"Not really."

"Damn fine example of what we in the business of restitution and rehabilitation refer to as escalation."

"This beating wasn't much different from the last."

"The last two."

"Okay, the last two. Gave her a shiner and she took a nap, but so what? The way she's going she should toughen up."

He paused. "You might have to take your own advice."

"Whatever." I looked for patterns in the concrete behind his head.

"You should know that three violent offences mean the judge may sentence you to incarceration."

"They weren't that violent."

"That is in the eye of the beholder, or in this case, that of your victim." Boyer shook his head. "Too bad, really. According to this file, at one time you showed a measure of potential."

"Maybe before my pops blew his brains out. A thing like that changes a person." I watched him for the usual sympathetic adjustment of tone. Instead, Boyer's blue eyes drilled into me so sharp I flinched.

"You only had two months left of your eleventh grade with a good chance of graduating high school next year with honours. Why'd you stop going?"

"I'm not a bad person, if that's what you're implying."

"Then why do you continually find yourself under arrest?"

"Wrong place, wrong time."

Boyer didn't blink.

"So what do you want me to say?"

"You admit what you've done, and that you know you were wrong. If you plead guilty, there may be another option for you."

"What kind?

"There's a program called Intensive Support and Supervision. An alternative sentencing. A condition for probation. It would allow you to attend classes, receive treatment and gain work skills in a more open environment than a juvenile incarceration facility."

"Sounds like bullshit."

"It's not."

"How come I haven't heard of it?"

"It's only considered in certain cases."

I looked him a question.

"Usually if there are mental health issues or other extenuating circumstances."

"No."

"You *are* guilty, Eugenia."

"Not like you mean. I'm not nuts and I'm not sorry. She had it coming."

"The girl is in hospital."

A sour taste rose in the back of my throat. I'd barely hit her! Except I knew that wasn't true. Something had happened, something I could hardly recall. It was like I'd been outside my body for part of it. Whatever it was, it scared me. But that was nobody's business but mine.

I itched to touch my bruised knuckles, press into them. I wouldn't give Boyer that satisfaction, not with the way he looked at me, triumph already bleeding through.

"No."

Boyer looked at me a moment longer, then closed my file. "Let's go, then."

The uniform had his hand back on my shoulder, like he thought I might get lost. The sheriff's office was now crowded, but it wasn't like I could make a run for it, even if I wanted to.

"Watch, it!" another cop snapped as I ploughed into him, maybe a little on purpose.

He stepped out of the way, and when I saw his prisoner my smartass response froze on my tongue.

"Jackson," I said.

Before he had time to respond we were each yanked away. I looked back at him over my shoulder, and he looked at me over his.

My heart lurched. *Jackson.*

He didn't look good. I probably didn't look so hot either, but he looked worse. His clothes hung from him like he hadn't eaten in a while. Dark circles under his eyes. Sunken cheeks. Gaunt. He looked like something risen from a graveyard, some broken person who slept behind trash cans or begged for cash outside the beer store.

Remorse came in waves, hit so hard my knees were knocked out from under me as I entered the court. Gasps as the uniform helped me stay upright. I shook him off, cleared my throat, took my seat beside Boyer.

"You okay?"

I couldn't speak. Nodded.

Words, words, words came next, all the usual ones. It was Judge Marg presiding, though I'd never call her that. It was "Judge Gordon" to the riff-raff, but one time I heard a bailiff call her Marg before correcting himself. She read out the charges, asked how I pled.

All I could think of was Jackson. What was he doing here? What had he done?

Memories from better days: *Jackson laughing, Jackson teasing, Jackson showing how life could be fun even when it was hard.*

Jackson changing, Jackson leaving and staying away.

He never used to be like this. He wouldn't be like this if Pops hadn't killed himself. If I hadn't ...

"Guilty," I whispered.

Boyer's head jerked up. His eyes drilled into me.

"Speak up, Eugenia Grimm," the judge said.

"I'm guilty, your honour." The black truth of it oozed through me, into my eyes, nose, every open part of me until I couldn't breathe. It had nothing to do with Justine, nothing anyone would give a second thought about now. They should have cared when it counted. They should have looked harder. At me.

Instead, they'd tut-tutted, put a bandage on it all, sent us off without a rudder. Forgot.

I'd done the same, put my brother from my mind, wrote him off. Fun Jackson, reckless Jackson, who made bad choices but charmed his way right side up and always, somehow, made out okay.

Not anymore. In one look, I saw everything. I saw too much.

I wanted to run after him, tell him that I loved him and that everything would be okay. But how could it? He was broken. I saw it. In. One. Look.

My fault.

Judge Marg asked if I understood the charges and I said I did and then she said something about a sentencing date and my lawyer said something back about a psychiatric evaluation but I barely heard and cared even less.

Move along, folks. Nothing to see here. Just another Grimm tale. Three Grimms, each fucked in our own special way. End of story. Only surprise was that it took this long to get here.

CHAPTER FIVE

The judge hadn't let me spend the night at Luda's, but home wasn't jail, and Darcy was driving truck, so no lecture. In the morning, back in a breakout room at the courthouse, Jen waited in the hall as Boyer sat across the table from me and explained how things would go.

"It wasn't about your program, why I pled guilty," I said.

"Want to tell me?"

"Nope."

"You can, you know. Anything you tell me is subject to what we call solicitor-client privilege—it stays between us."

"Unless I say I'm going to hurt someone and except what you decide to tell Judge Marg to get me into this bonehead program."

He frowned at me.

"Judge Gordon, I mean. Why you so keen, anyway? What do you care?"

"It's your choice, Eugenia, though I do believe this could make a difference in your life." He paused. "Maybe getting you in it will make me feel good, that I did a good job. Did all I could for you."

I locked eyes with him.

In the courtroom when I'd pled guilty, I wanted and felt I deserved the worst of the worst. That's all I was thinking. That was then, and I was over it. Shit happened, but we were each responsible for our own choices. My brother was no different.

I was the first to look away. "Fine, whatever. I want the program."

"Good." He blah-blahed on about psychological and psychiatric assessments and the people who would see me next. He let Jen bring me a coffee before sending in the court appointed psychologist, a slight woman in a wrinkled grey skirt with a yellow pencil tucked behind her ear.

"Can Jen stay?" I asked her.

"If you wish."

I did, though I wasn't sure why. Just an impulse. I turned to Jen. "Is that okay?"

Her eyes glistened as she nodded yes.

"If it gets weird you can go back out."

"Deal."

The psychologist sat and shifted the pencil from ear to hand, absently nibbled on it as she opened a folder and flipped through a stack of loose papers. She pulled one to the front, made a mark, then chewed again.

"Didn't anyone ever tell you that's unhygienic?"

She lifted eyebrows at me.

"Your pencil. You're chewing it."

She glanced at the pencil, laughed soft and looked back at me. "Didn't even realize. Does it bother you?"

"A bit. That one of your questions? Is this a test?"

She laughed again, said, "No," and went back to her notes. This time she tapped her pencil on the table.

I glanced at Jen who looked a warning back at me. She wanted this to go well. So did I. I guess.

It was hard not to flash back to the counselling sessions forced upon me when I was eight. Didn't have much to say then. What could I say now? Yes, please, put me in this program and I will be ever so good forever and ever amen.

Now that I'd warmed up to the idea, I wished that I'd asked Boyer for details.

The psychologist's name was Dr. Yolanda Bird. It suited her. Her hair was in tight black curls, which accentuated her shapely head and gave her a regal air. She had a pointy nose and moved in small, jerky movements to look or cock an ear.

Ever notice that thing about names? People are either born or grow into them, like Penny Stampe the mail lady on our street, or Dr. Butcher the surgeon at Fort St. Luke General. He'd taken out my broken appendix last year.

"Eugenia Grimm," Yolanda Bird said, still looking at her notes.

"My name and my mood," I said.

She glanced up. "Excuse me?"

"Nothing. Joke. What do you want to know?"

"You understand why we're here?"

"I guess."

She waited. I winced at a leg pinch from Jen.

"You're going to decide if I should go to the not-jail program."

"Intensive Support and Supervision Program. ISSP for short. But I don't decide. I assess and recommend."

Cop out. I was pretty sure my being accepted had a lot to do with what she thought of me. Was I a good candidate, or a lost cause? This ISSP was a good deal, if I got it. Boyer had been crystal clear that the alternative would be a youth facility too far away for visitors, not that there were many people I wanted to see. I let the echo of Jen's pinch straighten my back. "Yes, ma'am. Thanks for taking the time. What can I tell you?"

She smiled, and this time her eyes crinkled in the corners. Point one for me.

After a few baseline questions about home and family, stuff that must have been in my file, she asked about my school life until the inevitable: "Why did you quit?"

I bit back my inborn sarcasm. If I were going to get this thing, I'd need to amp up the bullshit. "I just didn't see the point, you know?"

"I'm trying to."

"I only"—my eyes watered just a little—"I can't explain it too well except that for a long time I thought I would make my father proud. You know? But then I woke up and realized that he won't be proud. He won't be anything because he's fucking dead." Actual tears now, as Yolanda Bird handed me a tissue. I reminded myself I was faking and felt bad about Jen's hand on my knee. Damn, I should get an Oscar. I scrunched the tissue. "And then I just didn't care."

"Eugenia," the bird twittered, "do you feel you are a danger to yourself."

"What? No! I just ..." think, think. "I used to know what I wanted and now I need some time to think about it. I'll go back to school once I know. I promise."

That one she didn't buy, I could tell. But she took something from it, tapped her pencil, made a note.

"Sexually active?"

The hell? "I believe a person's sexuality is a personal thing, but no. If you have to ask for your report, I have decided I would rather focus on my own self rather than deal with someone else's shit. I mean stuff. Sorry. And sorry about the eff sharp earlier."

"You're talking about relationships. Being sexually active doesn't necessarily mean you are in a relationship."

I heard Jen huff softly. She found this as awkward as I did.

She asked me about friends and bullies and church and sports and music and all kinds of stuff. Keeping my attitude in check and tossing just enough truth in the ring to keep her believing felt like twelve rounds of brain boxing. Where was the bell? *Parry, block, whiff.* She probably saw loads of bullshitters, but none as sharp as me. I had brains. I just wasn't inclined to show them off. It was a personal thing, like my sexuality.

Finally, she finished.

My relief was short lived. As she flew out the door, she told us to hang tight. There would be another so-called expert. It was clear they were going to keep me so busy with interviews before my sentencing that I'd have no time for trouble, even if I wanted it. Which I didn't. There was a time for everything. With any luck I'd be in and done with this get-out-of-jail-free program in a few weeks and Luda and I would party like never before. Then maybe we'd finally blow this town.

This was a lucky break. A wake-up call. I was too known here and needed a fresh start.

Next interview was with a psychiatrist. Jen said that was different from a psychologist in that they were more about the science and didn't much care about feelings. That suited me fine. The card Dr. Simon Mogeldev handed me was pretentious with its artsy scrawl and string of gobbledygook degree letters.

"I'm not dead yet."

"Pardon me?"

Out the corner of my eye I saw Jen crack a grin, which made the corners of her mouth *pop*. She ducked her chin low.

"Card says you're a forensic psychiatrist."

He looked amused too, but not in a way that made me feel bad. "Don't worry, you're not the first young person to think that. I enjoy crime shows as much as anyone, but I can assure you this not that."

"What is it, then?"

"I'm going to assess you for potential underlying factors and make recommendations regarding a treatment program."

"What kind of underlying factors?"

"Developmental issues, mental illness, that sort of thing."

I blinked at him. "I already told Boyer. I'm not nuts."

"No one said you are." He snapped open a briefcase and handed Jen a sheaf of papers. "Fill these out as best you can. We'll meet next week for formal evaluation."

My blood rose along with my voice. "For what?"

"Depression, Oppositional Defiant Disorder, ADHD. That sort of thing. Fill out the forms and I'll see you Monday."

Jen tapped the edges of the papers on the table, gave me a reassuring smile.

Dr. Mogeldev said his goodbyes, held open the door as Dr. Bird fluttered back in.

"Miss me?" she chirped.

Her next set of questions were of a more personal nature. I think Jen was relieved when I asked her to go.

CHAPTER SIX

The flutters in my gut were unfamiliar as I took my seat for sentencing. Same old courtroom. Nothing new but the nerves. I tried to dissect the source, like a Bird or a Mogeldev would.

It was because I'd let myself want this program. Stakes were higher.

Deep breath in, let it out. Boyer gave a reassuring wink.

"What do I tell the judge?" I whispered.

"With a bit of luck, yes please and thank you should suffice." Boyer glanced at his watch and pushed back his chair. "Now stand straight and keep your mouth zipped unless spoken to."

For much of the proceedings the prosecutor and Boyer said what they had to, as did Bird and Mogeldev, who finished with: "Medication not required, but the subject would benefit from structured support and cognitive behavioural therapy."

I kept my eyes fixed on the coat of arms above Judge Marg's head, listened as she recapped my criminal past. Today's sermon was more detailed than usual, her expression more severe. I felt a trickle of sweat on my forehead and wiped it away. Boyer's face was stone.

"According to your file," the judge said, "your petty theft began at age twelve and got steadily more serious."

It was around then that I'd started hanging out with Luda, not that I put any of this on them. I took responsibility for my own muck. Besides, Luda was plenty good at making their own.

They were also one of the few people in my life I could count on, no matter what. Like today. The bailiff hadn't let them in the courtroom, but they were here, like I knew they would be, waiting just outside. Banged up and bandaged, but present. We had each other's backs. Jen was inside as my official guardian, all tired and sad-eyed. No Darcy. Probably still on the road, not that he would have come. He'd washed his hands of me.

"Speak up, Miss Grimm."

I'd missed something. Judge Marg asked one more time if I had anything to say. I shook my head and the judge spoke louder, her words weighted. "Eugenia Grimm, do you understand how this could go today?"

"My lawyer says it could be bad, Judge. He said something about escalation."

"That's right. Given your steady progression from shoplifting, to—what's this, lawnmower theft?—to repeated attempts at causing serious bodily harm, not to mention your sudden disregard for education, I am not very confident that you are heading toward a life of law-abiding citizenship. This Court's concerns are grave."

That idiot Justine had had it coming, but Boyer insisted the judge wouldn't find that reasonable motivation or excuse. I bit my lip to keep words inside.

Boyer glanced at his watch, then the door. I looked that way too, and as if on cue a man filled the doorframe and let himself in. He had broad shoulders and a bulldog face.

All air was sucked from the room and I began to sweat.

It was the guy from last winter. The one Luda tried to run down.

If he remembered me, he didn't let on. Instead, he removed his Stetson and spoke to the judge. "Sorry I'm late, Your Honour."

"That's okay, Noah," said the judge. "I know you had a ways to come."

I turned to Boyer, whispered even though I wanted to shout. "What is this?"

"Hush."

"But I don't—"

"I said, hush."

This man called Noah stood between Boyer and the prosecutor.

"You've had a look at Miss Grimm's file?"

"I have, Your Honour."

"Do you agree she's a suitable candidate?"

"I do, Your Honour."

The judge cleared her throat and turned back to me. "Eugenia Grimm, there are extenuating considerations as outlined by a number of folks we've heard from today. Mr. Danby runs a sanctioned Intensive Support and Supervision Program. Has your lawyer explained what that is?"

I glanced from judge, to the man, to my lawyer, back to the judge. Nodded.

"Please state yes or no for the record."

"Yes, Your Honour."

"Under certain circumstance we consider this program an alternative to incarceration. To say it plainly, I am sentencing you to a six-month probationary term to be served at Mr. Danby's ranch. Do you understand?"

I nodded again.

"Over the next six months you will perform a variety of chores as assigned. You will also continue your interrupted schooling through distance education and attend regular counselling sessions. At the successful completion of this program, you will return to your previous high school." She must have seen the protest building inside me as she held up her hand to cut me off. "Three months after that, we will evaluate your progress. Does this seem a fair proposition to you?"

What? I don't … Huh?

If this *Mr. Danby* did in fact remember me, the idea of hanging out at some ranch with him was not appealing. But there was nothing in those ice-chip eyes that hinted at anything more than what had been said.

"I will add, if it becomes apparent that your time at the ranch is not moving you toward a more productive and positive state, you will be incarcerated at a youth corrections facility. What is your answer, Eugenia Grimm?"

Boyer leaned close. "Remember what I told you?"

Clearly, I would not get a better offer. "Yes, please, Judge. And thank you."

Goodbyes were not Luda's thing, but they gave me a shoulder-punch before ducking down the hall and out. If they recognized Danby from last December, they didn't let on, and they were gone before the man got a good look at them. If Danby recognized me, I still couldn't tell.

Jennifer handed me the tuck bag I'd packed that morning.

"Can we have a moment?" Jennifer asked Danby. He nodded and moved away. Jennifer looked tearful. "I feel like I should have a going away gift for you. A box of chocolates or something."

"I'm sweet enough."

"You shouldn't joke. It could have gone bad for you in court."

"I know."

We looked at each other until the quiet got loud. "Where's Darc?"

"On a job."

"Right." I knew that, but a part of me thought he might come back for this. I'd forgotten one of my life rules: keep your expectations low. I stuck my thumbnail under a paint flake along the door trim. "I'm sorry, Jen. I know it hasn't been easy for you."

"It's been fine, Genie. I'm not complaining." She said it matter of fact.

"You never do. I'm talking about Darcy."

She frowned. "Darcy's a good man."

"One that should be around a whole lot more than he is."

Her face hardened, and I kicked myself. This wasn't the time. I shoulda said something a long time ago, but never felt it was my place. Still wasn't.

"Sorry. It's none of my business."

"You're right." She sighed and her voice softened. "What's up with you, Eugenia? It's not like you to talk about personal stuff."

"Don't know. Nerves, maybe. The unknown."

"You going to live your life better now?"

"I'll do what I'm told. Stay out of jail."

"It's a start, I guess." She hugged me and I hugged her back. It was hard to let go. "You've had a tough life, you and your brothers. No one can help with what came before, but you have to find a way to deal."

She locked arms with me, and we started up the hall toward Danby.

"That night your dad died it was rough on you. It was rough on everyone, but you didn't talk for so long." *One month.* "I always wondered why."

"Nothing to say." *Lie.* "You and Darcy were new. You coulda turned around right then and got far away from us. Why didn't you?"

Jennifer shrugged. "Darcy opened up about what he was going through. It brought us close." She stopped, stroked my hair. "You should talk, next time you get a chance. Really talk. Jackson too, if you can find him."

I swallowed. She didn't need to know about how we'd seen each other outside court. Jackson would be back in jail by now, which meant her fantasy of us all sitting down together wasn't likely to happen. "You're probably right, Jen."

"You get yourself straight, Genie. Maybe you've got a shot."

With my head too full of bad history, I was ready to get gone, off into my uncertain future. Could be that Darcy drove truck for the same reason. In some ways being near Jen kept the bad stuff close. She did like to talk.

CHAPTER SEVEN

Noah Danby was not much of a conversationalist. For the first ten minutes on the highway he stared straight ahead, which left my stomach uneasy as I wondered what he was thinking. When he finally spoke it was to point things out as we left the industrial trappings of civilization: a moose in the bush, a lynx crossing the highway so far ahead I turned cross-eyed trying to see. "Guess my eyes aren't so good."

"You're just not used to looking. Town life makes you blind."

"I'm not blind."

"Short-sighted, then."

"Town life is all I know," I admitted, "other than some ranch work with my brothers when I was a kid."

"What kind of ranch work?"

"I was too young to be more than a pest."

"Maybe some of it will come back. You'll do your share up at Reason's Wait. That's the name of my place, if you didn't know." He glanced at me. "You ride?"

"A little." My keeper had wind- and sun-beaten skin, looked like he just stepped out of a Wild West theme park. "Look, Mr. Danby—"

"Call me Noah."

"Okay. Noah." I peered into the bush. "Thing is, if what I did was so bad, why do I feel like I'm going on vacation?"

"There's no place I'd rather be than Reason's Wait, but it's no holiday." Noah tapped his thumb on the wheel. "Judge and a few others think you're worth more effort to get straight."

"Am I?"

"That's up to you. I need workers, and you need to work. You'll find out soon enough what you're made of. You'll either take to it or land back in Fort St. Luke and a nice, comfortable cell." He glanced at me. "I don't think that's going to happen." He looked like he actually believed that.

"Okay. There's something else." Had to be said.

"What is it, Eugenia?"

"You recognize me? From last winter?" I looked for surprise or a flinch or some other give in that poker face. Nothing. "I think you do."

"I do. Guess that means you remember me too."

"You expect me to apologize?"

"You want to apologize?"

"I wasn't driving." No reaction. "So why take me in? Aren't you pissed?"

He didn't answer. Had he heard? Maybe this was his plan for payback. He would torture me with mind games.

And then abandon me in the woods.

Don't be an ass, Eugenia. The guy is official. And probably monitored and stuff.

Didn't mean he wouldn't go hard on me.

An hour up the road we turned in at a truck stop marked by a sign that warned travellers that this was the last chance to fill up tanks and bellies before a long empty stretch. We did just that and carried on. As the blacktop wound around bends and over hills, we passed fewer vehicles, then none, and I saw the blue haze of distant mountains. The haze gave way to cuts of grey and green against sky. Where in the hell was this place?

With eyes forward and one hand on the wheel, Noah reached around to a cooler on the back bench, pulled out a bottle of water, offered it.

"No thanks."

He twisted the top off with his teeth, drank half the bottle in two swallows, the rest in two more.

"This program. How many other kids are in it? At your place, I mean."

"A few."

"That's no answer."

He crumpled the plastic bottle, tossed it in a small blue recycling tub beside the cooler. "They come and go depending on their sentence. Right now, four. Five with you."

I chewed on that as we turned off the highway. Luda and I had been a team for so long, I always thought when we left Fort St. Luke it would be together. Instead I was going someplace I never heard of to be thrown in with a crew I didn't know, like a whacko first day of school, Hogwarts for demon spawn.

No, probably not that. A work camp; an old-timey shackled chain gang.

Maybe not that either.

It appeared Noah had said all he was inclined to about his place. I kicked myself again that I hadn't grilled Boyer when I had the chance. I was his client, which meant he worked for me, which meant he had to tell me. Pretty sure it was the law.

The new road was little more than a rough track through a short stretch of trees into a clearing. We stopped beside a pile of crates. "Keep your eyes peeled west. Ole will be here any minute."

"Who's Ole?"

"My pilot."

The hell? I heard a buzzing not unlike that of a dirt bike, and a speck appeared against the blue. The speck grew into a small red and white aircraft, which flew over the grass strip then circled around to land. "Where is this place?"

"Not too far by air. Two days by horse."

"No roads?"

"That's right."

That made escape an unlikely option should I feel the need. Location probably figured into Judge Marg's consideration.

"How come you don't just fly out of Fort St. Luke?"

"We do sometimes, but by using our own strip we can park a truck as long as we like"—he gave me a side eye—"and not worry about some young punk vandalizing or making off with it."

Noah Danby was a smartass. I liked him a little better for it.

"Plus, it's cheaper." He pulled the first of several taped-tight packages from the back of his truck, indicated I should help. "Saves on fuel and landing fees."

"I've never flown before." I said, pulling a box marked "TP" in black marker from the truck, then a lumpy bag, and on and on until the truck was emptied.

"Nervous?

"Course not." Not really.

The aircraft taxied close and shut down. We loaded the cargo, and I sank into one of four comfortable seats behind the cockpit, cardboard boxes and plastic tubs stacked behind me.

"Welcome to Reason's Wait Airlines," Ole said with a goofy arm flourish. His accent sounded European, but I couldn't tell from where. "Here's your safety message: buckle up and watch your step to the bathroom. It's a long drop."

Another joker.

"Where are you from?" I asked.

"Right here in God's country." He took in my eye roll and laughed. "Oh, you mean before? Norway. Not far from Oslo." He turned to Noah. "Hiring me was the best decision you ever made, right boss?"

"You put a dent in the food supplies, but I wouldn't call you wrong."

"Nor late for dinner."

Ole started one engine, and then another, said the airplane was a Piper Navajo. My stomach pinched during takeoff, tilted with the sky as we banked west. I worried I might lose my lunch. We levelled off and my guts settled while below us the forest changed to marsh, then forest again with grassy-topped mountains. In a valley beside a twisting river a small cluster of buildings were set next to a round pen. Inside the pen there were animals, though from this height they looked like brown boulders. Horses, maybe. Or cows. I squinted. Probably not cows.

"Out-camp!" Noah called over his shoulder. The buzz of the engine made it easier to look out the window than talk, but from time to time Noah would point things out, much as he had on the highway.

The Navajo cut between steep rock-sided mountains and others with meadows melting in easy downslopes into trees. Grazing elk dotted the slopes. An appealing location for an outfitter, and for the hunters who paid big bucks in search of a prize. I doubted many would come all this way just to fill their freezer, which was the only good reason I could think of to take out some of these beauties. Not that I was one of those save-the-animal PETA types, but what's the use of a head on a wall?

My own head was smoothed and soothed by the vibration of the engine. I nearly dozed or maybe I did until Noah's voice cut through: "Home sweet home."

It was a green valley right out of a storybook. We dropped between mountains, circled around a collection of log buildings and more pens. Ole landed the Navajo on a grassy field, then taxied toward a waiting red quad hitched to a flatbed trailer. As we climbed out of the airplane, a scarecrow with a straw hat hopped off the quad and met us. He was lean like a zipper with a boy's freckled cheeks and old man creases around his eyes. Guess that put him somewhere in the middle.

"Good to see you, Noah." The zipper-man's eyes flicked toward me then back to his boss. "I take it all went as expected?"

Noah stretched, cracked a muscle in his back. "It did. Eugenia, this is Melvin, our office manager. Most of the time I'll be around, but when I'm not and you're not assigned to a supervisor, he can answer any questions."

"Ok." But I was hardly listening as I gaped at what lay behind the quad. The ranch looked like something out of Lives of the Rich and Famous. The main lodge was two stories high with a red brick chimney rising from a sloped roof, three separate balconies under stained glass windows off the top floor. Neat wooden decks stained cedar red wrapped around the main level.

"Welcome to Reason's Wait." Noah smiled like he knew I was impressed, then turned to his right hand. "Melvin, I've got to make a call. Bring Eugenia up to the house as soon as the supplies are seen to."

"Sure thing."

Unlike his boss, Melvin liked to talk. While we transferred packages from airplane to trailer, I learned that Noah had only had the place five years. He'd given up being a paramedic after his uncle, Reason Danby, had a tragic encounter with a bear. Noah was one of his few remaining relatives, and the only one willing to take it over. According to Melvin, the Danbys weren't known for their longevity. Melvin said Noah decided to change the family luck by turning the ranch from a hunter's paradise to a multifunctional destination, whatever that meant. Not for hunters, anyway. The "Program," Melvin said—using air quotes—was a more recent addition. Besides Melvin and Ole, Noah employed two cooks and two guides. Each of those other employees coincidentally had degrees in social work and/or had worked in prisons. The program participants, aka prisoners, served as wranglers.

"I hope you appreciate how lucky you are. Folks spend a fortune to get to a place like this. Nothing in the world like riding a trail through these mountains and woods."

"If you like it so much, how come you're not a guide?"

Melvin shot me a look.

"Because he never ate his vegetables," Ole teased.

Melvin smiled sweetly and called Ole a name that would make a trucker blush. "I'm delicate like my mother, you Nordic freak. Not that size has anything to do with the job."

"It helps."

"I started four years ago as a wrangler," he said. "I'd just quit my job at a bank and was looking for a change. Noah could see pretty quick that I had more of a knack for paperwork than the outdoors and made me his right hand, which suited everyone fine."

"So how come you're out here unloading this cargo?"

"We all pitch in. Besides, I had to meet you."

While Ole taxied the Navajo toward the tall shed, Melvin hopped on the quad and motioned for me to get on the trailer. The barrels and plastic tubs were packed tight, no place to sit. He gunned it like he thought I was aboard, but I knew it was a lie. Just a test of some sort, or a hazing. I was puffing pretty good by the time we reached a cluster of sheds.

After stowing supplies, Melvin led me up to the big house, where Noah relaxed on the covered porch, boots and hat free, coffee mug in hand. A yellow dog, gone white around its snout and eyes, lifted its head, thumped its tail twice, then lay back down.

"She's all yours, boss," Melvin said, and disappeared inside. Through the kitchen window I heard the breathy squeal of steam escaping a kettle, and pots clattering in a sink.

"Nice dog."

"His name's Copper. He's a good boy, but nearing his best before date."

"So I see."

"Come on, then. Take your hat off when you're entering the big house," Noah said, rising and opening the screen door.

"House rules?"

"Good manners." With a blue folder in hand he motioned for me to follow. I set my hat on a hook beside two others, pulled off my boots, and dropped my gear. Down a short hallway there was a laundry room to the right, and a large bathroom with shower next door. Across the hall, two women in crisp, linen butcher aprons were busy in the kitchen. One scrubbed a pot in a white enamel sink while the other was elbow deep in dough. How stereotypical.

"Merry and Heather, meet Eugenia."

"Our new slave," Merry teased, pulling her hands out of the dough. She was slight, with silver hair cropped so short it was almost a buzz cut. Her sleeves were rolled, showing off healthy biceps. "You probably thought Noah was boss around here, huh?"

"Isn't he?"

"Here's the truth of it," Noah said. "If Merry and Heather tell you to stack wood, you do it. If they tell you to peel potatoes, paint a hall, or take care of the garbage, you do that too."

"So *all* wranglers start out in the kitchen?"

If Noah caught my meaning, he ignored it. "Wranglers start out whichever way they're booted out of bed each day, Eugenia, but if one of these ladies tells you to do something in the kitchen or otherwise, you'll do it." His lips quirked as he added, "If you know what's good for you."

"Oh, now, you just go away, Noah, and leave her with us." Merry waved one floured hand in the air and took the blue folder with the other.

"But it's true," Heather said. "No one crosses the cooks unless they want grit in their porridge or habanero peppers in their pudding." She had pale blue eyes and a heart-shaped face with a wide smile that curled toward her eyes. Her hair was the colour of a moonless night. There was a softness to her, a sparkle.

The loose kitchen banter reminded me of family. Not mine, but someone's. "Good thing I like habaneros." The joke fell flat. "Awkward," I mumbled into my collar.

Noah turned to me. "We have a few hours before dinner. Merry will go over house rules and show you where you're bunking. We'll catch up later."

Somehow this man with the bull-dog face could smile without smiling. Something to do with his eyes. He gave me one of those non-smiles and left me with the ladies. A few seconds later he passed outside the kitchen window, hat back on, headed toward the empty pens.

"He gonna put animals in there?"

"Soon enough," Merry said, climbing into a tall chair at the kitchen island, chin-nodding for me to do the same. She wiped her hands and offered one to shake. "Merry Franz," she said. "House mother and educational supervisor." She nodded toward Heather. "Heather Gobbet is our psychologist. She'll be meeting with you for individual as well as group sessions."

"Wait. What?"

Her eyes were laughing, though she kept a straight face. "We don't just bake scones, you know. Everyone does double duty."

"Sometimes triple," Heather added.

"Sometimes more than that."

"Pleased to meet you," I stammered.

Merry opened the folder, tapped at the top of the list, flour scattering about the page. "Rule one, drink or drugs and you're out."

"Obviously."

Another tap. "Fighting or threats, and you're out."

"Okay."

"Smoking only in designated smoking sheds."

"Don't smoke."

Tap. "No gambling." Tap. "Be respectful." Tap. "No use of firearms, hunting knives, or anything that might be used as a weapon without supervision." Tap. "Staff may search your bunk at any time."

"Anything else?"

"Lights out 10 pm, rise and shine by 6."

"That hurts."

Merry grinned. "You'll get used to it."

I took the sheet and read a few additional notes about listening to staff and doing as I was told, plus guidelines for visitors and phone calls, all with the dire punctuation of "do it or you're out."

"Okay. Doesn't seem so bad."

"Good!" Flour poofed into the air as Merry slapped her knee then slipped off the chair. "You've got the summer off from schooling, same as regular, but if you'd like a head start or a refresher, I'm here. Right now, you can chop us some fuel for the stove."

"Shouldn't someone show me where I'm sleeping?"

"Later," Heather said as she scraped a spoon inside a bowl and dumped its contents into a larger bowl. "Right now, we hustle for dinner."

Merry slid dough into a cast iron stove right out of an antique shop. How long before the dough baked into fresh bread? My mouth watered in sync with a stomach rumble. Lunch wasn't that long ago. Maybe it was the mountain air.

A wet dishrag thunked my shoulder. "Get going!" Heather's voice rose like she was exasperated, but her smile told me she was not. "The woodshed is out back."

Assured my bag was fine by the door, I set to work in the yard. Chopping wood was hard, but I'd done it before and liked it. It didn't take long to get into a rhythm, and swinging an axe seemed a good way to get the kinks out. It did cross my mind that in most circles an axe might also be considered a weapon. Apparently Merry's idea of supervision was to occasionally stick her head out the door and call, "You good?" I kept at it until a clanging bell called me to dinner.

I sucked the sting from a fresh blister. Time to meet the other inmates.

Boots off, hat on a peg beside half a dozen others, I washed up in the bathroom and entered the dining hall. Two long oak tables stretched below the mournful gazes of mounted heads—a sheep, an elk, and a grizzly bear. I wondered if any of their brethren were on tonight's menu.

Noah invited me to sit across from him. "Eugenia, you already know Melvin. This is Hayden, and this is Tammy. They are guides, and along with the cooks their word is law. Understand?"

With the exception of his red T-shirt with the words, *Kiss me I'm Nisga'a*, Hayden looked like he could have stepped right out of an old western movie. Over the shirt he wore a leather fringed vest and had long silver hair pulled back in a ponytail, but it was mostly his handlebar moustache crouched upon deeply weathered skin that made me think of the movies. It looked like it might jump off his face and run off. Tammy's hair was also pulled back, but it was dull brown with swaths of grey and looked as dull and tired as her face.

I nodded toward the middle table where Ole was tucking into a heaping plate. Next to him there were assorted wranglers: short and stocky, tall and tough-looking, tall and goofy, short and slim. "Those my roommates?"

"More or less," Tammy gruffed.

"Our short-term guests room with staff," Hayden explained.

"Am I short-term?"

Hayden winked in answer. I guessed that was a yes.

"Where's your manners?" Tammy bellowed into the room. "Sound off and introduce yourselves to our newest resident."

"And who might that be?" tall and goofy asked.

"Eugenia," I said.

"Pleased to meetcha, Eugenia. I'm Nathan."

"Rick," said short and stocky, who then punched tall and tough in the shoulder. "This is my brother Jimmy."

Jimmy grinned, elbowed Rick.

"I'm Frankie," said short and slim. She smiled, and it was like the room got a little warmer. Didn't look much like a trouble-maker. Neither did Nathan.

I nodded hello and turned back to my meal. I'd get to know them soon enough, figure out friend or foe and all that.

Like she'd been watching through the wall, the moment I set my fork on my empty plate Heather called me into the kitchen. She handed me a pair of yellow rubber gloves splashed with gaudy pink flowers and pointed toward a sink full of pots. "Scrub."

If Luda could see me now they'd probably laugh and say, "See ya, wouldn't want to be ya." As the sink drained my eyes drooped.

Merry clapped her hands. "Wake up, Eugenia! You're not done yet. We need you to bring in some of that wood you chopped, or you won't like what we serve up come morning."

"I'm guessing that if the wranglers don't like their breakfast, they won't be blaming you."

"Smart girl!"

"That's what my Ma used to think."

"The others are getting things ready for the camps," Heather said. "You don't know about the camps yet, so right now you do what we say." She waved a wooden spoon in mock threat. "Don't make us tell you again!"

I plucked the spoon from Heather's grasp, slid it back in its drawer and winked. "You've got no argument from me. I'd rather be with you than any of that lot, anyhow."

Merry cackled. "You trying to butter up the cooks, Eugenia?"

I grinned back. "Not really. Didn't you hear? They sent me here because I'm a badass."

"We'll be the judge of that."

I grinned. Somewhere in the back of my mind I realized I'd become part of the banter.

Arms aching, I dropped the wood in the box and whispered hallelujah when Heather pointed me past a rustic hot tub, a no-electricity-required kind warmed by a wood-fuelled burn box, toward one of two visible bunkhouses.

"Yours is on the end."

The bunkhouses sat on either side of a creek with water that rippled and glowed pink in the waning light. Silhouette cut-outs, one with a skirt, one without, indicated a separation of space per boy-girl gender. How very last century. It irked me on principle, but I liked that mine was about as far away as you could get. It wasn't yet lights-out, but all I could think on was quiet and sleep for the next eight to ten. Slinging my pack over one shoulder, I crossed a two-board bridge spanning the creek and pushed open the bunkhouse door.

Inside, just a soft glow from a lamp. No one home. Perfect.

"Hey," came a voice from the other bunkhouse. It was the tall, goofy looking wrangler, Nathan. His red hair was slicked back, ears sticking out like wings. "Not joining us in the hot tub?" He spoke with an East Coast lilt.

How was this not summer camp?

"Not tonight." There were three sets of bunk beds, plus a single. "Hey, Nathan, how do I tell which bed is free?"

"That one against the wall looks like someone made it up nice for you." He grinned, flung a towel over his shoulder and made his way to the hot tub, skinny legs shining white inside his cowboy boots.

I dropped my bedroll by the door, put my hat on the hook, kicked off my boots, and stumbled across the room toward the single, too tired to even change. It was nice, a thick quilt on the mattress, and a pillow. Puffy. Just how I liked it. Since Merry was house mother, that probably meant she looked after our dorm arrangements. She must have got it ready as an acknowledgement of my hard work and effort. I wasn't used to nice gestures like this and felt a tightening in my throat.

I sank in, eyes closed before my head hit the pillow, and then just ... fell.

Until a bear roared and ripped me from my vague but comforting womb of dreams. Full consciousness found me somewhere on my way toward the floor.

Another roar, neither dreamed nor a bear: "What are you doing in my bed?"

"What do you mean?" My tongue felt slow and thick. The floor was hard, but not as hard as the boot to the backside I anticipated would come next. I scrambled backward on all fours trying to get away, whacking my head against a table and chairs I couldn't see.

Using the chair as aid I pulled myself to my feet and backed toward the door. "Give me a break!"

"I don't gotta give you nothing."

"I didn't know—"

"You were in my bed!"

"But I thought—"

"Just what we need, another golfurnaking slider!"

It was the guide named Tammy. Her presence was a stink blot of a snarl and I knew that if I didn't get out of there right that instant I'd start punching, rules be damned. But some part of me, some shining sliver of self-preservation refused to get booted out of the program my first day in.

I lurched out the cabin door and slammed it behind me.

Before I could blink, the door opened and out came my bedroll and gear. I caught the full force with open arms, and fell backward—

—over the lip of the creek bed.

My innards were instant ice with the cold shock of it. I pulled myself up and out, gasping, retrieved my sopping gear and bedroll.

Crap. At least my boots were dry.

The door opened one more time. "Don't forget your stinkin' boots."

"No, don't—" My reflexes were sluggish with the sure onset of hypothermia, and the boots sailed over my head into the creek.

"Stay outta my space!"

"Wait, where am I suppose to—"

The door slammed shut.

"—sleep?" I stared at the closed door, its message loud and clear.

The water came down cold off the mountain. Numbed skin gave way to violent shivers as I gathered my soggy gear and boots and stepped carefully across the moonlit two-board bridge. The wood-fired hot tub offered up remnants of steam though the logs had burned down. I stripped off my icy-soaked jeans and shirt, and wearing just my bra, tank and panties, lowered myself into the water until I was warmed enough to get out, spread out my things to dry, and reload the burn box. I climbed back inside, exhaling in steamy relief as warmth thawed and soothed my aching everything. Maybe I should have joined Nathan and the others after all.

Nathan! I'd deal with that asswipe tomorrow.

Stars popped high overtop mountains and my soul filled with the green, pink and purple of Aurora Borealis whispering and shifting against the cosmic carpet of the Milky Way.

CHAPTER EIGHT

A female voice: "That's my towel."

"What?" I rubbed the sleep from my eyes, saw it was one of the wranglers. *Frankie.* I shifted against a hard surface, aware that I was no longer in the hot tub. Must have crawled out during the night. "Sorry. I don't even remember. Must have grabbed the closest."

She looked amused. "Forget it. Just leave it in the laundry room. While you're at it you can toss your wet gear in the dryer."

A dryer. Of course. I sat up, squinted at her. "You're not surprised I'm out here. Were you in the bunkhouse last night when … um?"

She nodded. "I woke up. Thought you woulda slept in the house."

I glanced at the main building. "I seriously didn't think of that. Nor the dryer."

She laughed and shrugged.

I couldn't decide if I should feel grateful at her for not rubbing in my lack of horse-sense, or furious for not helping me last night.

"If you're smart, you'll watch your step around Tammy," she continued. "Least 'til she gets to know you."

"I was set up."

She cocked her head to the side, eyes twinkling. "Were you, though?"

"Damn straight."

She grinned. "Everyone gets pranked in the beginning. Just our way of saying hello."

"I might say hello right back."

"You might want to find some clothes first."

I adjusted the towel.

"Eugen-ia!" Merry's voice rang out.

With my gear in the dryer, I wore Frankie's towel like a skirt with a windbreaker from Heather to complete the look while I peeled potatoes on the back porch.

I moved stiffly, my abdomen aching from last evening's wood-chopping—aggravated, no doubt, by my awkward sleeping arrangement. Felt like I might break in two. I was about to ask Merry and Heather for an aspirin, but snickers from Rick and Jimmy as they passed the kitchen were enough to get my back up and the job done.

Out the corner of my eye I watched for the chucklehead that led me down last night's garden path.

"Hey, buddy. Nice to see you dressed for breakfast."

That lilty accent would be lodged in some dusty corner of my brain forever. I looked hard at him. "I ain't your buddy."

Big-eared Nathan, with a chin full of peach fuzz trying to be whiskers, answered with a grin, then disappeared into the dining room while I thought about future revenge. Except everything I thought of would get me booted me out of this place, and I wasn't so angry to forget this was a sweet deal.

Ma would have been disappointed in my arrest. We'd watched Jackson drift deeper into the land of lost cause. She'd wanted better for me; thought I could *be* better. *You're a special child, Eugenia. Don't ever think otherwise.*

Not special enough for her to stick around.

Whenever I thought about Ma, a buzzing in my brain got all mixed up in my heart. I shut those emotions in a box, locked it tight. I knew sure as maggots on roadkill that they would otherwise swallow me whole. Better to remember Ma as she was before everything changed, when she would take me by the hand and tell me about all the wonderful things in the world, like hotels made of ice, and tour-rockets to the moon. Back then, there were dreams.

That all stopped when I turned fourteen.

I remember waking that morning feeling like something different was in the air. I thought it'd be something good. Ma had made pancakes and told me I was grown and that she was proud of me, more or less. She'd had to add that: *more or less.* I went to school all puffed up and glowing, particularly as I'd been in trouble for taking a neighbour's bike. All was forgiven, I thought. Ma believed in me, and everything was going to be okay.

Two months later there was a letter explaining that she'd left to get her head straight, and how sorry she was. I burned it, and every letter that followed. They'd stopped coming when I turned fifteen. One year. Guess that's how long guilt takes to fade for someone like her.

"Your clothes are dry." It was Heather. "Come in and eat." She handed me my laundry, neatly folded.

"Thanks. Boots?"

"Still wet."

The dining hall smelled of maple bacon and strawberry jam. Everyone else was already seated. As I loaded a plate there were nods and easy g'mornings as if I'd already been there more than a day. Tammy was scowling.

"Good morning," I said, sweet as pie, daring her to admit what she'd done. As my bunk supervisor I was pretty sure she'd stepped over a line.

"Morning," she grunted, eyes slitty. I took a wide berth and moved to the other table.

"Over here, dear," a voice rang out.

Dear?

It was big-ears, clearly not done getting my goat. He nodded toward the seat next to his, like he expected me to take it. Frankie sat across looking happy and relaxed. Fine, I'd mind my manners—for now.

I'd landed in the middle of a conversation about ranch business. Nathan and Frankie had been out counting horses in the hills yesterday. Nathan insisted there were a few missing. I listened with interest and Nathan had the gall to wink at me.

"Last year we found a few strays up by the Wendy," Frankie said, then shovelled beans and runny egg into her mouth.

"The Wendy?" I asked.

"Wendy Robinson Creek, new girl" Nathan said.

"Call me Eugenia." I bristled, imagined punching him in the nose.

"Come on now," Nathan says. "You're not still pissed about last night, are ya? Consider it your initiation. We all get pranked in the beginning."

"So I heard."

He lowered his voice and glanced at the other table. "Christ on a cracker, Tammy went a bit overboard, din't she?"

"You call that an apology?"

"I apologize."

I gave him a hard stare. "Whatever. She was drunk."

"Not likely."

"Then she's psycho." My eyes were still steady on him, but he didn't blink. I sat back. "You a Newf?"

"Newfoundlander," Frankie corrected.

"Nah. I'm from the Bay."

"Glace Bay," Frankie clarified.

"Where's that? You sound like a Newf."

"Newf is disrespectful," Frankie said.

I glanced at her. *Seriously?*

"I'm a Caper—"

"Cape Breton Island—" Frankie shovelled in more food.

"Nova Scotia, but I weren't born there."

"So when he calls you 'buddy' he doesn't mean you're best friends."

"But maybe I do."

"Maybe you do."

"You don't believe me, Frankie? I keep telling ya, I'm a nice guy!"

"Tell that to Eugenia."

Nathan looked at me with mock hurt, and again spoke quietly. "Tammy can be a right arse at times, but give'r a chance. We're good now, yah?"

"Guess you'll know when you know," I said. Nathan looked uncertain. My lips twitched, then I smiled. Couldn't help it. "Let's just say you owe me."

Nathan's face split wide in a grin. "Not quite how it works, but no worries."

After breakfast the others scraped their plates and stacked them beside the sink. Merry handed me the scrubbing gloves while Heather held out a bottle of bleach.

"Again?"

"You did such a fine job yesterday, Eugenia."

"I suppose it'll be more wood-chopping after this."

Noah appeared from around the corner.

Merry laughed. "No, I think we have enough for now."

"I've got another task after you're done with the dishes." Noah said. He turned to Merry and Heather. "Thank you, ladies. Breakfast was delicious."

"What task?" I asked. He didn't answer. Instead he chattered on with Heather and Merry like he hadn't even heard me.

I scrubbed the plates in one soapy basin, and then dipped them in scalding hot rinse water. "The bleach'll kill anything the soap doesn't get," Merry said.

Holy hot-stinging pain, Batman! I was glad to finish.

Another wet dishrag to the shoulder from Heather. "Don't forget the pots and pans!"

While I worked, Noah sat at the kitchen island with Merry and Heather, sipped coffee and shot the breeze.

"Don't worry about the drying, Eugenia," Merry said. "If you're finished washing, you can go with Noah."

Noah and I walked out onto the porch where Copper climbed to his feet, tail wagging. "Wait here, Copper," Noah said, and the dog sat.

Noah looked at my sock feet.

"My boots are wet."

He didn't ask why. He'd probably already heard Tammy's version. "We have a collection of old boots in the tool shed. I'm sure we can find something for you."

I raked fingers through my tangled hair. My head felt naked without my hat, which I hoped was still hanging in the bunkhouse.

Jimmy pulled up on a quad with a flatbed behind it. Noah took over the driver's seat as Jimmy stepped out, gave me a sidelong look and a smirk. What in the hell was that about? In another life I'd wipe that look off of Jimmy's face. Noah waved me toward the flatbed. "Hop on."

I tried not to fall off as we bumped toward the tool shed on the far side of the still-empty pens. The boots I pulled on were stiff and dusty. I felt a pang for home and my familiar if imperfect life.

"Sometimes guests forget them, and sometimes we recycle our old ones," Noah said. "We try not to waste anything up here."

"Guests," I said. "Don't you mean prisoners?" He flicked me a look but didn't respond.

We loaded the flatbed with rope, saws, hatchets and axes. "What are we doing?"

"Clearing brush. That's step one."

This need-to-know act was getting old fast.

Back on the flatbed, I hung onto tools in addition to keeping myself upright and on board. Across the field, through a stand of pine trees, I saw an occasional glint of reflected sunshine off water.

The river was wide, grey-blue like distant mountains, its shores mottled with multicoloured rock rubbed smooth by years of erosion. Not far upriver, limestone cliffs cut skyward. A broad wingspan drew my eye as an eagle folded onto a skeletal tree branch hung low over the river.

"Over here, Eugenia." Noah pointed to where a portion of the fence had fallen into the river. "We'll tear this apart then clear a space in the brush for a new, stronger fence, connect it to the still-good portion."

"I heard you're missing horses. They escape through this?"

"Our horses are free range when we're not using them. The game fence keeps elk and deer off our meadow and landing strip."

There was twenty feet of brush to clear. Noah handed me a pair of leather work gloves and a hatchet.

"This isn't going to do much."

"First we clear the shrubs and lower branches. We've got other tools to take down the trees."

"It's going to take forever."

"Put your head down and keep working, Eugenia. We just push through."

We clipped away the fallen portions of weathered chain-link, pulling the submerged portion out of the river. Where the ground was mossy and strewn with dead branches, we hauled until pain in my lower back burned white-hot. Along the new line marked by Noah, I reached through tangy boughs to lop off lower branches. Soon I was scratched like a bugger and sweaty. My good nature slipped away.

I was unpaid labour. If Noah wanted to work me into the ground, who would stop him? An inner growl seeded anger, took hold, grew, fuelled another kind of energy.

We backed and forthed on a two-person saw, made kerfs to make the trees fall. By the time Noah handed me an axe, I wanted to swing it at his head.

Noah read what was crawling under my skin. "You got something to say, Eugenia?"

"If we were in Fort St. Luke, no way you'd be allowed to work me like this."

"This isn't Fort St. Luke."

I clamped my lips shut. It wasn't like youth justice could pop by when they were in the neighbourhood, make sure he treated me right. This was about last winter, it had to be.

"I've got rights."

"Sounds like you've got attitude."

With more force than Isaac Newton explored, I dropped the axe and stomped toward the river. Where the hell else was I going to go?

On a wide, sloping boulder beside our pile of dead and recently cut underbrush, I sat. The eagle was still there and I glared at it and it stared back as if to say … nothing, because it was just an eagle. That didn't stop my brain from imagining. If an eagle could talk, what would it say? *Breathe. Look. Listen.*

My pulse slowed to the dance of water over stone, wind rustling boughs, the chitter of a squirrel, the squawk of a jay. I unclenched my fists.

The buzz of an approaching quad snaked into the moment. It was Heather. She gave Noah a cloth bag and something else I couldn't make out. After a moment she kicked the machine back into gear and left while Noah made his way to my boulder. He handed me my hat. Heather must have retrieved it from the bunkhouse, or someone else had. I settled it on my head and felt right again.

"Lunch." Noah opened the cloth bag and handed me a chicken sandwich. From a thermos he poured me a cup of ice-cold lemonade, which I immediately drained. He refilled my cup and poured one for himself. If he was expecting an apology, he didn't say so. Instead he chewed on his sandwich, watched the river.

I bobbed a thumb toward it. "So what's it called?"

"Rubicon."

"I think I've heard of it."

"Maybe you have. Maybe you've heard the saying, 'crossing the Rubicon.' It means you're passing a point of no return."

"Sounds prophetic."

"Big word for a ranch hand," Noah teased.

I let my vision go wide, looked at everything and nothing all at once. Something about the sounds of this place got right into my core. It felt ancient and powerful. But I wasn't ready for a point of no return. I wanted answers, and not about the geography. "When we left the city you admitted that you remembered me, but you didn't say why you took me in. I want to know. I have a right to know."

"There you go about rights again."

"At least tell me if you're pissed about that night, what we did to you. I mean, you gotta be."

Noah flicked a glance at me. "I was."

"What about now?"

A pause, then: "No."

He could have been lying—what else could he say? But I believed him. I felt something fall away. "Why am I here? Anyone else we did that to would've been happy to see me rot behind bars."

"Told you, I need workers."

"So why have this place at all? As a program, I mean. Sounds like it was doing okay as a hunting lodge."

He shrugged. "It's not a secret. Just life, I suppose. The natural progression of what you want and need at different stages. When I was your age, I was a scrapper, fighting for my future, figuring out who and what I wanted to be. Normal teenage stuff. As I got older, I began to think back on the things that made a difference. Or would have if they'd existed. When my uncle passed, I saw an opportunity for a more peaceful life up here." He paused to watch the eagle spread wings wide and fly back up into the blue. "Then I got to thinking about how the ranch might help others in some way. Doing good makes a person feel good. Ever notice that?"

"My lawyer said something similar."

"Sid's a fine man."

"You know him? Boyer?"

"He's been coming up here every summer for as long as I've been here. Longer."

"He calls his business, 'retribution and rehabilitation.'"

Noah smiled. "Yeah, that sounds like Sid."

My turn to pick up a stone and toss it. I considered telling Noah about my warm welcome to the bunkhouse the night before, but I couldn't think of any way of doing it without sounding like a snitch. Maybe he already knew. Maybe it was all part of the Program.

I'd told Boyer that the girl I'd beaten up should toughen up. *You might have to take your own advice*, he'd said.

Fine. Point taken.

For the rest of the afternoon we worked steadily, the aggravation I'd felt during the morning long done and distant. The sound of the river and the rhythm of our efforts loosed thoughts and memories, some good, some not. Trees were felled, trunks yanked, land cleared, holes dug. By the time we were ready to sink posts my stomach growled again, fierce enough to scare away small animals.

"We're done for today, Eugenia." Noah tipped his hat up, wiped his brow. "Good job."

At the big house my boots were sitting pretty on the mat, dry and polished.

"Cutting it close," Merry teased as we filled our plates. The others had finished and were headed out to evening chores and relaxation. Nathan had a rag in his back pocket. There was no mistaking the sharp scent of Dubbin boot wax that clung to him.

"Thanks, man."

Big goofy grin. "I'm not sayin' I felt bad."

Much as I wanted to, I couldn't hold my grudge. Not with a heaping plate of savoury beef stew and dumplings in front of me. After dinner, I began rinsing plates, but a towel flick from Heather stopped me. "I've got it. You go relax, take a look around." She handed me a sheet of paper with a schedule.

"What's this?'

"Group sessions every day except when you're away, one-on-ones once a week, more if you'd like. I'm here for you anytime, but these times"—she tapped the sheet—"for sure."

The sheet had blocks for meals, chores and recreation, with a slash in the recreation blocks to indicate one-on-ones. "I missed today's group session."

"Special dispensation while you were settling in."

Building a fence was settling in?

"Come on," Noah said, filling the doorway. "I've got something to show you."

We took two quads across the clearing and over a hill. Noah stopped, pointed. "Look there."

"Holy ... where'd they come from?" In the valley beyond the hill there were horses as far as I could see. White, grey, brown, and patched, big and sturdy looking, chunkier than the average quarter horse.

"Second largest free-range herd in North America," Noah said. "They run wild for eight months out of the year, living as they were meant to in nature. We bring them in every spring, clean them up, trim their feet, put some training on the ones that need it."

I whistled. Hard not to be impressed.

"The mares are for breeding, same with the studs. I spend more time training the geldings we use for riding, but we keep some others for packing."

"Do you really need so many, now that you're not a hunting camp?"

"Probably not."

One thick-necked stallion circled what might be his family group, judging by the shades of blue roan on the young ones. A curious brown yearling from another group wandered close and was charged by the stud for his efforts. The younger horse bolted away, and the stud, seemingly satisfied, snorted, shook his head and trotted back to his herd where he touched noses with one of the mares.

"When will you start working with them?"

"Few days. We'll finish with the fence, then get you sorted with a horse."

"You mean to ride?"

"If you're going to spend time here, you're going to ride. You'll also work the horses that need it."

"I'm no horse trainer."

"Relax, you'll do fine." He looked amused. "You'll watch for a while, and then dive in. It's the best way. Every day you'll watch a little more, learn a little more, do a little more, and at night we'll talk about what you're going to do next. Good?"

"Okay."

As we drove back to the lodge, a buzz of excitement wrapped around my nerves, but as Noah wished me a good night, thoughts of tomorrow were set aside for something more pressing: my sleeping arrangements. I stopped on the path. There were only two bunkhouses, and a room in the main house hadn't been presented as an option.

Something Noah said when we were clearing brush echoed as if the man were standing right behind me: sometimes you just had to push through.

Fine.

Across the bridge and up the wooden steps. Hand on handle, deep breath. Open.

Tammy was at the table with Frankie, playing cards. Frankie grinned hello. Tammy did not. "Well?" she asked.

"I have to sleep here."

Tammy stared hard at me. "Course you do," she growled. "Sit down. We'll deal you in."

I left my gear next to the door, just in case I felt the urge to dash. "Poker?"

"No gambling, slider! Crazy Eights. My rules. No eights as last card."

"Same card changes suit?"

"Yep."

Frankie made most of the small talk while we played. Tammy didn't outright welcome me to the bunkhouse, but her mood seemed lighter. Twice, she even smiled.

Frankie called last card then game over. Tammy gruffed at me as she walked to her bed, "This time, stay outta my space."

"No problem."

She let her back say her goodnights.

"You can take this bunk next to mine," Frankie said. "Top or bottom, it's all yours." There was a lightness to her that seemed out of sync with our situation. What had landed her here?

I took the bottom, parallel to hers. Leaning in, I kept my voice low. "Any chance I'm going to get dumped out of bed again?"

A returned whisper. "Probably not."

How reassuring.

There was a creak of springs from the other side of the room. "Shut up, would ya?"

I slept like the dead.

CHAPTER NINE

The work was no easier my second morning. After breakfast we separated the geldings from the mares, babies and studs, and herded them into a separate field. Afterward, Frankie, Nathan and I were left to clean the pens while brothers Rick and Jimmy went off with Hayden to weed a garden.

"I don't much mind the smell of horse crap," Nathan said, shovelling it onto the trailer.

"Do tell," I drawled.

Frankie smirked.

"I mean, don't get me wrong, crap is crap, I'm not saying that cleaning pens is my preferred chore around here, but compared to other kinds, horse crap is a pile of roses."

"Or clover," I said.

"That's what I'm saying! I mean, it's all natural, right? Not like pig crap, or cow crap."

"Or human crap," Frankie added.

"Yeah, that'd be the worst. It's all about the feed. The more bad stuff you put in, the worse it comes out."

"Hang on," I leaned on my shovel. "Are you calling Merry and Heather's cooking bad?"

"Oh, sweet Jesus, no, but animals that stick to grasses and the like are a joy to shovel up after."

"A joy," I deadpanned. "Really."

Nathan raised his brows at me. "Oh, I get it, you're hacking on me." He looked back and forth between me and Frankie. "The both of you."

"Clearly we've not spent as much time as you have contemplating crap," Frankie teased.

"Maybe you should. You don't want to think about what they must be feeding those cows and pigs to get the stink that comes out of the other end. It's not natural, that's for sure."

"Neither is this conversation," Frankie said. Unable to hold back any longer Frankie and I doubled over, laughing.

"You're quite the educated fella, Nathan," I said, removing my glove to wipe away my tears.

He gave me a funny look, then glanced at Frankie, who stopped laughing, coughed.

"I say something wrong?"

Nathan grinned, slow and wide. "Nah," he said, and turned back to his shovelling.

That was weird. Any awkwardness was soon wiped away by Nathan's continued chatter, which had now turned to dung beetles and fire ants.

"You ever get bit by one of those, Genie?" Only my family called me Genie, but before I could sort my feelings about that he was into his story. "This guy up here a few years back, two years maybe—"

"Longer than that. It was before you and I got here," Frankie said.

"Three, five years, maybe. The way Tammy tells it there was this guy who really loved eating, never stopped even though he was skinny as a zipper."

"Turn sideways, stick out his tongue—" I said.

"—and he looks like a zipper, yeah, you heard that one, Genie?"

"I guess."

It was a good moment. Nathan's sunny nature lightened the air, and Frankie sweetened it. They were nice to be around, even while shovelling shit.

"Anyhow, the way Tammy tells it he wasn't the brightest bugger, and on the lazy side."

"A slider?"

"You been talking to Tammy. She calls us all that at first."

"Not me," Frankie said.

"Aren't you special, then? Anyhow, this guy? Not a slider neither. Well, maybe. Anyway, he was eating peanut butter and honey sandwiches, and because he'd get all in a panic if he didn't have snacks with him at all times, he had another one in his pocket. The way Tammy tells it he was lipping off about taking a break and sat himself down on top of a hill, not realizing he was sat down on a nest or whatever. Tammy kept trying to tell him and this guy kept lipping off and lipping off until Tammy finally said … well you know Tammy—"

"—that we do—" Frankie said.

"—so Tammy said 'whatever,' except not in those words, and went back to work. Wasn't thirty seconds later before this guy was screeching like three crows on a bagel and heading for the hills. Those ants crawled all up the inside of his legs and got at the honey, which had leeched through the wrapper and into his pants."

Frankie grinned. "So the moral of the story—"

"—is don't talk shit to Tammy," I finished.

Job done, we stored the dung for later use in gardens, and washed for lunch. After baked beans with cold cuts on fresh-baked bread, the guides made a show of clearing plates and taking over kitchen duties while the ruffians and Heather settled in the great room in front of the fireplace. Time for "Group."

There was groaning and laughter when Heather grinned and pulled out a roll of toilet paper. "You've all been through this at least once. Who wants to tell Eugenia about our welcome game?"

Jimmy put up his hand, caught the TP as Heather tossed it. "You're supposed to take as much as you think you'd need if you're going to spend a night in the bush, then for each square, you say something about yourself."

"Sounds like a shitty way to get to know each other," I said. "Pun intended."

Nathan guffawed. "You're on a roll there, Genie!"

More laughs from the group.

Maybe I should have felt weird or annoyed at forced participation in a woo-woo sharing circle, but I didn't. Maybe it wasn't so woo-woo. Just a chance to get to know everyone a little better. I watched and listened as Rick said he like the colour blue, movies, jelly beans, and the book about birds he stole from his brother Christmas morning when he was ten and Jimmy was twelve; as Jimmy said he liked playing guitar, real cowboy music like from Hank Williams Senior, smoking weed, and his brother even though he was a thief; as Nathan said he liked beach parties, cooking, olives with garlic in them, and shovelling shit with friends. Everyone laughed, and it was my turn.

I'd watched as everyone took a length shorter than their arms and did the same. It had all been easy, until now. At least I wasn't last, like the punctuation at the end of long sentence everyone waited for because then you knew it was done. I just had to say some stuff, and we'd move on. I took a deep breath, noticed Rick and Jimmy were giving each other small and quiet thigh jabs while Heather's attention was on me. I took another breath. "I don't know. Ice cream, I guess. Tiger-tiger. Hanging with my friend Luda at the pool hall, except I don't even like pool." I felt myself blushing. "Sorry, we're supposed to say what we like."

Heather smiled. "It's all good, Eugenia. What else?"

"My nephews, Conner and Tip." That was three. I should have given Conner and Tip their own squares. Too late now. Three more to go. "That lichen you have on rocks up here. The mountains." I thought. What else did I like? "Lunch was pretty good." More laughter, and it was Frankie's turn.

"The colour green, which is probably obvious from my clothes, a game called Lemon Twist I had when I was a kid, I like lunch too, and honest conversations." She smiled at me with her eyes, and I knew we'd be friends. I liked honest conversations too.

It was hard to reconcile this easy conversation with the understanding that everyone here had done stuff bad enough that they'd been headed down the same road as me. Also like me, someone somewhere had thought they were worth another chance.

For the rest of the session I listened as Frankie asked Jimmy about playing guitar, Nathan talked about eating fresh haddock from the ocean and Frankie hopped around and tried to show us what a "Lemon Twist" was and how to use it. Then Heather headed to the office with Rick while the rest of us had free time.

"Come on, let's go for a walk," Frankie suggested.

"I'll pass," Jimmy said. "I'm working on a new song."

He headed to his bunk while Frankie and Nathan and I gave old Copper a pat and walked into the meadow. An eagle soared overhead as we scuffed at field grass, wandered up and over the slope toward where Noah and I built the game fence. We veered off onto a path lined with big-headed plumes of purple flowers that resembled starbursts, honeybees touched from one to the next, and juvenile pines reached for the sun filtering through a canopy of poplar. I tripped along the Rubicon's stony beach, exploring clumps of washed up and sun-bleached driftwood while Nathan and Frankie kicked off boots, rolled up pant legs.

"Come on, Genie!"

"Looks cold."

"S'pose it is," said Frankie.

Fine, whatever. I stifled a gasp as I dipped my bare feet into the wet, waded in up to my calves. "Not so bad," I said through gritted teeth, treading careful over the stony bottom.

"Sure, for some," Frankie said. I glanced up. She and Nathan were back on the shore, boots on, big toothy grins.

"Keep at it, you guys." I hopped back to shore. "There may come a day when the prankers get pranked back." That made them laugh harder, and I laughed too.

Re-booted, we carried on along the shore as it curved back toward the ranch. From there we took a less-travelled path heavily crowded by larch and willow, but we were soon through. In the open space just beyond, a weather-worn shack, and beyond that, a slope that led back to the meadow and the lodge.

"What is this?"

Frankie shrugged. "Library. Used to be for storage."

The outer walls were made of split logs and mortar, and still looked strong despite the building's age. A rack of deer antlers hung above the door, which was held shut by a simple hook. Inside there was just enough room for two faded willow chairs and a folding card table, a latched cupboard against one wall. Nathan glanced at me like he was about to unveil a secret stash of hooch, then pulled open the hinged doors. No whiskey. Instead there were four shelves with books, a couple of notebooks and a glass jar with pencils.

"A quiet spot to get away should you feel the need," Frankie said. "It's not like it's a secret. Nothing here is."

"Yeah, about that. This is supposed to be a sentence, an alternative to juvie, right?" Nathan nodded. "So why all this freedom? I mean, I'm not complaining, but it doesn't make sense."

"Noah believes that you get trust by giving it." Frankie said.

"Also, we're not exactly unsupervised," Nathan added. "From Noah's office window you can see pretty much every place around here. The meadows, the river, Hayden's garden."

"Hayden's garden?"

Nathan grinned. "What do you think we saved the crap for?"

"Okay, but what about here? Unless Noah's got a hidden camera he can't see what we get up to though these walls."

Nathan shrugged. "Used to be that Merry would check in, but she trusts us."

"What about me? I mean, to be honest I have reputation for violence—"

Frankie and Nathan exchanged a look. Nathan frowned, "No, Frankie—"

But before he could finish, I was on the ground, winded, Frankie's face inches from mine.

"What the hell?" I gasped once I was finally able to sit up again. "Is that what you call 'honest conversation'?"

Frankie looked miserable, backed away.

"Frankie has training," Nathan said.

Frankie held up a palm. "Don't ask."

"Seriously?" I sputtered. "So what was that. A warning?" I felt my blood rise. "You want me to know you can take me? You're the tough girl?"

She turned to the window. "I'm sorry. I don't actually know why I did that."

I'd caught the anguish on her face just before she turned. The fire inside of me fizzled. "I guess maybe I asked for it."

"No you didn't." She turned back to me. "When you said you were all violent and shit I did that without thinking. I suppose I wanted you to know I was tough too. We're all here for a reason."

"I know that—"

"—I know you know that, and clearly, I still have some stuff to work on."

I wondered again what she'd done. This didn't feel like the right time to ask.

"I'm sorry," she said again. "I really am."

Something in her look made my heart hurt.

She came close, held out her hand. "Friends?"

What choice did I have? These were close quarters, even with miles of wilderness surrounding us. I nodded and we shook. "Maybe you can show me that move? I mean, self-defence and all that?"

"Sure."

Nathan whistled. "Am I going to have to watch my back around you two? You gonna go all super ninja around this place?"

Frankie grinned. "Ninjas in the mountains. Could be a movie."

I looked at the shelves. "Or a book."

Frankie and Nathan each settled into chairs with books already dogeared. I found a thin paperback by Louis L'Amour, and because there were no more seats, decided to take my quiet time outside.

On my way up the slope I waded through puff-topped cotton grass, wild oats, and tight, ball-like flowers red as raspberries. Under a spindly stand of paper birch, I settled, cross-legged, surrounded by sweet-smelling wild strawberries, several fat fruits already ripe for plucking. I popped one in my mouth while examining the book I'd grabbed. It had caught my eye because of the cover: cowboys gathered round a table of an old-time saloon. Made me think of how things used to be with me and Luda. Not that we were hanging around saloons—not legal ones, anyhow.

I wondered how they were doing. We'd been through a lot together, and not always the sort of activities that landed us in trouble. Before we started truly punching back against this suckhole of a world, sometimes we'd just hang out. Luda was my best friend, would always be my best friend. I'd finish this summer, and then everything would get back to normal.

Beyond the shed, the river curved eastward through green mountains. I marvelled again at my lucky break. Even Group was okay. I liked how no one judged me, or if they did, they kept their opinions to themselves. Here, we could let our pasts disappear and imagine another life. As long as we didn't throw each other on the floor.

Through the window I saw the gloss of Frankie's hair as she tilted her head over her book. She had a sweet nature with a powerful and unexpected wallop. Maybe I wasn't angry about what she did. Maybe that just made her interesting.

Frankie shifted slightly, and I saw Nathan lean in. At first, it looked like he was making a move on her, but then I saw it was about a book, the one Frankie was holding. She ran her finger along a line, sharing it with him.

Move or no, it was an intimate moment. For the first time I noticed the fine shape of Nathan's jaw, the pleasing, tawny glow to his skin. I looked closer, searching for some sign that there was more between them than reading.

"So, Nathan?" I whispered that night to Frankie, after Tammy had begun snoring.

"What about him?"

"Something going on?"

She was quiet for a moment. "Not in the way you mean. That'd be against the rules."

I thought about the litany Merry had put me through. "I don't remember that one."

She yawned. "We got each other's backs here, Eugenia."

"Mine's a little sore right now, thanks."

"I'm really sorry. I feel like such a shit for doing that, I can't even tell you."

"No, I meant my back is sore from all the work. Not what you did."

She reached across the space between our beds, touched my arm. “You okay? Seriously.” I could see she was genuinely worried.

“Nothing hurt but my pride. It was unexpected.”

She nodded, quiet.

“So where’d you learn that?”

She opened her mouth to answer but was cut short by a string of admonishments from Tammy. Instead she mouthed, *Goodnight.*

We’d be fine.

CHAPTER TEN

Four hours past sunrise, mist clung to the valley as if reluctant to leave. Once the cloud overhead moved on it would burn off, but for now it gave the feeling of being somewhere *other*, far away from a damaged world. The air was soft, my companions, silent, and horses waited calm in pens. Thanks to Rick and Jimmy.

"They're good boys," Noah had said to me at breakfast as Rick and Jimmy played a game that involved exchanging punches to the jaw with escalating force. Each punch was followed by loud guffaws. "Not too complicated, and hard workers."

"You stop that before you brain-damage each other!" Merry scolded, and sent them to scrape their plates.

I was pretty sure any damage had long since been done.

But as mist turned to memory, I saw the truth of Noah's words. They'd moved a lot of horses while the rest of us had a second helping of pancakes.

"Salt-licks help," Jimmy said, pointing to the blocks in each pen.

A simple trick, but a smart one. Salt was a treat for the horses, not easy to come by when they were running free.

Nathan and Frankie followed Tammy into the tack-shed while the rest of us perched high on fence posts to count.

"I don't see Dusty," Hayden said.

Melvin took off his hat, wiped his brow. It was going to be a hot one. "He was moving stiff last year. Guess he didn't make it."

One by one the youngsters buckled their legs and sank to rest beneath the canopy of the family herd. Noah chewed a toothpick as horses nickered back and forth. “I count 167,” he said.

Melvin put his hat back on. “Me too.”

“163,” I said.

All eyes on me like question marks.

“Hayden, what’d you get?” Noah asked.

“I stopped when you and Melvin both got 167.”

“Nice try, kid,” Melvin said.

“I’m sure there are 163,” I said.

“Rick and Jimmy?” Noah asked. But Rick and Jimmy were back at the punching game.

“Okay,” Noah said. “Let’s count them again.”

I waited this time.

“163,” Hayden said.

“Rick and Jimmy?”

“163,” Rick said.

Jimmy shrugged. “Lost count.”

“I got 163.” Noah said. “Melvin?”

Melvin looked uncomfortable. “Yeah, 163 here too. Couple of them must have moved.”

“For both of us,” Noah agreed.

If anyone had asked, I’d have said that Melvin got lazy and hadn’t counted in the first place, but no one did, and what did it matter anyway?

“We’ll go with 163,” Noah said.

“Nice catch, Eugenia,” Hayden said. “That’s down some, isn’t it?”

“A few,” Melvin said.

“Five,” Noah said.

“We still need to check the Wendy,” Hayden said. “Could be there.”

“Maybe.”

We followed Noah into the yard between the pens. Melvin was looking at me weird. "I'm good at numbers," I said by way of apology, though I didn't know what I was sorry for. That I'd embarrassed him, maybe. "It's like they jump out at me or something."

"Nice trick," Melvin said.

I shrugged. "Makes math easy. Got me extra credit working in the office at school."

"Maybe we should get you working the desk with Melvin," Noah said.

I couldn't tell if he was joking. "No way! I mean, no thank you. Not my thing. Besides, it was a long time ago."

Hayden drawled, "Kid, I got socks older'n you."

We hauled out saddle-pads and trees, anchored them on horses. The "trees" were rigs strapped over the saddle-pads in order to hook packs, which were plastic boxes meant to keep vermin out and contents airtight and dry. Within the hour, Rick, Jimmy, and Hayden were off to Far Camp while Tammy, Nathan, and Frankie prepped to go to Crooked Camp. With or without guests, the camps needed cleaning and maintenance.

As Noah disappeared into the shed, I watched Hayden's line of packhorses snake through the meadow then over the hill. The ringing of horse bells faded to an occasional clang, and then nothing.

I asked Melvin, "How far is Far Camp?"

"Three-hour trail ride. We call it Far Camp because it's our farthest away out-camp."

"Boy, somebody put a lot of time into thinking up that name." Melvin gave me a baleful look. "Ah … so Far Camp and Crooked Camp. Any others?"

"Just the two. And before you ask, it's called Crooked Camp because of how the river goes there."

"When do I get to go to the camps?"

Melvin looked annoyed. "You'll have to ask Noah." He spun on his heels and walked up to the house. Who peed in his cornflakes?

"Come on," Noah said. "Big day today."

"Oh good. Yesterday was way too easy." Noah and I had finished putting up the game fence after dinner while the others relaxed with board games and the hot tub. "We'll check the horses for health, get started on gentling and training the young ones."

"Thus begins my re-education."

Noah grinned. "Thus it does. We'll get you comfortable around the horses, then you can ride."

"I'm comfortable around horses."

"You said it had been a while."

"I guess." I watched Frankie and Nathan tie a couple of horses to the fence. "So why keep the camps if you don't have hunters?"

"No point in letting them fall apart. You gotta look after what you have, Eugenia."

I rolled my eyes. "Like turning that old shed into a library."

"Something like that. Besides, we do get the odd visitor. There's some paperwork to get through, but the ones who really want to stay don't mind. Mostly we get artists, writers and scientists, people connected to nature in some way through their work."

"That gives you enough dollars to run this place?"

"Not really, but we're diversified. Horses are a large part of our operation, breeding and selling at auction."

"Plus you get government dollars for the program."

"Speaking of, let's put you to work."

I studied a bay-coloured horse looking sideways at me through the bars of the first pen. "It seems big. They all do."

"They've got some draft horse in them. We change studs every few years." He lifted his hand to the horse's nose, let him have a sniff, then stroked him. "This is Packman. He's a nice old gent. Good to learn on."

"I told you, it's not like I've never been on a horse."

"Trim his feet and we'll go for a ride."

My rising indignation hit pause. "Hang on, I don't know anything about feet."

Noah looked amused. "You know they're important, right?

"Course I do. I just don't know anything about trimming."

Noah glanced at his watch. "I've got a call to make," he said, walking away. "Watch what the others are doing, then take a brush to this guy. Get to know him."

I leaned against the shed and considered my new friend. "Hello horse, nice to know ya."

"What in the hell do you think you're doing, slider?" Tammy emerged from inside with a mouth full of bitter. She let loose a string of not-quite-cuss words, more *golfurnacking* mixed in with what sounded like a *pinchinoff* and *wakapomping*, as if she had to get them out of the way before she could get to the point of whatever it was she wanted to say. "You get in there and start bringing those packs out."

"But Noah said—"

This took her a notch further. "Noah didn't say nothing that's gonna save you from me kicking your ass!" Her face turned the shade of beet soup as she moved in close. Too close.

"Pretty sure you can't touch me. Specially not with witnesses."

"When a guide tells a turd to move, the turd moves!"

I wiped the woman's spittle from the side of my nose. My fists clenched, my heart pounded, but I knew that if I smashed her ugly face, my time here was done.

Somehow, I choked back the impulse, stepped sideways into the shed and willed my pulse to slow.

"Over here, Eugenia," Nathan called from the shadows.

I worked with Nathan while Frankie checked and trimmed feet. Soon enough, the horses were ready to go. Tammy grunted as she walked by, which I read as approval, which made my blood rise all over again.

Her *golfurnacking* approval was not one of my life goals.

I held the gate open as the supply train was led away, anchored by Frankie. "When will you be back?"

"Soon enough," Frankie said, which was no answer at all.

Noah found me. "Ready to trim feet?"

"Didn't see how. I was hauling gear," I said, willing him to ask me why. He didn't.

"Follow me."

In the shed Noah chose hoof picks, double-handled tools he called "nippers," and rasps. Back outside, he set them on the ground and retrieved Packman from his pen. "Glad to see this old man is doing well. A lot can happen with these guys in eight months."

"You don't check on them?"

"Not until spring. They run as nature intended, sometimes for their lives. See this?" Noah stroked four curving scars on Packman's rump.

"Looks like something took a swipe at him."

"Cougar, I expect." I must have looked alarmed. "Don't worry, they tend to stay away from humans."

"I'm not worried," I scoffed.

"There are all manner of animals out here. Some are predators, others are prey. Some we see often, others we don't."

Shifting my line of sight toward the mountains, I contemplated the open, grassy areas, good for grazing animals like the horses, elk, and mountain sheep. There were also forested areas where all manner of long-toothed dangers might hide.

Gently, Noah ran his hand down the back of Packman's left

foreleg, and the horse lifted its hoof. "Atta boy." Grabbing hold, Noah first scraped the mud off the bottom, then clipped the overgrown edges with the nippers, which looked like super-sized nail clippers. Next came the rasp, which Noah used to smooth the edges. He stood up. "Got it?"

"I think so."

I'd used a variety of hand tools in my life, mostly on home repairs after Pops died. This was the same thing only different. As I bent over the hoof, my back end toward Packman's head, I glanced over my shoulder more than once just to make sure the horse wasn't inclined to take a bite.

I heard Noah chuckle even though he was being quiet about it. "Relax," he said. "Packman is a good old boy."

"In some parts, it's the good old boys you want to watch out for."

"True enough." He finished with the horse he'd been working on, moved on to the next.

"Guess I'm slow at this."

"You'll get the hang of it."

I had a feeling "getting the hang of it" might take some time, but I kept at it and got the job done. Packman had his eyes closed as if napping. "Okay, finished. When are we going to ride?"

Noah was picking out the feet of a black and white Paint. "Soon as the horses are looked after. Why don't you get one of those fellas from the last pen?"

"They look wilder than Packman."

"You can handle it."

Noah's faith in me was misplaced. Some of these horses had hardly been handled, and with every hour I became more aware of all I did not know.

At the gate of the pen, a red horse, neck gleaming in the sunlight, stuck his nose between the posts as if trying to get the smell of me. He was different from the others in that there wasn't a speck or a blaze of another colour on him, not even his mane and tail. He was smaller than most of the others, but bigger than a few. "How you doing, boy?" I crooned at him and moved to stroke his nose.

The horse squealed and gave little buck as he trotted head and tail high to the middle of the pen where he hid himself amongst the others. A moment later I saw him, head low, peering at me from between the legs of his pals.

"In the wild, if an animal swipes its paw at you it isn't saying hello," Noah called out. "To that young horse you were attacking." He returned to his task. "Just go easy."

Noah was soft in the head to send a green wrangler into a pen full of half-wild horses. He was either trying to build my confidence or setting me up to fail. When I was a kid my brothers employed that particular technique more than a time or two, especially when they thought I was getting too big for my britches.

In my head, I heard Jackson: *Suck it up, buttercup.* Jackson and Noah were nothing alike, but the sentiment was the same. Just gotta push through.

I climbed through the bars of the gate, felt the horse watching me. "Hey, there." I kept my voice level, soft. "Don't be afraid. I'm not going to eat you."

A half dozen beasts stood their ground as I come close. Eight or ten others—the smaller, younger horses, including the red one—moved away.

Noah probably expected me to halter an older horse. Instead, I went after Red. I was green when it came to horse care and training, but I'd been around them enough to know that as long as I moved slow, Red would too. I was prepared to follow him around this pen until he wore out or decided I wasn't a threat.

Forty-five minutes later, I haltered a fat, grey horse and led him out of the pen.

Noah might have remarked on my failed effort. He did not.

After I finished with the grey's feet, I moved on to a next horse, then another. Each time, Noah checked my work and turned the horse out into the clearing where it rejoined the larger herd. All except Packman and a muscled, blue roan with a black face, which Noah tied to the fence.

Finally, there were only the young ones left in the pens, including Red.

"What about them?"

"Later. Let's go for a ride."

As we saddled our horses, I noticed that Noah used rope bridles with no bits. "Pressure goes on the nose rather than the mouth," he explained. "Go easy, and these boys will want to keep it that way."

"That's what I thought when I tried to catch the red horse."

"You missed something."

"Let me guess," I drawled. "Trust. I would have got it, just needed more time."

"More than that, Eugenia. Trust is important, but so is respect. It goes both ways."

I kept my eye roll on the inside.

CHAPTER ELEVEN

"No. Just, no." The grueling grind had caught up with me. My denial was in part directed toward morning sunlight streaming through curtains someone had so cruelly opened wide. The other part was my body. It refused to move. Even my fingers hurt, every segment.

A pillow hit my face. "Chow time," Frankie said.

More cruelty.

Slowly, I twisted my head sideways and saw Tammy had already gone. Small miracles. "I don't need food. I don't need anything, except a new body. Just let me die."

Frankie laughed. "Didn't peg you for a wuss."

"Do you even know how much pain I'm in?"

"Course I do. It gets easier."

With effort I turned my head back toward Frankie just in time to see the door shut behind her. I groaned, rolled onto the floor.

Okay. Let's do this, Eugenia.

The pancakes made hauling myself to breakfast worth it: thin and stacked high with homemade strawberry jam, and something called clotted cream. Afterward, my body was even less inclined to move. Was it too early for the hot tub?

"Come on," Noah said, pushing back his chair. "You and I are working horses again this morning."

"What about Nathan and Frankie?" Hayden, Rick, and Jimmy had spent the night at Far Camp and were expected back around noon.

"Another run to Crooked Camp."

"When can I go to a camp?"

"Soon."

"When?"

"Soon enough. You any good with a rope?"

"Not really. Played around with one as a kid."

"You'll want to practise. But first we're going to let everyone but the two- and three-year-olds out to play." He rambled on about the day's plan as I followed him out, hoping today wouldn't be so frustrating.

A low buzz in the distance grew louder until the Navajo appeared above one of the surrounding mountains and circled to land.

"Mail call," Melvin said, heading for the landing strip.

His movement flushed out a beast grazing at the forest edge. It bolted from leafy hiding into the clearing. "Is that an elk?" I asked.

Noah frowned. "More than one." Two more followed the first.

My stomach clenched. "What about the airplane?" Noah didn't respond, but I relaxed as Ole buzzed low over the animals, ensuring their continued dash toward the river. He circled once more and set up for landing.

As Noah and I pulled gear from the shed, I watched Ole taxi to a stop. Melvin accepted a small stack of envelopes and headed back our way.

On reaching us Melvin said, "Ole says the game fence is down."

"Which part?" Noah asked.

"The one you repaired the other day." He turned a baleful gaze on me. "Must have been a weak link."

I didn't like that look. "What are you implying?"

Melvin shrugged. "Nothing at all."

"You think it's my fault the fence came down."

"Hang on," Noah said gently. "He's not saying that, are you Melvin?"

Was there a warning in his tone? It was subtle enough I may have imagined it.

"Course not, boss. Just saying there must have been some flaw in the repair. Maybe it was the materials."

I heard him loud and clear: the newbie had failed.

"I'll go right now and fix it." I tossed the brush I'd been holding back in the bucket.

"No, no." Melvin's voice was silky. "You're learning other skills today. Ole and I will do the repair as soon as I take care of some bills."

"Thanks, kindly," Noah said, as if he hadn't heard anything untoward.

I stared lasers into Melvin's back as he made his way up to the lodge.

"Come on, Eugenia. Full day ahead."

"The fence was strong, Noah. You checked my work."

"Let it go, Eugenia."

But I knew what he was thinking: I'd screwed up.

Noah passed me a halter, put his hand on my shoulder. "I mean it, Eugenia, let it go. Horses can tell if your mind is elsewhere."

He removed his hand and I took a deep breath. "Okay."

Moving slowly, I entered one pen while Noah slipped through the bars of another. Soon the only horses left were ones already weaned from their mothers and too wary to let us get close. A blue roan stood on his own in one pen, while a dozen others, including Red, were in another. Noah approached the blue roan. A white number 132 was freeze-branded on his left shoulder.

"We mostly just leave them alone until they're two," Noah said. "This fella is three, which means he began his education last year."

"Want me to help with anything?"

"For now, just watch. See his ears?" The horse wasn't looking at Noah, but its closest ear followed him as he came near. "And his eye?"

"Looks worried."

"He's not too sure about this. He kind of remembers, but he's spent the winter in the mountains just looking to survive. He's ready to move if he needs to."

When the horse turned his head toward him, Noah pivoted and walked away. "As a reward for looking at me, I took the pressure off by walking away."

He repeated the exercise, but this time when the horse looked at him, instead of walking away, Noah stood and fiddled with the halter he was holding, as if he were there minding his own business, nothing to see, nothing to see. The horse dropped his head to the ground, sniffed, as if he wasn't watching either.

The next time Noah approached the horse its eyes looked calm. He walked all the way up and rubbed its neck. After an initial flinch, the horse relaxed and Noah fastened the halter.

"Guess he remembers," I said.

Noah rubbed the horse all over his neck, then his nose, and then moved on to his body. After a while the horse stopped flinching and sighed. Noah ran his hands down a front leg, and the horse picked up his foot. "He's really remembering now."

The horse gave Noah a playful shove with its nose. Gently, but firmly, Noah put his hand on the horse's nose and pushed until it stepped backward. "He was testing me with that shove. It was his way of saying he's the boss of me. He tried to move my feet—that's what horses do to each other. Instead, I made him move his feet."

"You made him respect you."

"Me and my space. Every herd has its pecking order. This horse and I make a herd of two. If he doesn't respect me, he won't listen to me."

Noah made horse-gentling sound like the most natural thing in the world. I was so completely drawn in that I jumped when Merry appeared with a note.

He read it. "One of those occasional guests I mentioned," he said to me. "Writer from Winnipeg."

"Anyone famous?"

He shrugged. "Anita Daher."

"Never heard of her, but I don't read much."

"I told her you'd get back to her about dates," Merry said.

"Sounds good. How long until lunch?"

"Any time you're ready."

Noah handed me the lead line. "Set him loose and come up for a bite."

I breathed deep as Noah and Merry left me, gazed out at the wide meadows, the woodlands and the encircling mountains. The horse next to me pawed the ground.

"Getting bored, buddy?" I led him through the big gate to the clearing. As I lifted my hand to unknot the halter, he flinched. I'd moved too fast. I tried again, slower, like Noah had. No flinch. Ears forward, his attention was locked on his herd. I slipped off the halter, watched him trot away.

With everyone else gone someplace else, Heather had scheduled our first one-on-one in place of the usual afternoon group session. While she searched through a file cabinet, I watched curtain edges rustle at a touch of breeze through the open window, wished myself a bird that could fly up, out and away, anywhere but in this office talking about stuff that either didn't matter or was best left alone.

I thought back to the sessions forced upon me after my father died. The couch had been huge, or maybe it only seemed that way. The memory of yellow walls with an alphabet border was stuck in my mind like shitballs on a cat's ass. The couch had been scratchy, covered with looped nylon fabric, like the kind you see in old people's basements. I'd kept my hands tucked under my knees, pulled at the loops with my small fingers. The man in the room, a child psychologist named Dr. Boom, must have been used to that, as every time I came back the snags had been trimmed away.

"How're you settling in?" Heather asked. Instead of tucking herself behind the desk she chose a wide-armed chair in another part of the room, motioned for me to take the sofa. It was firm, blue. A box of tissues sat within easy reach on the small table in between.

"People use those?"

"Sometimes."

I nodded and wondered who. She'd never tell. "Settling okay, I guess. Sore from all the work."

"It is hard work."

I had my guard up. It was a physical thing, like extra starch in my back. This was different from Group. She wanted to get inside my head. She had to. It was her job.

Heather tilted her head. "Is this weird? Talking this way?"

"Kind of. You do a lot of this? Sorry, of course you do. Dumb question."

"It isn't at all."

"Sorry."

"Why are you apologizing, Eugenia?"

"Sor—I mean, I don't know. I think I'm nervous."

"Any idea why that might be? We've known each other a few days, and I think we like each other."

"It's just that this," I motioned between us, "brings back some stuff I don't like thinking about." I told her about Dr. Boom. She probably already knew.

"A difficult time, but did those sessions help?"

"I mean, I was eight. I mostly remember that I hated it."

She nodded slowly, scratched something in her notebook.

"He did that too. I hated that a lot."

She smiled. "My turn to apologize, then. Not for making the notes, because I won't stop. I'm sorry it makes you uncomfortable, but if I don't make notes I might forget something important. I might ask you the same questions over and over again, which would get pretty annoying."

"We had a neighbour who did that. She'd ask me something and I'd answer. Five minutes later she'd ask me the same thing again." I frowned. "We used to make fun of her, but now I wonder if she had Alzheimer's or something. She was pretty old."

"I can show you what I write."

She turned the notebook so I could see. It was exactly what I'd told her, but in short form. No big insights into my psyche, no statements about control issues or anything like that.

"Better?"

"Maybe. I don't know. Not really." I thought about it. "Inside my body right now it feels like what Noah showed me with the horses. They spend the winter free range in the mountains, always ready to run, and when they get here, they're still ready to run until they get used to things, figure out it's okay."

"You're ready to run?"

"No. But that's what it feels like."

"Your reaction is natural."

"I'm not a horse."

"You're uncertain what might happen, despite your experience when you were eight. Your instinct is to protect yourself."

I shrugged.

"We all feel anxious sometimes, Eugenia. It can be a good thing if we're walking alone late at night or driving in traffic. We need to be aware and alert for danger in order to stay safe."

I looked around the room. "I don't have a car."

"Other times we feel tense even after our brain tells us it's okay, the danger has passed. That's what we'd like to diminish. What do you do to relax in those situations? Have any techniques? Deep breathing? Visualization?"

I snorted. "I drink."

She didn't miss a beat. "You feel like drinking now?" No shock, not even a scolding look.

"Couldn't if I wanted to."

"Do you?"

"Maybe. What does it matter, what I want?"

"It matters."

I folded my arms. "I want to go home."

This time, an admonishing eyebrow.

"Fine." I uncrossed my arms. "I haven't actually thought about drinking until now. Too busy working." I leaned back, took one of those deep breaths. "When I got here, I thought Noah was one of those backwoods rednecks that believed women belonged in the kitchen." Heather chuckled. "No offence about the kitchen work."

"None taken."

"Anyway, that changed pretty quick. You ever do any of the outside work? Mucking pens and herding and stuff?"

"Not yet. I'm a city girl through and through. Before coming here, the closest I'd been to a horse was when someone rode down main street while I was stopped at a red light."

"In Fort St. Luke?"

"Maybe he thought it was a parade day."

There was only one person I knew of that rode through town. Most people drove pickups or quads. "Big, black horse? Hairy feet?"

She looked surprised. "How did you know?"

I grinned. "That's old Mr. Wuzik. Me and my brothers used to work out at his ranch. Well, my brothers did. The cops took his license away a couple of years ago, so he rides in sometimes to pick up his prescriptions."

Something weird happened then. It was like I was sucked out of the room through time and space and transplanted into Mr. Wuzik's living room, drinking sweet tea and eating crumbly cake. I could smell the cake, warm and buttery. My brothers looked too big for the room and their smiles were even bigger. We were all laughing, I don't know why.

"Sounds like a character," Heather said.

"I guess."

We sat quiet then and I wondered how much she could see of the memories wafting beneath my skin.

"I think I'm done for today. That okay?"

She nodded and said something about relaxation and coping strategies for stress, but all I heard were echoes of my brothers and better days.

CHAPTER TWELVE

After my session I wanted to work, to sweat off a mix of happy and melancholic emotions that would have been better left unstirred.

Noah was in the pens working the horses, this time with Melvin, who met my return with an annoyed expression, gone in a blink and replaced with something neutral.

It was possible that I had messed up with the fence, but he didn't have to be so two-faced about it. I hated it when people said one thing but implied something else in such a way you couldn't even bring it up without looking like a jerk.

The red horse, my nemesis from the day before, jogged along the far side of the pen, nostrils flared, tail high. He was fire from the inside out, and I couldn't look away.

"Why don't you start with him?" Noah suggested. "See the brand? It's from last year when he was two. That means he's had some work on him, just needs a refresher."

"No sweat then." Noah had made it look easy. Now it was my turn. "Let's do this, Red."

I walked toward him and he moved off. Fine, I expected that.

From outside the pen, Noah watched but offered no comment.

"Time to change the pattern," I mumbled. At the center of the pen, I intersected Red's path and turned so that he was suddenly moving toward me. Red stopped short, swung his head. "Weren't expecting that, were you?" I turned my body, took the pressure off. After a moment, Red sighed and looked away.

Blow me down. This crap really worked.

My pulse quickened as I readied the halter and moved two steps closer. Red held his ground. One step closer, I lifted the halter. Red snorted, turned his back to me.

His body language was clear. If Red had a middle finger, it would be raised sky high.

My first impulse was to throw the damn halter as far away as it would go. Instead I sidestepped around his kicking zone and touched his side. He flinched but stayed put. It didn't last. As if slapped, the horse bolted, and I was spitting dirt.

I repeated the process. "Come on, buddy. Let's get this done."

After a third try, Red finally let me touch his neck. I walked away, rewarding him by removing pressure.

Noah and Melvin were in the next pen working two unbranded horses, smaller than Red. I leaned against the fencing to watch.

"You're doing well," Melvin said.

He looked like he meant it. People were way more complicated than horses.

This time when I returned to Red, he let me slip on the halter.

"Coming to dinner?" Noah asked.

I looked around, saw the other horses were already back with their herds. Somehow, I'd missed the passage of time.

"Not quite finished here."

"We'll save you a plate."

Obvious much? Noah was showing me he trusted me alone with this horse: today's big lesson in the re-education and rehabilitation of the prisoner known as Eugenia Grimm, aka *slider*. Faith was Noah's modus operandi. Big mistake. In time, I'd let him down. Faith meant you had something to live up to. It was both a challenge and a trap.

Red no longer minded my rubbing around his neck and head, even leaned into me. Something warm flickered in the general area of my heart, spread as I scratched behind Red's ears, smoothed the sweat-damp hair under his forelock. His eyes drooped like a little kid gone sleepy.

Another memory, vivid, like before. I was five or maybe six, sick in bed, and Pops wiped my forehead with a cool cloth. It was the best feeling in the world.

Something hard built in my throat. I wrapped my arms around Red's neck, pressed my cheek against him. After a minute, he lowered his head, rested his chin on my shoulder like he was hugging me back.

Red jerked his head up and snorted. A hint of sound grew into a tinkle of horse bells and a string of horses emerged from the forest trail. It was Tammy, Frankie, and Nathan back from Crooked Camp.

A minute later, another string appeared from over the hill—Hayden and the boys.

The gang's all here.

Tammy cursed under her breath as she strode past and was spitting vinegar by the time she reached Noah and Melvin, who'd come down from the lodge to help unload. "Someone's messing with me."

"Come on." Frankie grabbed my hand, pulled me toward the lodge. Nathan sprinted past, muttering about needing the biffy.

"Tammy's not happy."

"And that's unusual, how?" Her eyes sparkled with the same hue as the late afternoon sky. "Someone left Tammy a special gift up at Crooked Camp."

"What kind of gift?"

"She knew something was up when she saw the pen swept smooth. Unnatural smooth like someone was trying to hide their tracks. Inside, set in the middle of the table and as pretty as you please, her coffee mug."

"That's bad?"

"Special one shaped like a horse's ass." She grinned. "Special to her anyway. Said she lost it a few years back, always blamed it on a pre-program wrangler named Jack."

"Why?"

She shrugged. "Tammy talks about him sometimes as a bad example. They didn't get along."

"A slider?"

"The original."

"Long time to hold a grudge. Or care about a cup."

"This is Tammy we're talking about."

I grinned. "Right."

Frankie leaned in like she was about to say more, but Merry stepped out on the deck, cupped her hands and shouted that dinner was still on the table for any who wanted it.

CHAPTER THIRTEEN

An overnight storm turned paths into rivers, rattled windows and carried anything not well battened into the clearing in front of the lodge. Usual chores were put on hold, and after breakfast it was all-hands-on-deck retrieving boxes, a barrel, errant cups that had been left outside, a few soggy towels and other odds and sods.

I leaned against the porch, mopped my brow as Nathan and Frankie drove up in a quad, flatbed hitched behind. Mid-morning heat rose moist with a heady scent of Labrador tea mixed with swamp weed, and just a hint of dog piss. Oblivious, Copper snoozed by the door. With eyes closed he thumped his tail. "Hop on, Eugenia!" Nathan called. "We got trails to clear."

"Can I grab a drink first?"

"Gotcha covered." Frankie grinned and tossed me a flask.

"Whiskey?"

Frankie snorted. "Lemonade."

"That'll do." A lie. I'd told Heather that I hadn't even thought about drinking, but since our session I'd thought of nothing but. I'd been here six days. No whiskey, nor beer, which I missed even more—especially on a morning hot as this one. Could be this forced dry-out was good thing. Addiction wasn't part of my life plan. Not that I'd actually made life plans, but when I did, it wouldn't be that.

I climbed onto the trailer and we bumped down to the shed. After loading up on assorted implements, we started up the path that led to Crooked Camp, while Rick and Jimmy rode toward Far Camp. The way they were messing about, they wouldn't get far, not that it was a competition or anything. Our guides/guards assured us they'd be by on horseback every half hour or so, make sure we weren't up to no good. Meanwhile, they'd count horses, search for strays.

Clad in thick, cowhide gloves, we fell into a rhythm, took turns driving the quad and walking beside, tossing loose and broken branches onto the trailer. We hauled debris back for burning in the firepit, but as we got farther away, we dumped it in clear spaces away from the path. "Let nature take care of it," Nathan said.

The banter was mostly light. When Nathan fell backward trying to heft a particularly stubborn branch, Frankie put on a Nova Scotia accent. "Too much for ya, b'y?"

"Ya'll are gonna to be sorry ya'll mocked me," Nathan mocked right back.

Frankie laughed while I offered Nathan a hand back up.

"Thanks, buddy."

"You're welcome buddy," I said.

Frankie thought this was hilarious.

With the sun high and my back soaked with sweat, my stomach rolled out a complaint loud as a ten-pin bowling ball down a hardwood gutter. Nathan and Frankie looked at me as if I'd shouted. "So I need fuel. That make me soft?"

Frankie grinned. "That makes you timekeeper." She glanced at her watch. "Let's take a break."

The creek we'd stopped at burbled cool and bright where sunlight filtered through the canopy. Nathan opened a zipped backpack, retrieved wax-wrapped sandwiches and three short thermoses filled with sweet tea.

I peeled back the paper. "Peanut butter and banana."

"You allergic?" Nathan asked. "There's tuna in there too."

"No, it's good. Reminds me of when I was a kid."

Frankie crumpled her wrapper, stored it in the backpack. "Never grow out of the good stuff."

"That an order or an observation?"

"Definitely an order," Nathan said. "Haven't you noticed how bossy she is?"

"Definitely an observation, you doofus." Frankie pulled a mossy clump from the forest floor and tossed it at Nathan. "Or maybe it's a wisdom. It's like, I don't know, jello or making a snowman."

"Does anyone really ever grow up, or do our snow forts just get better?" Nathan asked.

"You're encouraging her now?" I asked.

My turn to be pelted by moss.

"If you like something why do you have to give it up just because someone expects you to?" Frankie continued.

"Like knocking over liquor stores?" I tried but failed miserably at keeping a straight face. "Jeez, you guys, I'm joking! You should see how you're looking at me."

Nathan frowned. "We don't actually know why you're here, Genie."

Frankie gave him a look. "We usually don't talk about our pasts outside of Group."

Nathan gave her a look right back. "It's not a rule."

Frankie considered this.

"Noah must have said something about me though."

"Nope," Frankie said. "Just that you were mostly a good person in a bad situation."

"Mostly?"

"Maybe he didn't say mostly."

"It's what he said about me too," Nathan said.

We munched sandwiches while water tumbled over stone, adding melody to the thrum of a breeze pushing through treetops. A pulse started in my head, like a tattoo. The desire to talk, to *share*, bubbled past my natural inclination to push it back down. “You wanna know? Don’t have to wait for Group.”

“You wanna tell?” Frankie asked. “You don’t have to.”

“It’s just that I shouldn’t even be here.” Birds twittered, a blackfly buzzed near my ear. I slapped at it. “I’m not talking about being arrested. I guess I had that coming, probably for a while. Everyone thinks I’m better than I really am and so they give me chances.” I hesitated. It wasn’t like me to open up like this, but it felt okay. Natural. “I steal and I hurt people and truth is, I like it. When I’m getting crazy everything in my past goes away and I feel more in the moment than I ever do otherwise.” I shrugged. “This is me. I’m not going to change just ‘cause I’m here. I don’t want to change.”

“Is that what this is about for you?” Frankie asked. “Changing?”

“Isn’t it for you?”

Frankie tossed a pebble. “I’m sure it’s what they hope. But maybe it’s just a chance to take a breath. See something other than our miserable lives.” She sounded melancholy.

“Maybe I shouldn’t have said anything.”

“You trusted us, Eugenia. Nothing wrong with that.”

“No judgement here,” Nathan added.

Except I hadn’t told everything. “Hey, we all got something, right?”

“We do,” Frankie said. “It’s your life. It’s all of our lives. They can’t tell us what to do forever. What is it you want?”

This was too somber for comfort. “Another sandwich,” I joked. “Another PB and B if you got one.”

Frankie flashed a grin, reached into the pack. “Tuna. Take it or leave it.”

"I'll take it."

"I'll have one too," Nathan said.

"What am I, your servant?" Frankie tossed him the pack. "Get it yourself."

Nathan feigned the pack being heavy and fell backward, except he must have forgot the creek was there. He sprang back up out of the water with a shriek. Thankfully he'd had the wherewithal to hold the pack high and dry.

We laughed so hard my belly hurt. Frankie pulled a cloth from the back of the quad and touched it to Nathan's sopping forehead, still chuckling. Her touch seemed tender. What would it feel like to have someone touch me like that? No one ever had. Least, not since I was a kid.

Cut that out, Eugenia.

Still.

After lunch we packed up, readied to get back to the day's work. In the mud by the creek, I spotted animal tracks: paw prints showing a fat back pad and teardrop toes, narrow claw marks barely visible.

Nathan came up behind me. "Whatcha lookin' at?" I pointed and he bent close. "Looks like a mountain lion. Fresh."

Frankie searched the bush then called out, "Here's its scat."

Showing as much sense as a goose bedding down in a foxhole, we poked around further. I spotted an animal foreleg half hidden under a shrub. By its colour, size, and split hoof I guessed it was a deer, though much of the fur and flesh had been torn away.

Unease stirred in shadows, whispered through rustling leaves. I looked around for a guide. "Either of you gotta gun?" I knew the rules, but we were in the wildest of wilds, a long way from fields of cows or corner donut stores.

"Yeah, right," Frankie said. "Anyway, cougars are mostly shy. Good to tell Noah, though."

"Should we be worried?"

"Probably not," Nathan said. "But if you hear a baby crying in the treetops, don't look up."

"A baby?"

"The sound it makes to get you to expose your throat."

I couldn't tell if he was kidding.

CHAPTER FOURTEEN

"You've got five minutes, slider."

Tammy's mood hadn't improved since her return from Crooked Camp. It was a good bet she'd wolfed down her breakfast extra fast just to make me look slow. "Name's Eugenia," I growled, setting my coffee mug beside my plate. "Try it out."

Tammy narrowed her eyes. "Until I tell you otherwise, your name is dirt." If Noah or any of the others took issue with the way she spoke to me, I couldn't tell.

I clamped my mouth shut, scraped what was left of my breakfast into the trash, and followed Tammy outside.

At the shed she motioned for me to pick up a shovel, then led me beyond the bunkhouses to a flat space cleared of rock and shrubs not far from a weathered outhouse. "Start digging."

It had to be said: "What, my own grave?"

"We need a new outdoor crapper, and since you're such a shit I figure you're well suited. Dig a hole three feet deep, two feet square. When you're done we'll move the box from the old hole to the new one."

"There are two bathrooms inside the lodge. Why do we need an outhouse?"

The fires of hell gathered beneath Tammy's skin.

"Fine," I said. "No problem."

It was like she wanted me to take a swing at her, was pushing for it. Tempting, but I had no intention of getting booted. I would hold tight to days like yesterday, hanging out with Nathan and Frankie.

A break from my miserable life.

With a final glower she left me to my task. I imagined clocking her a good one, took the daydream a step further and saw her face shatter into a million pieces, like it was made of glass. Fuelled by anger, I placed boot on shovel and pushed. Time turned irrelevant, each moment marked with a satisfying stab and heave. I didn't notice Tammy's return until she opened her stinking pie-hole of a mouth. "Where'd you learn to use a shovel?" she snarled. "A two-year-old knows to put her back into it. What kind of soft life you been livin'?"

I felt heat rise up on my neck but kept digging. "Not soft."

Tammy walked away, cursing under her breath.

She knew nothing about me. No one did, not the truth of me. What I told Nathan and Frankie didn't even scratch the edge of it.

Dark thoughts lodged deep, simmered and stewed. Finally, the hole dug. I set the shovel aside, pulled myself out, and fell back against the freshly piled soil.

"Think you're finished?" Mid-morning sun radiated from behind Tammy's hat and made her appear faceless. Her words came from nothingness.

Painfully, I stood, brushed myself off. "Yes."

"I think you miscalculated."

"Two feet wide, three feet deep. That's what you said."

"Keep digging."

I muttered into my shirt collar, "I hope you die in the woods and that ravens pick out your eyeballs."

Tammy pushed her face close to mine. "What was that, slider?"

Mouth clamped, I took a step back.

Under Tammy's hateful watch I dug another half-foot deep. This time she grunted satisfaction. We sunk a prepared casing and moved the box over the hole, Tammy driving a Caterpillar tractor, me on the ground.

Finished. Hallelujah!

"I need a shower."

"That'll wait. Generator's down. Without the generator there's no water pump, and there's cooking and washing to be done."

"I'm not a mechanic."

"You got beans for brains?" She pointed to a flatbed loaded with five-gallon pails. "Noah will look after the generator. You bring the cooks what they need, then fill the troughs for the horses."

"The horses can drink from the creek."

Tammy's eyes bulged.

I threw my hands in the air. "Fine!"

After hooking the trailer to a quad, I climbed aboard and aimed for the creek, then immediately hit the brake as Tammy stepped in front. A shame my reflexes were so good.

"What kind of witless, scum-of-crow flesh-bags are they hatching in town these days? You're not going to get clean water from this part of the creek. Go farther up or get it from the river!"

My self-restraint deserved a gold medal. I hit reverse and chose the river.

There was something about the Rubicon, the sound, and earthy smell of moss and damp soil, that slowed my pulse, took me someplace else. I read somewhere that water symbolized rebirth, like a baptism. Whether or not you were into all that Jesus stuff, from the beginning of time folks had emerged from water transformed in spirit. Body too, if you considered walking fish and swamp creatures from those old horror movies.

I breathed deep.

Time to move my ass lest Tammy decided it needed kicking.

One by one I filled the five-gallon containers. Grunting under the weight, I placed each on the flatbed then made my way back to the lodge.

"Thanks, Eugenia," Merry said as I set them on the porch. "This should do us until Noah gets the generator back up and running. Shouldn't be long."

"Good, 'cause I really need a shower."

At the pens I filled the troughs, then paused to watch Rick as he worked a two-year-old. Envy twisted my gut. Horse training was way more fun than digging pits and hauling water.

"Slider!"

"Crap."

Kicking the quad back in gear, I returned to the lodge where Tammy waited. She motioned for me to follow, which I did, keeping the quad at a crawl as she walked behind the bunkhouses, past the new privy, and finally arrived at a pile of neatly stacked logs.

"Seriously? I've been working non-stop all morning. Don't I get a break?"

"You'll break when I tell you, slider."

But not on the inside. No way in hell. I focussed on keeping my pulse slow and steady, felt the earth beneath my feet. "You want me to turn this into firewood?"

"No, slider. You're going to skin these so we can use them to build a new woodshed. You think we'd burn fine, straight lumber like this? I feel bad for your mother, turning out a shit-for-brains kid like you."

"Enough!" I shouted. "I'm not a damn slider!" I pressed my knuckles hard into my sides as a reminder not to use them. "I worked hard today, and I'm done. You can take your woodpile and your bad attitude and go straight to hell."

Tammy didn't appear inclined to go to hell nor anywhere else as she continued, "We'll put up the shed in a day or two. You want a break? Fine."

I felt my mouth drop open.

"You can do this now, or after Group, but the sooner you finish the sooner I'm through with you."

"Through?"

"You burned through my list a lot faster than I thought you would." She tipped up her hat. "You're a good worker."

If there'd been any kind of wind, I'd have been knocked on my ass.

"Close your mouth unless you wanna catch flies," she gruffed, and left me to it.

I looked at the pile, decided I may as well get 'er done.

When the lunch bell sounded, I was halfway through. Merry brought me a glass of cool lemonade and a sandwich I swallowed in three bites. Finally, an hour later and twenty years closer to my grave, I dragged myself back up to the lodge.

As I collapsed into a tall chair at the kitchen island, Heather brought more lemonade and a cool, damp cloth. "Group in fifteen," she reminded me. "Generator's back up, if you want a shower."

"Thanks," I croaked. I drained two glasses of lemonade, held the cloth to my face, then pressed it against fresh blisters. I didn't even feel the sting. In fact, I felt pretty good.

Tammy was an ass, but I'd impressed her. How about that? Burned through her list, she'd said.

"After Group, join me at the pens," Noah called from the doorway.

I stared at him blankly, no gas left in my tank, certainly not enough to wrangle horses. Nodded anyway.

After a shower I felt somewhat restored, if semi-boiled. I pulled on a fresh shirt and joined Heather and the others in the Great Room.

"Ah, here she is," Heather said.

"Sorry I'm late."

Nathan grinned big. "We appreciates your washing the stink off."

"Heard you had a shitty job," Rick added.

"Not as shitty as your shorts," I quipped.

Jimmy guffawed and punched Rick in the shoulder.

"Seriously, does anyone else notice a theme here? I sense a fondness for conversations about shit."

Rick elbowed Jimmy. "Did she just say fondness?"

"Nah, she's too cowboy for that."

I grinned.

"Our conversations aren't always so shitty, I promise," Heather said, and everyone cracked up. "Rick was just talking about whether he wanted to go back to ranch work after this."

I sunk into a pile of floor pillows in the corner as Rick looked to his hands as if checking to see if they were clean. I saw him take a breath. "I don't know how we'd tell Pa if I don't go back. I'd be letting him down. Jimmy too."

If Jimmy had something to say, he kept it buttoned.

"This isn't about your father, nor Jimmy."

"I know."

Heather looked at Jimmy. "I'm sure you have some thoughts on this, Jimmy."

Jimmy looked serious. "They can wait."

"Is there a reason you don't feel comfortable sharing your thoughts with the group?" Heather asked Jimmy.

"It's not that. I just don't want him to stop talking." Jimmy looked at his brother. "I notice that sometimes. If you're talking about something and I say something different, it's like you change your mind. That makes me think I'm stopping you from saying what you really want to."

Rick looked from his brother down to his hands, loosely clasped between his knees. "I'm not saying I won't go back. I just want it to be my choice, you know?" He looked at his brother. "You're right, I change what I'm saying sometimes. I don't know why."

Heather looked to the rest of us. "Would anyone like to comment?"

"That's always the problem, right?" I surprised myself by speaking. "Sorry, I mean I don't really know you or anything."

All eyes on me. *Crap.*

"Eugenia," Heather said. "You don't need to apologize if you want to say something."

"I know, sorry." I laughed. "Yeah, I'm going to stop that now, okay?" No one laughed with me. Maybe everyone was nervous at first. Frankie reached over, rubbed a small circle on my back. I tried again. "I just wanted to tell Rick I know how he feels. About expectations. Feeling like you don't have a choice is like being stuck in a box and having it taped up tight. Maybe you like the box and maybe you don't, but you can't know if it's not your own choice to stay in or get out."

"Free will," Nathan said, nodding.

Rick looked thoughtful.

I'd surprised myself, not only that I spoke, but with the words that came out of me. I hated expectations, that was nothing new, but it dawned on me that the things that usually bugged me most, about how to be a sister, a good student, the daughter of parents, one dead and one gone, were eased here. I was just another criminal and way outside of the box I'd lived in back home. *Careful, Eugenia. You're not supposed to like this place.* But maybe I did. A little.

"Thanks, Eugenia," Heather said.

"Yeah, that's good," Rick said. "I'll think about that."

I felt my cheeks flush a little, but it was a nice feeling. Warm on the inside.

"Not to change the subject," Jimmy said, "but can we talk about our campout?"

"Campout?" Nathan asked.

"How'd you hear about that?" Heather asked Jimmy.

"I heard you and Merry talking,"

Heather smiled, her eyes twinkling. "Something new we've been planning. In about two weeks, weather allowing, you'll each be dropped at a spot on a lake for 24 hours solo camping. Noah will give you all the details once we've worked them out."

I whistled. "Sounds pretty outside the box to me."

The rest of the session dissolved into excited chatter.

CHAPTER FIFTEEN

Noah had two horses saddled and ready to go places.

"We're riding?"

"To the Wendy."

If my body had a choice it would have locked in place. I was sore from yesterday's digging, and the idea of bouncing around every ache didn't appeal. However, riding with Noah was a hall pass from morning chores.

My lower back burned as I mounted Packman, nudged him to follow Noah, who rode a spirited, black gelding named Spit. My fingers were so stiff I could barely grasp the reins.

Wild strawberries infused sweetness into the beat-down of morning heat as we rode toward a wall of lodgepole pine just beyond the meadow. The Navajo buzzed on takeoff, climbed skyward. In the clearing, horses grazed, popped up heads as we passed. I spotted Red in the centre of a small herd.

"Keep your eyes peeled," Noah said as we settled single file into an easy amble along the path. "We're still missing three horses."

"You think they're up at the Wendy."

"Maybe."

"How long are we riding?"

"You in a hurry to dig more holes?"

I grinned. "My body is so sore and slow I feel like my limbs are made of lead. If Packman bolts, I'm gonna eat dirt."

"He won't. Long as you don't point him into a hornet's nest."

"Tammy this hard on everyone, or does she have it in for me?"

"She's tough, but fair."

"More like heartless and mean."

As we rode out the gate, Noah tipped his hat at Melvin, who waved on his way into the lodge. "Sometimes people feel things more deeply than they let on, and some people have reason for being tough, even if they don't share it."

"We still talking about the same sharp-mouthed banshee named Tammy?"

Noah slowed and fell in beside me. "Meanness is different from tough, Eugenia. Mean is shallow. Just think on that."

"You think I'm being mean?"

"I'm not saying that. Besides, it's more important what you think of yourself. A wise woman once said that if you can look yourself in the mirror each morning and like what you see, you're doing okay."

"What wise woman?"

"Tammy."

I rolled my eyes. "This feels like one of Heather's one-on-ones."

"The whole program is a one-on-one, Eugenia. Remember why you're here. The mountains have a way of making you see things differently. If you want to change your path, this may be the place to do it. But only if you let it. It's your choice." He clucked Spit into a trot over a flat grassy stretch. "It's always your choice."

There was no pressure, nor admonishment in his tone. Noah treated people the same way he did horses.

Packman matched Spit's pace without my asking. My body screamed with every jolt until finally we slowed back to a walk and conversation resumed.

"Answer me one thing, Noah. Why does Tammy call me slider? Frankie and Nathan said she calls everyone that at first, but it's like she has it in for me."

Noah looked hesitant. "We had someone work here a few years back. He had an attitude. Tammy figured he was looking for an easy ride and called him slider."

"This isn't easy."

"He learned that quick enough."

Pops used to say that hard work never killed a person, and I knew that to be true. It was sitting around that could do real damage.

"What did he do to piss Tammy off so bad?"

"Jackson wasn't a good fit."

My head jerked up. The air shifted. "Wait. Jackson?"

"Yeah."

"I have a brother Jackson."

"That's right."

"My brother was here?"

"Yes."

Three summers ago, Jackson disappeared. It was the first time he'd taken off for more than a few days, and I took it hard. When he got back one month later, he didn't say where he'd been, but after that he was drunk or hungover most every time we saw him, which was less and less often. That's about when I started saying what the hell and Luda and I took to hanging out by the liquor mart waiting for someone to pull beer for us. Then Luda got big and we didn't need anyone else.

"So Jackson is the Jack I heard about. From before you started this program."

"It's how he introduced himself to the others. Figured that was what he went by now."

"What do you mean, *now*? You knew him from town? Before you hired him?"

He nodded.

"Why didn't Tammy like him?" The Jackson I knew, the one I remembered best, was a likeable guy. Easy laugh. Joy in everyday moments.

Memories of shoulder rides when I was little, reaching for pinecones and stars.

That was probably the reason. Next to Jackson, Tammy must have felt like her inner gargoyle was constantly on display.

"He didn't agree with the way Tammy worked the horses. Said she took too long over things."

"So it was Jackson who picked the fight." That I could see. "Taking a long time doesn't sound like Tammy."

"The woman is a hard worker, but she knows when to go slow. Some horses learn quicker than others. People too, I guess. One night, Tammy found Jackson in the pens working a young stud. The horse had bloody sores on his sides from misuse of spurs."

A moving image of torn and bloody flesh, a screaming horse, jumped into my mind. "No. He wouldn't do that." Not my brother. Not Jackson.

"He'd also tied him to a post with a long lead, forced him to run circles around it."

"Why?"

"Thought it would teach the colt to stop pulling on the rope. When Tammy got there, Jackson was shouting and looking like he was ready to do worse. Horses don't understand anger."

"Jackson wasn't like that."

"He had issues. You don't need me to tell you that."

I breathed deep, let the mountain air centre me. "I guess not."

"In the end he and Tammy agreed that he didn't belong here. Last I heard he found more trouble back in town. The legal kind."

"I saw him at the courthouse."

"Sorry to hear that."

The path opened wide into a gentle slope thick with knee-high flowers of yellow and purple, white and blue. We waded through, side by side, the hum of fast firing insect wings near deafening. Packman swiped bites of greenery as we went, grunting as he chewed. At the top of the slope we moved back into single file as the forest crowded in to reclaim the path. The scent of wild rose was strong. More climbing, then the path widened into another broad clearing, circled by grassy slopes rising like undulating velvet into mountains. There were elk the size of gophers halfway up the sides. This place played tricks with your eyes.

Noah called a halt. We tied the horses to a tree, dismounted and drank from a clear, mountain stream.

"Is this the Wendy?"

"It is."

I never knew water could taste so sweet. Noah dunked his head while I sat on a fallen log, surrounded by plants I'd never seen nor imagined. A gentle breeze carried mingled scents of sun-warmed pine and jasmine. I fiddled with knobby mountain grass, absently pulling it apart as Noah turned his face toward the sun, leaned back on his elbows and closed his eyes.

"I'm sad things didn't work out for Jackson here. Of the three of us, Jackson always enjoyed ranch work the most. I mean, I would have liked it, but like I said, I was little."

"You tagged along."

"Mostly because my mother made them take me." I pulled up more grass, watched it fall between my fingers. "I wonder now if it was to get me out of the house, away from Pops when he was feeling down." I glanced at Noah. "He had depression. You know that from my file."

Noah sat back up straight, eyes dark.

"Jackson was like the opposite, of Pops and everyone else I knew. Always had a joke, always made life light and fun." I felt a pain in my head. "He read books with me, played with me in the yard, spun me around in airplane rides until I had no breath left. He'd tickle me until I wanted to pee or puke or both."

"Sounds fun."

"It was, because he was changing things up. He did that when I was sad or mad about something. He showed me that even when I was so mad I wanted to break or hurt or crush or blow up everything and everyone around me, it only takes a second to turn it all around." I wiped wetness from my eyes, took a breath. "I can't imagine Jackson doing that to that horse. I can't imagine him angry."

"People change."

I just couldn't see it. "The Jackson you knew from town, was it the brother I remember, or this other version of him?"

Sunlight and shadow danced about his face as he turned to me. "I knew him like I knew you."

"I don't understand."

"I remember all of you: I used to be a paramedic."

"I know. Melvin told me." A buzzing began in my fingertips and ran through my legs. "Be straight with me, Noah. All the way straight."

"The night your father died. I was there."

My head whirled as a memory of Pops came to me. *Sirens, flashing lights.* I felt my throat tighten.

"Okay" I swallowed, shook off my thoughts, pulled up another handful of grass, let it fall. "That's weird, but why didn't you tell me?"

"You were resistant when we met. I thought it might complicate things."

"How?"

"That night is hard to remember and even harder to talk about. I can't know how it is for you." But he did know, or he thought he did. I could see it in his face.

I shook my head. "I don't think about it."

"This is a good place to think, Eugenia."

Nope. Wasn't going there. Not now, not ever.

Noah nodded as if I'd spoken. "Didn't work out with your brother, but that's what got me thinking about how this place could be good for someone in trouble. Boyer told me about these Support and Supervision programs for young offenders, helped me set it up. He's the one you can thank for being here."

"I'll remember that next time I see him," I said dryly.

"When I saw you last winter, it wasn't rocket science to figure out that what happened that night sent you down a road you wouldn't otherwise have gone." He jerked a hand through his hair. "It's a tough memory, Eugenia. For me too. It was the look on you back then, in your whole body. There was such a weight on you. I wished I could take it away." He paused. "I don't imagine it helped any when your mother left."

There was pain in Noah's face, deep in the creases of it.

"Anything else?"

"No, that's it."

"Looks like there's more."

"We all have lives, Eugenia, histories we've learned from. Some people spend their lives trying to atone for those histories. Think on that. Think on the choices you make, the life you want to look back on."

"Sounds like Heather talk."

He chuckled and stood. "Come on. No horses here."

"Tell Tammy I'm not my brother, okay? Not like that, anyway."

"She knows that. Give her a chance, Eugenia. She's a good person once you know her." Noah offered me a hand up. I needed it. My body felt like it might break in two.

As someone once said, what didn't kill you made you stronger.

CHAPTER SIXTEEN

After three hours in a hot saddle behind Nathan's buckskin gelding Buttercup, Hayden on the lead on Brownie, I was ready for a break. My body wasn't as sore today but had not yet fully recovered. Damned if I would complain, though. I could stand my thighs cramping.

Shit.

Maybe not.

The hot tub, I now understood, was not a luxury, but a tool to keep us functioning.

My hard work and general acquiescence had earned me a day trip to Crooked Camp to paint a pen. How I would clamp my hands around a paintbrush I did not know, but I was confident I would work it out.

"Dismount," Hayden called, halting his horse.

"Yeehaw," I drawled. Nathan grinned.

All around us there were trees, grass, mountains, more or less what we'd been looking at the whole way. There was that one paper wasp nest hanging out of a tree that broke things up, but even that was beautiful in its own way. Breathtaking faded into the background after a while.

If we'd arrived at the camp, it was cleverly hidden. "We there?"

"Nearly," Hayden said. "First we have to get over this hill. Too steep to ride."

We dismounted and led our horses zigzag up a steep incline, then down the other side where we stepped over a narrow stream.

Nathan watched as I contemplated the stirrup and hoisting myself back up. "Ya can ride if ya wants, but it's just around the corner."

"That's what they all say."

He grinned and made a grand show of sweeping his arm for Packman and me to go ahead of him. Around the sunny side of a heavy-boughed pine, there is was. In a small clearing, a tidy collection of buildings nestled near the Rubicon.

"Crooked Camp," Hayden announced.

It looked as it had from the air, but with greater definition: green meadow, river the colour of wet slate edged with glistening white stone, all surrounded by blue misted mountains. Above, flat-bottomed clouds bunched upward like whipped cream piled too high.

After settling our horses in the pen, we made our way past a brick barbecue into the log cabin. A low deck encircled the building. It reminded me of the main lodge, but in miniature, and only one level. The inside was spacious, with four wood-framed couches for lounging, a fireplace, two dining tables with bench seats, and a large kitchen. Doors led to bunkrooms, and there was an indoor biffy with a composting toilet, which Hayden immediately excused himself to use.

"Not really roughing it," I said.

"Back when the place was open to hunters, Noah's uncle poured big money into the place. Got to spend in order to get, yeah?"

"I don't get why Noah changed it. Run out of goats to shoot?"

Nathan shrugged. "Lots of game here." He dropped his pack.

"Let's get to work," Hayden said, exiting the biffy.

We were meant to be back before dinner. Gallon cans of paint were stored and waiting in the shed behind the cabin. As we pulled out what we needed, Hayden pitched right in. His style was the opposite of Tammy's and more like Noah's in that he worked alongside his crew and left the barking to the dogs.

"Weather's changing," I said. The tops of the whipped cream clouds had begun to spread into storm anvils. "Should we wait to see if it's going to rain?"

"You our resident storm chaser?" Nathan teased.

"Nothing to worry about," Hayden said, but I wasn't convinced. He added, "Heather is making strawberry strudel for tonight, and no way I'm going to miss it."

"It's that good?"

We freshened the paint, gently pushing away the noses of curious geldings when they got too close. I swatted flies as they bit my neck and buzzed my sweaty ears. The cloud darkened, blotted out the blue. We were three quarters through our task when the first fat drop fell.

"Looks like I called it," I said.

"Few drops won't hurt." Nathan looked skyward as a second drop smacked him in the eye. "It's fast drying paint," he said with less confidence. The wind picked up and a gust sent his hat flying.

"Break time," Hayden called as Nathan chased his hat. "I could use a nap anyway."

Back inside, Hayden teased, "No parties," and headed for a bunk. Nathan and I pulled out packed sandwiches and brewed up a pot of coffee, which burped and steamed as the storm arrived in earnest. Rain punched against window glass in waves. I looked out at the horses huddled behind a lean-to.

"Glad I'm not a horse."

"Don't worry about them," Nathan said. "They're in the weather most of the year."

Except running free in the mountains they could shelter in the trees. I joined Nathan at the counter, helped myself to a sandwich. He looked glum. "We may not be back for that strudel."

I took a bite. Tuna. "There'll be some left."

"I guess. Not fresh."

"This wasn't in the forecast."

"Weather can change pretty sudden out here, and forecasts are hit and miss." He flopped onto one couch. I settled onto another, brushing breadcrumbs off my jeans.

We listened to the wind and the rain, watched lighting flash and listened for the crack.

"One Mississippi, two Mississippi ..." Nathan counted. "Sounds like it's right over top."

He had to be thinking of all that paint washing away. I know I was. Or maybe he was just thinking of strudel.

It was dark as night. From down the hall, Hayden let out a particularly loud series of snorts and snores. We snickered and Nathan lit the fireplace, giving the room a cozy feel. It felt good to be alone. I glanced at the open door to where Hayden slept. Almost alone.

For the first time I noticed the fullness of Nathan's lips, the curve of his jaw. He was a good-looking guy, and we were two, hot-blooded, hormonal teens. Hayden should have thought twice about leaving us alone.

Unless, like my brother, he assumed I was a lesbian.

A twittering warmth spread through me, and with shock I realized I was attracted. I'd made fun of those kind of feelings for so long, I never actually thought one would catch me. It felt kind of nice. Maybe I didn't want to fight it. Maybe I would just let myself feel, see what happened.

Nathan was no longer the annoying goofball with the big ears I'd first met. I tilted my head. Still had the big ears, but there was a whole lot more to this guy that was pleasing. His humour. His freckles. I even liked his ears. I licked my lips, imagined nibbling on them.

"You staring at me?" Nathan asked.

Or he could reject me, and it would all end awkward and awful. *Shut it down, Eugenia. Abort!*

I coughed. "I was just wondering about you." His eyebrows shot up. *Oh, God, please don't read my mind!* "I mean, what brought you up here. I know this isn't Group or anything." I was talking fast, my voice high. Totally transparent.

He looked amused. "That's okay. Not a rule."

"Right. Otherwise it would be written down."

It was his turn to stare. "Lots of things not written down," he said. "Ya just gotta figure it out."

My heart began thunking in my chest. Was he thinking what I was thinking? He held my gaze with an intensity I wasn't used to and I felt a fluttering again. This time it was nerves. We were totally on the same wavelength. Those lips …

He looked away, and I remembered to breathe.

"I quit school soon as I was old enough to work with my fadder in his store."

"He was okay with you quitting school? Sorry, that sounded judgy."

"It's fine."

"It's just that I never heard of a parent being okay with that."

Nathan shrugged.

"You said you weren't born in Nova Scotia."

He scratched his chin, as if deciding how to tell it. "That's right. Born in Maine, a village you never heard of near Bar Harbour." His voice went soft. "My mudder was sick. Bipolar disease. She didn't believe in medication and had a hard time getting a handle on it. When I was three, she sent me to live with my fadder until she felt better."

"Sorry, Nathan." My father had depression, not bipolar disorder, but it was still hard to live with. Especially for my mother. "Sorry you had to go through all that."

"Hey, it is what it is, right? She did get on her meds, but it took a few years and by then she didn't have the heart to take me away from my fadder. Anyway, his store wasn't doing too well, so last fall I moved west to work in the oil patch. Thought I'd take some of the pressure off him and earn a few bucks." His brow furrowed. "Didn't work out."

I waited, but he stayed quiet. "It's okay. You don't have to tell me." I shouldn't have asked.

"It's just that it still don't make any sense." He glanced at me and away so fast his eyes barely locked on, then took up the fire poker and moved around a log. "I told all this in Group before you got here. I was at a party, stole a truck, smashed it into the supervisor's shack."

"Got caught, got sent here," I finished gently.

"Except that I don't remember any of it."

"On something?"

"No. I mean maybe, but not intentional. They didn't find me right away. For five days I was walking around in the snow and I don't remember any of it." He looked at me again, his face twisted with anguish. "Five days! I keep thinking about that party and the stuff we passed around." He shook his head. "It seemed pretty regular. What would make me black out like that?"

His eyes were wide and seemingly without guile. But that first quick look made me wonder. Was he telling the truth?

I shrugged. "I mostly just drink, bit of weed, don't know about anything else. I blank out parts of stuff sometimes, but only for an hour or two. You think someone slipped you something?"

"That's what I'd like to think. I mean, my mudder, you know? What if I got some mental illness like her?"

"You get tested for drugs?"

"They didn't find anything, but after five days I'd probably pissed it out, hey?" His voice got quieter. "I talked to a psychiatrist."

"Psychiatrist say you were sick?"

"Inconclusive. I check in with Heather and chart my moods." He brightened. "The more I think on it, the more I'm sure someone slipped me something."

"I'm sure that's right." Maybe he was telling the truth. Drugs you could kick, if you were lucky. Mental illness was something you lived with. If you were lucky. He gave me a slow wide smile, and I felt another flutter. Nathan was definitely one of those people who grew on you.

"Anyway, that's why I'm here, even though they don't know for sure why I blacked out. Don't worry about it though."

"Not worried."

"Most people do when they're around someone with a mental illness, not that I'm sick, not for sure, but fear of the unknown and all that."

"Not so unknown to me. Depression, anyway. My dad had it before he died. Suicide."

"Ah, jeez. Sorry, Genie."

We sat quiet for a while, watching the logs shift and burn.

It was a comfortable silence. Nathan sounded far away when he spoke again. "My mudder has this saying she got from somewhere. She says, 'There are two things children should get from their parents: roots and wings.' We gotta make our own way, hey, Genie?"

"Goethe," I said.

"What's that, now?"

"Read it on a meme, so you know, might not really be him.He was a German philosopher, lived a couple of hundred years ago."

He chuckled. "You're a lot deeper than I thought."

"You too."

All this sharing was making my neck itch. I got up, wandered the room. No television, not even a computer. There was a shelf with books. I touched the spines.

"You can help me with this one, if you want." From his pack Nathan pulled the Louis L'Amour I'd found in the shed back at the ranch. "Looked interesting," he said. "And short."

"Help?"

"You heard me say I quit school, right?"

"You don't read?"

"I do, just not very well. Merry's helping me. Frankie too. Plan to write my GED this winter."

So that was what I'd seen through the shed window. Frankie was helping him read.

We settled at the table and I followed along as he read out loud. Every now and then he stumbled over a word. I waited for him to sound it out, and if he had difficulty, I helped.

"Storm's letting up," Nathan said.

I moved to the window. The cloud had brightened, the rain eased to the odd spit. "Hopefully it'll dry fast so we can redo the paint and still get back for strudel," I said.

"Now you're talkin'!"

A noisy yawn from the other room made us grin. Hayden was awake, stretching in the doorway. "I miss anything?"

A cursory survey out the front door suggested we still might miss that strudel. The storm had been fierce enough to pull open the gate. The horses were gone.

"They won't have gone far," Hayden said. "Not likely, anyhow." Above us the cloud was already breaking up and scattering. "Let's go have a look. Nathan, take the trees, I'll follow the river, and Eugenia, you head back up the trail a ways."

The humidity wasn't as oppressive as it had been before the storm, and the woods smelled green and cool. It was also bugger-wet, and I slipped in the mud twice before I found my feet. Beyond the piney boughs, I heard a nicker. At least, I thought I did. It could have been a squirrel, or a bird, or most anything. It hadn't been that loud. In search of the source, I crab-walked up a slope not far off the trail.

Definitely a nicker. There he was, in a clearing at the base of the slope, ears pointed my way, grazing with his buddies. At least they'd stuck together, plus they'd been joined by one more. One of the missing horses? "Found them!" I called out, then mumbled, "Stupid buggers," as I contemplated the slick and muddy slope before me.

One careful step, then another, I angled my body sideways, placed my boot heels on jutting stones, crushed pungent clumps of yarrow.

"Hup—nope!" I cried out as I twisted and slid on my ass all the way to the bottom.

"Great." I wiped muddy palms on now filthy jeans and reached for my hat. Movement made me shift my head. My blood turned ice.

It was a mountain lion.

A motherfucking cougar not three feet from where I sat, vulnerable.

She stared at me, yellow eyes rimmed thick with black, like the kohl you see on those hieroglyphs of Egyptian princes and princesses. Her tawny fur with its darker shadings down the sides of her nose and around the snow-white kiss of her mouth and chin gave the impression of a skull. Her bunched muscles screamed power. And my imminent demise.

She looked pissed.

Her mouth opened in an oddly silent yet menacing hiss. Two

more seconds of that unblinking stare, and she was gone. Like she'd never even been there.

My heart pounded so hard I thought it might burst out my chest.

Feeling returned to my body, my knuckles pressed into mud, and I looked around. The horses still grazed, as if unaware of our recent mortal danger. Maybe they knew she would go for me first.

In a trance, I joined the horses, then waited on Hayden and Nathan. No way I was going to go back into the woods alone. I for sure wasn't going to look up, especially if I heard a baby crying.

After we redid the paint on the posts, I finally told. It took that long to find the words.

"Holy crap, Genie!" Nathan said. "You had the angels looking out for you today."

If the angels were really looking out for me, they'd have poured me a drink.

CHAPTER SEVENTEEN

At the end of his rope, Red jogged circles around me, his movement effortless. His coat gleamed in the afternoon sun as if oiled, his hooves kicked up tiny puffs of dust. He was a smart bugger, learned a lot in just a few hours. So had I. He slowed, then stopped. I invited him to come close for a neck rub.

Thup-thup-thup.

A helicopter came into view, settled into the clearing, cut engines. Two cops spilled out. Noah and Heather walked out from the lodge to meet it, Heather carrying something wrapped in a red-checked tea towel.

"Looks like it's going well."

I turned to see Frankie at the fence, unclipped the lead from Red's halter and joined her. "Hardly feels like work. What are they doing here?" I nodded toward the cops.

She shrugged. "You've got the right disposition. Not everyone does."

"No?"

"These horses survive by instinct eight months of the year. They bring that same attitude back here with them and if you don't have what it takes, forget it."

"I'm mostly going by instinct myself."

Her eyes shone as she watched Red move about the pen. "He wants to know that he can trust you as a leader, that if he follows you, you'll keep him safe."

"Not sure I want that responsibility."

She bumped my shoulder with hers, laughed. "He's going to judge you by how you stand, how you move, and even by what's going on inside your head."

"He can read my mind now?"

"Body language. Horses can read the tiniest shivers and twitches. It's all words to them. If you're mad on the inside, there are signs on the outside he can see and smell, even feel on your skin. Like a vibration. He's going to have more confidence in a calm person than someone who's uptight."

"You think I'm a calm person?"

"I don't know. Ask your horse." She jumped from the fence. "You finished here?"

The helicopter lifted off and Noah headed our way. "Not quite."

"Okay, see you later."

I turned back to Red. Ask your horse, she'd said. *My* horse. I felt a glow inside. Red came over, snuffled my hand. He trusted me, maybe even liked me, who I was in this moment. Maybe I did too.

Last night I was in the hot tub, something my brothers would have disparaged. Darcy would call it a waste of time, while Jackson would tease, "Cowboys don't hot tub." These cowboys did. We'd talked about solo camp, now officially a go, what we would need, how it would feel being alone in the wilderness.

No one mentioned the cougar. I tried not to think about it.

Later, lying in our bunks, Frankie and I told each other ridiculous "dad jokes." They made no sense but we giggled like little kids until Tammy came in and told us she needed her beauty rest, which made us laugh harder. It was funny because it was true.

"I forgot to tell you," Frankie had whispered. She mouthed, *Tammy's Mug.*

I let my eyebrows ask the question. She pointed to herself, then mouthed, *Nathan*. And *Prank*.

I let my eyes tell her she was insane.

"Found it in the library," she whispered.

Ten days in and it felt like I belonged. Not that I wasn't looking forward to being free again. Nor did I believe this place would change the deep-down person I'd always been. We were shaped by our environments, and my same old, same old awaited my return. This was a time-out, plain and simple. A break from my miserable me.

Noah leaned against the gate as I released Red to his herd.

"Looks like you're doing good work," he said as I joined him.

The compliment warmed me. I *was* doing good work. "What did the cops want?"

"They were just passing by. Courtesy call."

"Heather gave them something."

"The pilot is her brother-in-law. She brought him some muffins."

"That's why they stopped."

"Maybe."

Noah looked like he had more to say.

"What's going on?"

Noah tipped up his hat, rubbed his forehead. "They mentioned your brother."

"Why would they do that?"

"They know my interest. Passed along the news that he'd got parole. He's been living in a halfway house."

"Okay." When I saw him at the courthouse he must have been heading out, not in.

I felt an ache in my chest, realized it began when I saw Jackson and never quite faded, not completely. Like it was waiting, for what I did not know. "You know where the halfway house is?"

"No."

"I'd like to talk to him, if we can find a number. If that's okay." I didn't know what I'd say. *Hey, bro,* maybe. Maybe that was all. Just to hear his voice.

"I'll see what I can do." Noah glanced over his shoulder. "Come on up to the house. You've earned a break."

We heard Melvin on the HF radio in the kitchen as we shed our hats and boots. The voice on the other end was obscured by hisses and pops. "We've been trying to reach Hayden and the boys," Noah explained. "Let them know we've got weather moving in."

Hayden had gone with Rick and Jimmy at sunup and they weren't expected back until tomorrow.

"They find those last two missing horses?" I asked.

"Not yet."

In the kitchen, blueberry heaven took the form of Heather's remaining fresh-baked muffins, those not given to her brother -in-law.

"Hey, boss," Melvin said. "Got through to Hayden."

"What'd he say?"

"They're finishing repairs to one of the pens. There's a lot of static."

"That'll be the weather."

I reached for a muffin, only to have Heather playfully slap my hand away. "Wash up first."

"Yes, ma'am."

Nathan, Frankie, Ole, and Tammy were already seated in the dining hall. A pot of coffee surrounded by mugs waited on the table, and after Merry brought out muffins and soft butter, she and Heather settled in too. Tammy prepared Heather's coffee for her—two sugars and one drip of milk. She even smiled. Hard to imagine Tammy being that way with anyone, but there you go.

Noah took his coffee black, and I decided to drink it that way too. I drew in a scalding mouthful, trying not to grimace at its strength.

The conversation turned to other matters: the upcoming election, continuing controversy surrounding the Calgary stampede, whether Ole's sister, Liv, would come for a visit, and the camp-out.

"We've picked out spots on Turtle Lake for each of you," Tammy said. "Not too close, as this is meant for quiet reflection." She glared at each of us in turn. "We'll be patrolling the whole time by canoe, checking in on you."

"Where's Turtle Lake?" I asked.

"About a five-hour ride," Frankie said.

"Water like glass," Ole said. "You'll love it."

"You're not meant to love it," Tammy said. "You're meant to think on your damned lives."

"Lives of the damned," I muttered, which earned me a look from Tammy. "Sorry. You weren't supposed to hear that."

"Then save it for when you're on your own."

"We'll all ride out," Noah said. "Including Melvin, Heather, Merry, and Ole."

"For us it's a holiday," Ole said.

"Plus we'll be close by if you need anything," Noah said. "You shout and we'll hear you. Sound carries."

"It's like the bottom of a bowl," Ole said. "A saucer sunk between mountains. Beautiful."

"But you're not meant to love it," Tammy insisted.

"On the way we can look for those missing horses," Frankie said.

"There is that," Tammy allowed, then glowered at me as if I had something to do with their absence.

Noah broke apart a muffin, slathered it with butter. "Except for a few nicks and bruises, the herd came off the mountain healthy."

"So they didn't starve," I said.

"Not likely."

I remembered the claw marks on Packman's rump. "What about mountain lions?"

Noah took a hankie out of his pocket and wiped his nose. "Could've lost a couple that way, especially if they got sick or injured."

"There was that toad-wipe move with my mug at Crooked Camp. I feel in my bones it was Jack come back to mess with me. Wouldn't put horse thieving past him."

Frankie looked an apology at me, as by now she knew my brother and Jack were one and the same. She hadn't meant to stir up trouble for me. She also didn't set Tammy straight by admitting the truth, I noticed, not that I could blame her.

"Oh, stop it, Tammy." Heather's scolding voice didn't match the twinkle in her eye. "The horses will turn up, and never mind about Jack. My brother says he's just got parolled, which means he would have been locked up when those horses went missing, not that he'd had means to get up here anyway."

"Funny that Eugenia is his sister, hey?" Melvin asked.

Conversation stopped.

Faces turned toward me, and I felt my cheeks redden. I waited for Tammy to call me slider one more time.

I dare you.

It didn't happen. I forced relaxation down though my shoulders, breathed deep and unclenched my fists.

"That is interesting," Tammy drawled.

"I'm not my brother." *My beautiful, misjudged brother.*

"I know it," said Tammy. With a start I realized she hadn't called me slider since I'd worked my ass off digging that hole.

Noah pushed his chair back, stood. "Nathan and I will head back to Crooked Camp tomorrow afternoon, maybe stay the night so we can have a proper look around. Frankie and Eugenia, you stay here, do some work in the yard, maybe weed the garden."

"That won't take long," I said, trying not to sound disappointed that I wouldn't be joining them on the trail. I reminded myself that no one cared if I was having fun, and the judge would likely prefer that I was not.

"You're doing good work with that colt, Eugenia," Noah said. "Keep doing what you're doing. Frankie'll give you a hand if you need it."

Frankie grinned at me, winked like she had a plan. Okay. Might be fun after all.

CHAPTER EIGHTEEN

Red stood with all four legs locked. "Let's go, boy, move over." I tapped him like Noah showed me, tried to get him to step sideways. *Tap-tap.* "Let's go … over, over …" *Tap-tap.*

Finally, a step.

"That-a-boy." I rubbed his shoulder to let him know he did good, then moved to his other side. *Tap-tap.* "That-a-boy." When I tapped his back leg, Red flattened his ears.

What was that all about?

"Okay, boy." I moved back up to his shoulder, watched his ears flick forward again. I rubbed his neck, then under his fore-lock. He closed his eyes. "You tired, boy?"

Overnight there'd been rolling thunder, but little rain. This afternoon a ceiling of cloud still hung low over the mountains, textured like grey stucco. I'd wanted to hold off working with Red in case it rained, but Merry assured me it wouldn't. Said her knees told her it would move out soon. Her knees were bang on. Within the hour the sky brightened and cloud cover fragmented like pulled-apart dryer lint. With the break in weather, Ole took off back to town for supplies. Tammy joined him, saying she needed to see to something. I wondered if she might look up my brother, see for herself that he hadn't stolen any horses or moved her damn mug.

I returned to Red's flank, placed my hand on him. He flat-tened his ears, but only for a second. Working with horses wasn't rocket science. Just took some time. I went back to tapping the spot that had been trouble. Once again, his ears flattened. "Come on, boy, what's it going to take?" This time instead of tapping or rubbing, I pressed two fingertips into his flank, pushed, gently at first, then harder. His ears hung off to each side as if he were unsure. I laughed softly. Horses could talk pretty well with their ears. I kept the pressure firm until finally he took a step. "Good boy!" I moved from one side to the other, celebrated each step with a rub and praise.

Time for a break.

My chest puffed like a rooster's as I quick-stepped to the house, set my boots on the mat and hung my hat. In the kitchen I hooked elbows with Heather in a do-se-do as Merry kneaded bread dough, chuckled and shook her head. Frankie was at the radio. "You win the lotto or something?"

I helped myself to an apple from a large bowl of fruit. "Had a good session with Red."

"That'll do it."

"You reach Hayden?"

She nodded. "This morning. He and the boys are on their way back. I'm trying to get through to Noah at Crooked Camp."

Melvin emerged from the stairwell leading up to the office. "Any luck?"

"Not yet." Frankie dropped the headset beside the radio. "I'm tired of sitting here. Let's go weed the garden."

Spending time with Frankie was fun, no matter what the task, but, "Can we do it later? I'm kind of on a roll with Red." I turned to Melvin. "If that's okay, I mean."

Melvin shrugged like he couldn't be less interested. "Do what you want." I had an inkling that the real reason Melvin wasn't a guide had nothing to do with a preference for being inside.

"Might be ready to get a saddle on him soon."

"Don't work him too hard," Frankie said.

"I know. Slow and easy."

Heather lined up carrots, onions, and celery beside a chopping board, waved a chef's knife at us. "Why don't you change things up, take him out on a trail?"

Frankie's smile widened. "Good idea! You can pony Red beside Packman."

"That allowed?"

"Long as you don't go far," Merry said.

"I've never done that. Ponying."

"And that's different from every other thing you've been doing here how?" Frankie asked.

I laughed. "Fair enough."

It was funny to watch Red get a feel for walking while attached to Packman's saddle. At first he kept his head high, took short, stiff steps as we rode around the pasture. Once he got comfortable, we followed Frankie and her big bay along a wide path into the woods.

"Might as well learn the trails." She flashed me a smile over her shoulder. "Maybe you can stay on after your sentence."

"Didn't know that was an option."

"Maybe not, but Noah likes you, I can tell. Maybe he'll make you a youth councillor or something. Who better help the newbies adjust than someone who used to be just like them?"

"Like you, you mean. You've helped me a lot."

She paused before answering. "I'm still in custody. Will be for another year."

And she'd already been here the longest, I remembered. Group sessions had been focussed on how we would handle Solo Camp, coping techniques for loneliness and the like. Her story, why she was here, hadn't come up.

A silence opened between us. Awkward. "Anyway, I have a condition attached. Gotta go back to school in the fall."

She dropped back beside me as the path widened, opened her mouth as if she had something to say, then closed it.

"What?"

"You seem like a good person. Hard worker, fun to be with, easygoing."

I snorted. "Maybe now." Fort St. Luke was ten days and a lifetime ago.

"You made out like you were a gangbanger or something."

"Not really a joiner."

"Well, violent, anyway. But I haven't seen anything like that. You don't seem at all like—" She broke off, looked away.

"What?"

"Your brother. Sorry. Now that dude sounded mean."

A swallowed a desire to shut her down, to defend him. There was also that thing about her letting him take the heat for the mug prank, but it wasn't like I'd called her on it. I breathed in mingled scents of warm horse, leather saddle, and tang of the forest. "I'm different here, I guess."

"I get that," she said.

"Honestly, everyone here seems pretty normal. I haven't seen a single act of badassery."

"You calling us wusses?"

"If the fuzzy slipper fits."

"I have fuzzy slippers."

"I know."

She laughed, then got quiet. "There have been incidents."

"Like?"

"Guy named Steven was a thief. He's the reason the office stays locked when staff isn't there."

"Booted?"

"Course. And there was a girl, Roxanne, she and this guy named John would sneak off in the bushes every chance they got." She snorted. "Gangster dude thought he was gonna be a hip hop star. She bought into it hook and sinker."

"They were having sex?"

"No. At least I don't think so—she's the type that woulda bragged about it. They were in love. Couldn't stand to be away from each other. Then Roxanne thought Merry had a thing for him, went after her with a knife."

"Seriously?"

"She got the boot, and John was inconsolable. His music took an interesting turn." She laughed again. "Love-sappy hip hop. Anyway, he left voluntarily. It meant jail for both of them, but I guess he figured they were closer that way."

"Did it work out?"

Frankie shrugged.

I thought about Nathan, the feelings he'd stirred in me up at Crooked Camp. "So relationships are allowed?"

"Nope."

"You said that before, but I looked and it isn't in the rules."

"Not officially. But if they see something they'll give the people involved a talking to and keep them far away from each other until one or the other finishes their time."

"That would suck."

She must have heard something in my voice, as she fell back until she was riding beside me, narrowed her eyes. "What's going on?"

"Nothing."

"Yes there is."

"Nothing!" I insisted. "It's just … I don't know." I glanced shyly at her. "Nathan."

"What about Nathan?

I felt my cheeks redden. "He's a good-looking guy."

"So?" Her voice was sharp.

"So, nothing. Except when we got stuck in that storm up at Crooked Camp, he got me thinking. I wouldn't mind if something happened. Not like that Roxanne and John, but something."

Frankie looked hard at me, then shook her head like she was disappointed, rode back on up ahead.

"Thanks for the support," I muttered. What the hell just happened?

The brush of leaves from wayward branches had become irritating. I swatted at flies with extra vigour, the patience I'd begun the day with gone. It was Frankie. "You wanna tell me what's going on with you?"

No answer.

Fine.

We rode in silence, the sound of horse farts and saddles creaks a percussive background to twittering birds and wind breathing through trees. Far off a moose bellowed. At a narrow creek we came upon a fallen log wide enough to make a good bench. There was a circle of rocks indicating the occasional campfire.

This was bullshit.

"You mad at me?"

Silence.

"Definitely mad, and you won't even tell me why." I chewed on my lip at the injustice of it all. Tried another tack. She was here long term, which meant whatever she'd done must have been big. Maybe if she remembered how tough she was she'd take that stick out of her ass and lighten up. "What's your story, Frankie? What got you here? I'm guessing everyone else already knows. Care to enlighten me?"

She carried on riding and I was about to wash my hands of her drama when she looked back. "Let's stop."

We hitched our horses and sat side by side. Frankie picked up stones and tossed them one by one into the creek. Then: "Short version is that I killed a man."

Whoa.

Whoa, whoa, whoa.

She glanced at me. "I know. It's a lot. Shocker that they'd let a murderer loose in the mountains, hey?" She sounded wry. A joke, but not really.

I had no quip. "Maybe. I mean, I don't know. I was surprised they sent me here, so."

She shrugged. "I still don't get it. I mean, why me? Why not someone else? Most of us don't plan on this life we get, or any kind of life, really. But then you wake up one day and you're down some path you don't know how to get off. If you even want to."

I didn't know what to say. What was the appropriate response? *Gee, sorry about that.* Or, *Lucky you, you sure got a big break*. Or, *Bet he had it coming*. I settled on, "You're different here too."

She shrunk in on herself. "I know."

"Sorry. It wasn't my business. I was just trying to understand."

"I still am. I mean, two people can start off just the same, maybe at a party, for instance. Someone's passing something around, they take a hit. One spirals, the other just takes the moment and moves on just the same. Why, Eugenia?" She looked at me like she really wanted to know.

"What happened?"

She focussed back on the creek.

"I mean, you don't have to tell me. But you can."

"Where do I start? My father died when I was ten years old," she said. "Car accident. He didn't die right away, and in the hospital he told me that it isn't easy choosing the life you want, but it's what you've got to do. If you don't have the guts to make things happen, you've got no right to do anything but take whatever comes at you, good or bad."

My breathing turned shallow and I gulped air as memories of my last minutes with Pops came hard and fast.

I was eight years old again, waiting for Pops to tell me, hey, great idea. It's your birthday and we'll go hunting. I was such a good daughter, a thoughtful daughter.

I could see him. For the first time in a long time, he was there. I saw the creases in his face, the shadows under his eyes, the way his hair was just a bit too long and would catch in his shirt collar.

"You okay?" It was Frankie. She sounded far away.

The forest came back in a rush. "Yeah. Good."

"Looked like I hit a nerve or something."

"Maybe. I don't know. Doesn't matter. Go on, I want to hear."

She hesitated. "Okay."

It was a big deal, her telling me. I could tell it was hard. Maybe she hadn't shared this in Group. Maybe she hadn't talked to anyone, except Heather. Maybe not even her.

Friend.

"Two years after Dad died, I was in grade eight and my mom and I had pretty much stopped talking. About anything. Seemed like whenever we tried, we both ended up screaming. I mean, I was a kid so it's understandable, right? She was supposed to be the stable one. Anyway, as soon as I finished the year, I left."

We had more in common than Frankie knew. Maybe that was why I felt this connection with her. Except that when I was a kid, I wasn't the one who did the leaving.

"Grade eight. You were twelve?"

"Thirteen when I left."

"Must have been hard."

"Yeah, well, I was hard. Tough—thought I was. Things are good between us now, but back then I only wanted to get away. I wasn't making the best choices." She sighed. "Most of those bad choices involved guys. Older guys. To be fair, they thought I was older too. I went from one relationship to another. Soon as I broke up with someone, bam, I was with someone else. Girls too. Typical movie of the week stuff."

"Must have been some movie."

"After a while there was no one. I was alone on the street. Nearly OD'd."

I didn't know my mouth was hanging open until she gently placed fingertips under my chin, pushed it closed. "Sorry," I said. "It's just, you really don't look the type."

She looked deep in thought as she rubbed at the crook of her left arm. Were there track marks under her shirt? Had there been?

"Some scars take a long time to heal," I chanced.

She looked at me, eyes haunted. "Especially the ones inside. Anyhow, it scared me. Went to rehab and got clean. Placed in a group home. See? Movie of the week"

"Except for the murder part," I said softly.

"I should have stayed in the group home." She looked heavy. "Took karate when I was a kid, then Muay Thai at the youth centre. Turns out some skills don't go away, even when you get lazy and busy and stupid and think you've lost everything." She got quiet and this time I wasn't going to push.

I leaned back closed my eyes, let the sun soak. Her words echoed. *Lazy. Stupid. Lost.* They were the kind of words you took inside of you stamped with permanent ink. Like a tattoo, or track marks that never went away. I knew that well enough. But I wasn't an addict, drugs or otherwise, and I'd never lived on the street.

"I was at a bar with a friend. Some guy started hitting on her and before I knew it, we were going at it. I didn't mean to kill him."

And there it was.

I imagined her in the bar, dancing, drinking, protecting her friend, getting mad. Too young to be there, but that never stopped anyone. "That's why you looked upset. When you laid me flat, I mean."

"I shouldn't have done that. I still got work to do."

"We all do."

She took my hand, squeezed my fingers. "Yeah."

My hand felt cold when she let go. It was like in that moment, we shared something important.

"Okay, your turn. You looked upset when I told you about my dad. Yours died too, yeah?"

My throat tightened and I nodded. Why was I so emotional? It wasn't like it was yesterday or anything. "Yeah, but not a car accident." My eyes ached with the pressure of holding back tears. "I killed him," I choked.

Words I'd sworn I'd never speak. What was inside was now out. I took a deep breath, let it out slow.

"Are you fucking kidding me?"

The world went tilt and I couldn't see straight. She was angry, like a volcano spitting lava. "I don't under—"

She jumped up, startled the horses. "I tell you I kill a man, and you gotta play some sick game of one-up? What are you, some kind of fucking liar?"

"No!" I got to my feet, feeling my own blood rise. "You told me a big thing. I just wanted to tell you mine."

"Why?"

"I thought we were friends."

"We are not friends." She spoke through gritted teeth,

jaw clamped. "It's like you wanna be me or something. Wannabee tough, wannabee cowgirl, steal my boyfriend, steal my crime—"

"Whoa, wait. Boyfriend?"

"Nathan! You know I'm in love with him!" The horses stamped their feet, flattened their ears.

"Hang on!" I shouted back. "You said there was nothing going on!"

"I did NOT! I said it would be against the rules."

I'd lost my words. I stood still, let the air around us settle along with the horses. The forest was quiet. Then a squirrel chittered. A jay squawked. I broke our stare, looked at the decaying forest floor. Dead grass, bark, leaves. *And so it goes.* I looked back at her.

"I didn't know. And there is nothing going on with me and Nathan." I kept my voice as steady as I could make it. On the inside, I shook.

She laughed then. It sounded crazy, and I felt a shiver down the back of my neck.

"It's complicated," she said. "We should get back."

As we rode through thickets and over streams, I felt numb.

Just like that, something special was wrecked. What if she told the others about Pops? She hadn't even asked me how it happened, I realized. Didn't care to know.

People were never who they let on to be. You had to work away at them and never, ever reveal your own soul until you peeled back their scabs to something pink, vulnerable and real, even if you made them bleed.

I thought I'd done that with Frankie. Clearly, not.

The trail merged with the river's edge, and we eased alongside of it. The Rubicon, point of no return. On the far side of the river, rising above the forest, there were meadow-covered hills, green velvet, climbing, climbing until they met what remained of the morning's cloud.

From the cloud there emerged a line of horses.

"Hayden and the boys." Frankie said, not looking at me.

CHAPTER NINETEEN

"Don't look so pleased with yourself." I picked myself up off the ground, kicked at the dirt and retrieved the saddle Red had just thrown off.

Under the misguided assumption that I would have him saddle-trained by breakfast, I'd started with the sun barely risen, Frankie still asleep. We hadn't spoken since yesterday's trail ride, which earned us weird looks from Rick and Jimmy at dinner last night. If the adults in the room noticed, they hadn't let on, or maybe they were too entertained by Tammy's story of the buskers she'd seen in front of the Fort St. Luke library. Guess she hadn't found my brother after all, or hadn't looked.

Everything was awful between me and Frankie. Blown up. I hoped that throwing myself into hard work would dull the awkwardness, in the way a paper cut was sharp at first, then you forget it was ever there. At the very least, it would take my mind off things. Except Red wasn't cooperating.

The horse pranced around the pen, tossed his head like he was really something, which he was, but he was being an ass. It wasn't like I was gonna hurt him. He should get that by now.

"You can't stay wild forever."

Isn't that what the judge tried to drum into my own damn skull back in court? And Noah? Darcy too. They all wanted me to straighten out, straighten up, do something useful with my life.

"If at first you don't succeed," Hayden said.

Startled, I glanced toward the gate. “Didn’t know you were there.”

“Just got here.” He looked amused, and again I was stuck by how much he looked like a movie cowboy, except not as tall as they always appeared to be. Then again, everyone knew about how actors stood on boxes. That’s how it was in the world, people puffing themselves up into what they imagined was something better. Like Frankie. And like me.

We were who we were. No one changed. That was just a lie we liked to tell ourselves.

“You missed breakfast,” he said.

“Wasn’t hungry.” A quad started up from behind the lodge. Three seconds later it emerged with Tammy driving, Rick and Jimmy riding in the trailer, headed up the meadow.

“Where they going?”

“Checking the trail to Turtle Lake.”

“Nice. Guess it’s chore time. You have something you want me to do?”

“Keep doing what you’re doing.”

“Except I don’t know what I’m doing,” I admitted. “Not really.”

“Not what I’ve heard.”

I leaned against the rails. “I guess you guys talk about us.”

“Course we do. Discuss progress, strategies, make plans, fill out reports. Everything you’d expect.”

“Sounds weird, actually. This looks like a regular ranch. I mean I know it’s not, but it seems like it. And that stuff doesn’t sound very cowboy.”

“Because that’s not all we are.”

“Yeah, I know.”

His cheeks bunched into crabapples.

“Melvin said you all worked in either social work or prisons before here.”

"Not quite."

"What then?"

"I can only speak for myself. Everyone has a story, and it's theirs to tell."

"Okay, so what's yours?"

He climbed the fence, sat on the top rail, invited me to do the same. "'Spose you're too young to know about the Iraq War?"

"Which one?"

"Fair enough. I'm not going to give you a history lesson, but I was over there with my cousin, Parrot." He took on a faraway look. "His name was Peter, but from the time he was a little kid everyone called him Parrot. I don't remember why."

"You're a soldier."

"Was, and Parrot was our captain. Good one too. After a while, the powers that be took notice and decided to reward him for his services." He took a hankie from his back pocket, wiped his forehead, though it wasn't particularly hot. "On his return trip, plane crashed when the landing gear collapsed. Parrot hit his head and died two days later from bleeding in the brain. They called it an accident." He looked distant.

"That's a loaded way to put it. You think it was deliberate?"

"Used to. He was a rebel, my cousin. At the ceremony he refused to accept the medal. For a while I wondered if he pissed off the wrong person."

"You know that's crazy, right?"

He smiled. "Yeah, I do. The belly-landing destroyed the gear so bad they couldn't draw any firm conclusions. That's what got me hung up for so long. No closure."

"You don't think that anymore?"

"Time has a way of helping you see around the edges of things. There were more on board than Parrot, and at the time he told the medics he was fine. Just a bump on the head." He shrugged. "Just one of those things. Life, hey?"

And death.

"Sorry about your cousin."

He patted my shoulder, gave a solemn nod. "And I'm sorry about your dad."

Adults always did that. When they talked about people they'd lost, it was like they wanted me to know they weren't comparing their loss to mine.

I waited for more, but he'd gone back into his head. "So how does that get you here?"

His cheeks apple-bunched again. "Parrot had a garden centre in Terrace, and a wife and kid. All my mother's family were near there, so I figured I would go to work for Parrot's wife and get to know my relations a whole lot better. Helped out with Parrot's kid." He glanced up at me. "You been to my garden yet?"

"No. You didn't know your relations?"

"Knew my dad's better. He and my mom met in a botany class in Vancouver. That's where we lived. They still do. Hey, check out my garden sometime. Pull a few weeds while you're there."

"Okay."

"It wasn't easy for Parrot's kid," he continued. "Guess that's what got things started for me. Helping him made me feel good about myself. Won't fix the lumps life's taken out of me, but I'm better for it."

"What kinds of lumps?"

"Everyone has a story, and everyone has lumps. Some they share, some they don't."

"I get it."

"I know you do, Eugenia. Anyhow, I was a volunteer with Big Brother for a while, then trained to work at a Youth Custody Centre."

"Jail."

"We don't call it that."

"We do."

Apple-bunch. "Met Noah at a conference, and the rest is history. I like it here." He breathed deep. "I like the air, the easy pace of things."

Red trotted over, snuffled at me.

"There's your cue," Hayden said.

"Think he's ready for a saddle?"

"Do you?"

Next to Noah, Hayden was the second-most relaxed person I'd ever met. Maybe when people spent a long time together they got to be like each other, which didn't explain Tammy.

With a mock swagger I said, "It's not exactly rocket science." I sounded more confident than I felt, but Hayden had reminded me about a key piece of this puzzle: I had to go slow. *An easy pace.*

I took the saddle, dumped it in the middle of the pen. Red took a step toward it, then another, until he was close enough to sniff at it. He mouthed the edge, took hold and pulled. The stirrup clanked, which caused him to squeal, spin, and kick.

Hayden chuckled. "For every action, an equal and opposite reaction."

"He's a full party package."

Standing square at the far end of the pen, head and neck low, Red stared down the saddle. It was clearly a frightening thing. Then, as if a switch flipped, he walked to it, gave it a yank, and lost interest.

"I think it's time," I said.

"I'm here if you need me." Hayden hadn't moved from the rail.

"I won't."

Focus, Eugenia. Slow and easy, reward every try.

Red stood quiet as I put on the halter. "Hey, boy. Saddle's no big deal, right?" I stroked his neck, then lifted the under-blanket to his nose. Red sniffed briefly, mouthed it, then looked away.

So far so good.

"Better check the underside, way it was dumped there," Hayden called.

I did, found a small clump of twigs and burrs stuck to the woven cotton. I smiled thanks and pulled it away. Next, our familiar routine. I brought it close, took it away, repeat, repeat, same with touching his neck, and other parts of his body. Once he was thoroughly uninterested, I swung the blanket onto his back, stepped away. Red stayed put and did not look in any way uncomfortable.

Time for the saddle. Like he knew something was coming, Red opened his eyes and shifted his weight. I let him sniff the saddle as much as he wanted, then settled it on his back. He stiffened, jerked his head upright, but stood his ground.

Bet I was impressing the hell out of Hayden. Maybe after all was said and done Noah would offer me a job, like Frankie said. Maybe with Merry's help I would finish school with distance education. Could happen.

Except for that small matter of what was broken between me and Frankie.

Focus, Eugenia.

Underneath Red's belly, where I'd eventually fasten the cinch, I rubbed. Red flicked his ears back, flattened them, while I murmured sweet nothings about clover and mares, rubbed circles on his belly, shoulder, and neck until he relaxed.

It was time.

Cinch fastened, Red swung his head back to sniff, then lost interest.

I love it when a plan comes together.

Willing my pulse steady, I tightened the cinch just enough that it would stay put if Red decided to bolt. Time to climb on and accept whatever came next. A metaphor for life.

In one swift motion I had my foot in the stirrup and swung aboard. Red stood still as a statue, except for his ears waggling as he figured things out. I leaned back in the saddle, ready to jump off if I felt the need. Red twisted his neck to look at me, sniffed my boot, mouthed the toe of it, but stayed put.

I'd done it! This horse, this beautiful boy, trusted me as his leader. We'd bonded, and he knew I'd keep him safe. Time to remove the pressure and give this good boy a break.

I arced my leg backward in the dismount, except in doing so I brushed Red's rump with my boot.

He exploded. The world tipped and went black.

CHAPTER TWENTY

Something hard against my back.

The ground.

I opened my eyes, tried to rise. Mistake. "Holy crap," I croaked, and willed a return to pain-free nothingness. Didn't work.

"You're okay, Eugenia," Hayden soothed. "Stay still. Don't move your neck."

I did anyway, groaned, then screeched as Hayden pulled on my leg.

"Sorry." His voice was anxious. "Your leg was twisted, but I don't think it's broke."

Sharp pain as I raised myself up on my elbow. "What …" —shallow breath, gasp—"What happened?"

"You got dragged." Softer voice. Not Hayden.

Frankie. Where'd she come from? She looked pale.

Heather and Merry appeared. "Relax, honey," Merry soothed. "You're going to be fine." Cool cloth on my forehead.

It all came back. I was in the pen. "Red?"

Frankie moved and I saw Red standing a few feet away, head low, ears forward. Watching us. The damned horse bolted when I dismounted.

My foot. I remembered now. I'd scraped it across his backside. I could almost hear Noah say that to a horse that would've felt like a predator was jumping on him. *Shut up, Noah.*

"Don't worry about the horse," Hayden said. "He's fine. Tell us what's going on with you."

I shifted, winced.

Frankie's face was flushed with worry. She looked away when my eyes settled on hers. Why was she even here?

"Hurts to breathe," I gasped, then shifted again. "Better this way."

"Sounds like her ribs," Merry said.

"Where in the hell is Melvin?" Hayden asked. "Merry, will you radio Ole, tell him to turn around? We'd best get her to a doctor."

"Right away."

"When's Noah back?" Hayden called after her.

"Soon."

Noah. Shit.

My assurances that I was mostly fine fell on deaf ears, not that I expected anyone to believe me. I didn't believe me. Just hadn't wrapped my head around it yet.

Melvin joined us, argued that he should be the one to accompany me, being Noah's number one and all. Merry put an end to it, saying he was number one in business, but we had regulations. In other words, I needed Youth Corrections-type supervision.

Melvin grumbled, but acquiesced. "Guess I'll start the paperwork."

Ole flew us straight to the Fort St. Luke airport instead of the private strip. It looked strange, like a town I'd never been to, and only in part because I was seeing it from the air. In measurement of days I'd not been away that long, but when I thought about all I'd done it felt longer. I'd built a fence, painted a pen, shovelled shit, dug a pit, trained horses, and made new friends. Maybe lost one too.

Hayden accompanied me into the examination room and stepped to the other side of a privacy shield when the doc asked to unbutton my shirt. "Guess Heather or Merry should've come."

"Breathe in," the doctor said, stethoscope cool on my skin.

I tried and winced.

"Likely a fracture," he said. He shone a light in my eyes, asked me to follow it.

"Do I need an x-ray?"

"Not necessary. No concussion, nor signs of other injury. You were lucky."

"I have a hard head."

"You didn't hit your head, that's why you were lucky." He looked toward Hayden like it was his fault, except that Hayden was still behind the divider.

With some difficulty, I buttoned my shirt, told Hayden he could come back. The doctor wrote something on a slip of paper, handed it to him. Prescription, I guessed. "Got some good drugs for me, doc?"

"Just ibuprofen."

"Oh."

"Put some ice on it, get lots of rest. It should knit back together in a few weeks."

"That's it?"

"That's it."

CHAPTER TWENTY-ONE

Back at the ranch, I settled awkwardly on the office couch, trying to find an angle that offered the least amount of pain. "Shouldn't this be hot tub time or something?"

It was past dinner hour by the time we got back from Fort St. Luke, and everyone had cleared out of the dining hall. Heather had brought out leftover chili and buns along with an invitation to join her in the office after dinner. Refusal hadn't been an option.

"Special circumstance," she said.

"Seems to be a lot of that around here. I'm guessing this is about what happened."

"It's about whatever you want it to be. It was a shock though, yes?" As always, she was light and welcoming without coming on strong. She wanted to draw me in without making me feel pressured. There was a lot of that around here too.

"It was my own damn fault. I was a jackass to think I could put a saddle on Red only two weeks in."

"Hayden didn't seem to think so."

I stopped myself from saying that made Hayden a jackass too. "I suppose this is where you say I gotta get back in the saddle."

"From what I hear, you weren't in it all that long." I barked a laugh and she joined me, except she sounded like piano keys up and down, while I sounded like a coyote with croup.

She tilted her head to the side, waiting.

"Maybe I am a bit scared. I mean, the horse was half wild when I started working with him."

"And other half?"

I rolled my eyes. "Fine. He was already broke. He just needed a refresher before the next step."

"You gave him that. From what I hear you're good at it."

"Noah's been talking me through things, showing me things, and I guess I really did think it was no big deal, long as I was careful."

"Accidents happen."

"I know." I frowned. She waited. I was in a sour mood. It wasn't Heather, it wasn't even the accident. Everything went south when I went for that ride with Frankie. "It's just that I feel like a fake. I'm working at a ranch like I'm some sort of cowboy."

"Cowgirl."

"I prefer cowboy in the non-gender specific sense, like painter or writer." I was making it up, but so what.

"You're an artist."

"Yeah, a con artist."

She waited some more.

"It feels real familiar because of all that time I spent hanging out with my brothers when I was a kid, but they were the cowboys, not me. Before I got a chance to do any of the real work, Pops died and everything changed."

"No more ranch work."

"We blew apart. Our family. That's what I'm good at. Blowing things up." In my head I saw a mushroom cloud. *Kapow.*

"That wasn't your fault, Eugenia."

Wasn't gonna go there. "I blew up my friendship with Frankie, too." *Kapow.*

She tilted her head. "What happened?"

I couldn't tell her why we fought. If staff thought there was something romantic going on between her and Nathan they'd keep them separate and that would make things worse. Neither could I say she got mad because I said I liked Nathan, because that would lead to the same place. "I'm just hard to get along with, I guess."

"That's not been my experience."

"Like I said, con artist."

Gently, she took my hands. "Stop that, Eugenia. We are all mixed bags with many facets to our personalities. It's dangerous and wrong to pull out a label and metaphorically paste it on our foreheads. Leave it there too long and we talk ourselves into believing it." She let go, and I remembered the feel of Frankie taking my hand. The truth of it came to me, why it'd felt so special. For a brief minute it was like I'd had a sister.

Out the window I saw movement. Noah was on his way up to the lodge from the pens, Copper at his heels. I felt my pulse quicken as if I'd done something wrong. Maybe I had.

"I'll think on that."

She followed my gaze. Another head tilt. "Something else?"

"Noah's going to be pissed." He'd been out when we got back. He and Nathan had found one of the missing horses at Crooked Camp, so there was that. Maybe it would soften his mood.

"Why do you think that?"

"Because I screwed up."

"Remember the part where we agreed this was an accident?"

"Some people say there are no accidents."

"Interesting philosophy."

I shrugged and winced at the stab of pain it caused. When I looked again, Noah had disappeared from sight into the lodge. "I'm tied up in knots about seeing him, if you wanna know the truth."

"Break it down, Eugenia. How do you see the conversation going?"

"He'll call me a dumb shit and I'll know it's true."

She raised an eyebrow. "Can we try something? Close your eyes." She laughed at the look I gave her. "It'll be okay! Just try it."

"Okay." I closed my eyes.

"Imagine yourself outside the office door. What happens next?"

I could see it, the door, the brass lever-style handle. My hand on the handle.

My eyes snapped open. "Nothing. I can't go in. It's like I'm frozen." I rubbed my hands together. They were like ice.

She leaned forward so that her elbows rested on her knees, reached out and placed her hand on mine. It felt hot. My heart was racing. "Breathe, Eugenia. Remember those relaxation techniques we talked about last time. Deep breathe in and out."

"Kind of hurts"

"Go slow."

I did as she said. After four deep breaths I felt more settled. "I have no idea why I'm so scared about that."

"Have you considered …" She trailed off, then looked steady at me. "Is there a chance Noah reminds you of your father?"

What the? "No! Just because I was a kid when Pops died doesn't mean I don't remember. He was nothing like Noah. So it can't be that." I almost shrugged, stopped myself. "I think I'm just scared he'll send me home."

She nodded. "Okay, let's see what that looks like. I'm not saying this will happen, but let's go to that worst-case scenario. Imagine you made it through the door, and the worst of the worst has happened. Noah has said you have to go home. What then?"

I stared at my hands. "You ever look at yourself in a spoon, Heather?"

She considered. "Maybe. I don't know."

"I mean really look. Try it sometime." I held my arm out straight. "Hold it out in front of you. You'll see your reflection upside down, the background out of focus. And if you turn around slow in a circle, you're locked in while everything around you is dizzy and shifting. I guess that's how I feel."

"I'm not sure what that means, but it's beautiful."

"It means you're not really a part of it. It means I don't belong."

"Belong where?"

"Here."

"Good work, Eugenia. That's your deepest fear. You feel a connection to this place, the people you've built new relationships with, and you're afraid you'll lose that."

I felt my blood rise again, the old anger as familiar as grilled cheese sandwiches and macaroni. "You're not listening," I grumbled. "I'm telling you I don't belong here. I thought I did, but I don't. I blow things up, remember?" I laughed bitterly. "At least there's a freedom in that."

Heather frowned, opened her mouth to respond, but I cut her off.

"We done here?" I didn't want to talk anymore, didn't want to hear anything else she had to say. For sure I didn't want one of her comforting touches. I drew my hands in close and looked at the clock.

"If you like," she said gently. I got up to leave. "Hang on a second." She waved a notebook. "You ever journal, Eugenia?"

"No."

"Give it a try. You express yourself beautifully. I have a feeling that if you write things down, you may be able to work out some of what you're feeling. Explore that spoon metaphor. I'd like to hear more. You do belong here, you know. There's a philosophy that says wherever you are is exactly where you are meant to be. Maybe think on *that*."

There was a knock on the door, and Noah poked his head in. "Can I come in?"

"Of course." Heather gathered her things to leave. "We were just finishing up."

Copper followed him in. "Eugenia, would you stay a minute?"

Looked like I wouldn't have to face that door after all. Heather hadn't considered this scenario.

She gave me a reassuring smile and closed the door on her way out.

Noah settled behind the desk, pulled out some paperwork and a pencil, began tapping the pencil as he read. I moved from the couch to the chair opposite him. He looked hard at me with those intense blue eyes. I sat perfectly still, stifled an impulse to flinch. I met his eyes with a glower.

"You ever saddle break a horse before?"

"No."

His eyes narrowed. "Then why did you think you could saddle break one that's half wild?"

"He was broke," I said, allowing some gratitude toward Heather for that cue. "Just needed a refresher. I didn't do anything wrong."

"Doesn't have to be wrong to be ill-advised."

"You told me to keep doing what I was doing and get help if I needed it. I didn't need it."

"Clearly you did, and you know damn well I wasn't talking about putting a saddle on him."

My voice took on a sarcastic tone. "How would I know if you didn't say so?" I was pushing and I didn't care. "Had to try it sometime. You've been teaching me since I got here, and I have listened to every word. I paid attention to Red. I got him used to stuff and took my time, probably more than I have with anything."

"And yet here we are."

"You work around horses you're going to end up with a few bumps and bruises."

"Or cracked ribs."

"Right. So why are you mad? The ribs will heal. Doc said I'm going to be fine."

He rubbed a hand across his forehead and relaxed his shoulders, but he still looked upset, nodded toward the papers. "Your accident report. You're supposed to be working on my ranch. You can't work with cracked ribs."

"Sure I can."

"It'll take weeks to heal them up right, and I don't think the judge will agree to you spending that time sitting in the hot tub sipping lemonade."

"Yeah, like that's my style."

He shook his head, spoke softly. "Damn it, Eugenia. I don't want to see your time here cut short."

That got my attention. I'd been booted from jobs before, and this didn't have that feel. It sounded, despite everything, like Noah was on my side. "From what I hear, not everyone makes it through the program."

"I don't want that to happen with you."

Far off, a light. "There's still plenty I can do. I can wash dishes."

"There's a whole lot more you can't do until those ribs heal. No horse breaking, no wood chopping, no heavy lifting of any kind. But, yeah, you can wash dishes." He looked thoughtful. "More than that. Let me talk to Melvin. Maybe he can show you around some of the office business. If you can tally some of those numbers you're so good at, he can take over some of your chores outdoors."

"He'll let Tammy boss him around?"

"It won't be like that. Can you handle riding a desk for a while?"

I felt something thaw inside me. "Better than jail I suppose." It also meant he trusted me in a room that was usually kept locked.

"Better than jail." He tapped his pencil again. "Okay, let's see how it goes."

"What about Red?"

"I'll work with him. You can watch."

This was probably a good time to take my leave. "Want me to get Melvin?"

"Guess you better."

I looked at Copper and the phrase *let sleeping dogs lie* came to mind, but there was something I needed to understand. I stayed sitting. "Why, Noah? I mean, why do you even care if I go to jail? You gave me a chance. I blew it."

"You didn't blow it." He paused. "For the record, I care about every kid who comes here, but I told you, I was there the night your father died. I've thought of your family often through the years."

"I know. But you did your bit, more'n you had to. More'n anyone else would have. I also know about Roxanne who got booted, and some other guy I can't remember. Were you this upset with them?"

"Maybe. They broke the rules."

"I didn't break anything except my ribs."

"There's your answer."

I shook my head. "I think there's more. As grateful as I am to you, I never asked for special treatment, and that's what this feels like. Unless there's something else going on I don't know about. Just be straight with me."

He leaned his weight on folded elbows, looked out the window before turning back to me. There *was* more. I knew it.

"This isn't something I usually talk about, but I had a sister.

She died when she was about your age." Dark smudges appeared beneath his eyes like shadows.

"How? I mean, I'm sorry. That was probably a long time ago, right?"

He sighed. "Yes it was. Time pushes the pain of it in the background, but it never really goes away." He looked at me. "I guess you know that."

He laid his hands flat on his desk like he was counting his fingers. I was about to take my leave when he spoke again.

"There was just the two of us by then. Parents dead. I was old enough to be her official guardian, so we stayed in the house. But I wasn't ready to parent. Not to someone with addiction."

"Oh. What kind of addiction?"

"Back then crack was the street drug of choice, then heroin. She'd disappear for days, come back for money. After a while, I told her to stay away until she got clean. Changed the locks." Pain flashed across his face. "They found her behind a trash bin. OD'd."

There was something uncomfortably familiar about this. Older brother taking in the sister who turns out to be a screw-up. I felt my back stiffen. "I didn't make my choices because of Darcy, if that's what you're saying."

He looked confused. "Darcy?"

"You think back home I'll become an addict? Because Darcy took me in like you took in your sister?"

"I didn't take in my sister, Eugenia. We were both already there."

"Yeah, but I only drink sometimes. No drugs. Not serious stuff."

His jaw ticked. "I didn't tell you about my sister as a warning. You asked for extra reason why I cared, and I told you."

I felt my blood rise. "So I'm sort of a substitute for your sister. You think if you can keep me from becoming an addict, it'll make up for her. But I'm not like her, any more than you're like my father."

"Whoa! Where's this coming from?"

My face flushed. "Where do you think? Some psychobabble your resident psychologist planted in my mind. I am so sick of people trying to manipulate me into a mould, like I'm jello or something."

I jerked to my feet, ignoring the stab of pain.

He wasn't my father. Nor was he Darcy. Darcy would have got right back in my face or stomped out. Pops … I had no idea what he would have done. I wish I did. I wish he'd stuck around long enough for me to find out. Tears stabbed my eyes. I turned so Noah wouldn't see. Wiped them away.

Noah was Noah. He stayed silent until I was ready to face him.

"You okay?" he asked.

"Yeah."

"You want to talk to Heather?"

"No."

He searched my face. No hint of anything but concern in his. Didn't matter. I'd wrecked something just now. Just like I wrecked everything.

"Okay. You better get Melvin."

Kapow.

CHAPTER TWENTY-TWO

"Sit up, Eugenia."

Still prone in bed, I blinked in surprise. "Uh, thank you?" I'd feigned sleep until after Frankie and Tammy left, dreaded the moment I'd finally haul my battered and cracked self to the lodge. Frankie and I were still not speaking—except for just after my fall, but that had the feel of a dream. Not in a million years did I imagine Tammy would bring me breakfast.

"One time offer." She set a laden tray on the table.

I sniffed. "Is that bacon?"

"And eggs, and pancakes with Heather-made blueberry syrup. Get your sorry carcass over here."

There were plates for two. "You're eating with me?"

"Looks that way. Stop asking questions, it's getting cold."

I groaned as my feet found the floor. "Feels like I've been kicked around like a soccer ball." No sympathy from Tammy as I limped to the table, scraped back a chair, and sat. I looked warily at her. "This is nice of you."

"Yeah, well." She bit into a thick slice of homemade bread.

For ten minutes I shovelled in hot and smoky bacon, runny eggs and mouthfuls of cakey manna, washed it down with scalding coffee and pulpy juice. Finally, I pushed away my plate. "Done."

"No kidding."

There was nothing left. "I can't use the excuse of working up an appetite."

"I hear trauma can have the same effect." She looked a warning at me. "Not that yours was so bad. But I guess it could have been."

"That your way of saying you were worried about me?"

"Nope." But there may have been a hint of something else in her eye. She pushed back her chair. "Come on. We've gotta get you moving."

"I'm supposed to take it easy today."

"That doesn't mean sitting around. You need to walk to avoid any complications in your lungs."

We returned the tray of dishes to the kitchen and headed for the clearing. "Move your shoulders up and down," she said. I winced. "Hurt?"

"Yeah."

"Can you stand it?"

"Yeah."

"Good, let's go."

We walked side by side toward the Rubicon, then looped back up past the reading shed toward the lodge. Tammy grunted only the most necessary directions. She seemed preoccupied, but still barked at me at regular intervals. "Roll your shoulders. Deep breath in, and out."

"You get the short end of the straw, or something?"

Eyebrows up. "Why would you say a fool thing like that?"

"I'm not your favourite person."

She stopped. "And why would you say a fool thing like *that*?"

"It's obvious you'd rather be anywhere else."

She screwed up her face at me like I'd suddenly grown another set of ears, then resumed her march. "Keep up."

"Fine," I muttered.

"For your information, you're an idiot. Ever occur to you that people have things on their mind that have nothing to do with you?"

"Of course."

"Really? Cause it seems to me all your generation can talk about is how lousy everything is and how it's always someone else's fault. Bunch of gollfurnacking snowflakes," she grumbled.

"For *your* information, I'm not blaming anyone for anything. Putting a saddle on Red was my own idea. Tried to take some initiative. Shouldn't that be a good thing?"

Another screwed up face. I thought she might spew some more Tammy-isms at me, but she went back to her own thoughts.

"How long are we going to do this exactly?"

"Long as I say."

Super. Tammy wasn't one for small talk. Even at cards she mostly kept her comments on the game. Neither Frankie nor I asked her opinions on anything. I didn't even know what movies she liked, or if she liked movies at all. All I knew was that she enjoyed torturing me. "So which are you, Corrections or Social Work?"

"What're you talking about?"

"Most of the staff has a background in Social Work or Corrections. Which are you?

Another glance. "Corrections I guess."

"Not sure?"

"Hated it. Worst job I ever had, in the end."

"End of what?"

"Started out same as anyone, all full of piss and vinegar. There were only two women guards at my old job when I first started. Felt like I was doing a good thing, breaking down walls. But sometimes you can stay too long at a place. It turns you sour. And yes, I know that's what you and most of the other punks who come through here think of me."

It was like this woman who'd been such a thorn had suddenly

bloomed roses. "I like that you chose a non-typical career for a woman in a male-dominated environment. I respect that."

She looked interested. "That right?"

"Drives me crazy when people expect me to do certain things or act a certain way just because of my gender."

"I guess you and me got that in common."

Somewhere, a fox barked. A breeze bowed over yarrow, scented the meadow with sweetness and pine.

"If you hated it, why didn't you go back to school, learn something different?"

She was quiet for a long while. "I was ready to walk a few years back, but then my husband got real sick. Wasn't the right time to make a change."

Tammy had a husband? She was already old, which meant that he would have been too. And she was here alone. "He died?"

"He died." Her tone softened. It was like all her edges melted away. "We were married 37 years. Today's the anniversary of his death." She said it plain, no emotion, like she was rattling off a history lesson.

"I'm sorry."

"A month after the funeral, I handed in my resignation. Thought I might travel, though I had no idea where. Ran into Noah. He told me about this program he was starting, asked me to come work for him."

"Isn't this the same thing only different?"

"It was a change when I needed one."

"Noah know you hate kids?"

Amusement flashed across her face. "Hate smartasses even more. Besides, kids eventually turn into old goats. Just look at me."

"Tammy, was that an actual joke?"

"I won't quit my day job."

Movement caught the corner of my eye, pulled my attention back to the lodge. It was Frankie. She had some tools on the quad trailer. Started it up and headed down a trail beyond the pens.

"Weeding, I expect. Hayden's garden."

"That was supposed to be my job today. I haven't even been there yet."

"You should check it out." Another glance. "Work things out with Frankie, while you're at it."

"How did you—?"

"You got peas in your ears? Go talk to Frankie."

I smiled. "Yes, ma'am."

"And roll your shoulders!" she called after me.

As I passed the pens, I stopped briefly to watch Rick and Jimmy working with the horses. Rick was laughing as he hauled gear from the shed, like Jimmy had just told him a joke. Jimmy snapped a long lead on a horse and led him into a pen. The way he lived and breathed ranch life and twanged out country music in his spare time, Jimmy was the most cowboy of us all. Even more than Noah.

I left them, headed for Hayden's garden as slowly as I could go. Sure, I'd talk to Frankie. Didn't have much choice, and not because Tammy told me to. We were bunkmates. We had to come to some sort of understanding, even if we weren't going to be friends after all.

With a start I realized I hadn't thought of Luda in days, not even when I was in town getting my ribs looked at. I could have at least given them a call. Course, I hadn't called Jen and Darcy, neither. Jackson, the sharp memory of seeing him in the courthouse, had already faded like sidewalk chalk in the rain.

As I walked past his herd, Red nickered, came out to meet me. "Miss me, buddy?" He leaned in, grunted as I rubbed behind his ear. It was a wonder he didn't hold a grudge. Must've scared him, that saddle flapping on him and then slipping off his back. Course, Red wasn't the one with the rib damage.

Red walked beside me as I continued along the trail, chose the fork that led to the garden rather than Crooked Camp. I thought about Tammy's husband dying, and how Noah had been there the night Pops shot himself. It had been a day of revelations. Noah thought he knew everything about that night, but he didn't, and he never would.

I'd almost told Frankie. I wouldn't make that mistake again. If she asked me about it, I'd tell her she was right. That I'd gone temporarily crazy and it was a dumb lie.

Beyond a shallow creek, I veered onto a narrow trail into the woods marked by wooden signpost. Red left me, whinnying as he returned to his pals. Through a small stand of paper birch, I arrived.

"What're you doing here, Eugenia?"

Frankie didn't look upset that I was there, only startled. She sat on a stump, one of three set in a half circle, whittling a piece of wood. Gardening tools rested in a dirt patch sprouting neat rows of green things. Behind her there was a small greenhouse covered in clear plastic. All around there were oddities hanging from branches in surrounding trees: dangling stuffed animals, license plates, carved items, and placards. One of the signs read, "I SUPPORT THE RIGHT TO ARM BEARS." There was also a giant peace sign made from twisted willow branches, looped with Christmas tree garland.

I whistled. "Hayden, you are a complicated man."

"Hayden's Haven," Frankie said. "See?" She pointed to a painted signpost hammered into the ground. "I thought you couldn't work."

"Didn't come to garden."

"Noah send you?"

"Tammy."

A solemn nod. "Sit if you want to. Pull up a stump."

On the inside I was twitchy as all hell, but I sat—not easily, but I got there—found a semi-comfortable position. I had no idea how to start this conversation, only that it had to be done. But did it? I mean, if we both sort of mutually agreed in an unspoken way to forget our fight, wouldn't that be just as good?

"Look," Frankie said. "I feel like yesterday was my fault."

I jerked my head up. "How do you figure that?"

She hesitated, looked uncomfortable. "This feels really arrogant to say, but I'm worried that what happened on our trail ride, I don't know, distracted you or something."

I raised a brow. "You're right. That is arrogant." Then I felt mean. We weren't in a good enough place to tease like that. Everything was different. "Sorry."

"No, I am. Sorry, I mean. Really. I overreacted."

I searched her eyes, saw only sincerity.

"I think I was raw, you know? Talking about why I'm here. It's still hard for me." She bent and started fiddling with her boot. "Even when I was yelling at you, I knew I was wrong." She snuck a glance up, and then back to her boot. "I just didn't know how to stop." She sat straight again, looked at me full on. "It's like I said before, I still got work to do."

"How long you been here, Frankie?"

"Sixteen months, almost. I'll get out before I'm 18." She shook her head. "But I'll never get away from what I did."

She looked at her hands.

"How old are you now?"

"Sixteen. Seventeen, end of next month."

Sixteen years, same as me, and sixteen months in. It was

like some sort of magic number, except it wasn't. That was eighteen, when our past crimes were locked up, if not erased. If only we could lock up our memories like that. "And that's why I drink."

"What?"

I shook my head. "Nothing. I was just thinking about the stuff we do. What we've done. It's pretty hard." I turned to her. "I didn't mean to make you feel that what you did was anything like ... I mean, I know. I mean I don't know." I wiped my hand over my face in frustration.

"It's okay," Frankie said. "I know what you're trying to say." She grinned and then squinted. "At least I think I do. I also know that technically what I did was manslaughter, not murder. Doesn't make it any different in my head though." She reached into the bucket of weeds, grasped a handful by their wilting stalks, then dumped them back in. "His parents and his sister were allowed to read victim impact statements at my trial." Her face turned red and her eyes filled with tears. "Worse part is, they forgave me."

It was my turn to hold her hand. We sat there like that as she sniffled and wiped her eyes.

"What happened to your friend?"

Her voice turned bitter. "She called before sentencing. Said it upset her too much to visit me when I was in detention. Last I heard from her."

Not like Luda. They'd been there for me, out in the hall of the courthouse. "Not much of a friend."

"Guess not." She took a breath, let it out, spoke softly. "Want to tell me about your dad?"

My jaw froze. There was a pain in my chest and it was hard to breath. I couldn't look at her. She turned her hand in mine, squeezed. I'd forgotten I was holding it.

"It's okay," she said. "It's okay," she said again. "I'm here if you ever do. I'm sorry I was so full of myself the other day I didn't even ask."

I nodded my thanks.

She stood, picked up her bucket. "I've gotta get this done before lunch. Too bad you can't help."

"I'll entertain you with my wit."

She laughed. "With your stellar ability to not fully remember jokes, that won't make time go any faster. I'm so hungry I could eat the arse end off a squirrel."

I laughed hearty, holding the ache in my ribs. "The arse end off of what, now?"

Frankie grinned, no sympathy for my pain. "Just something Nathan says."

We both stopped smiling at the same time. Frankie kneeled between rows of potatoes neatly marked by someone's paintings on scraps of wood.

"I wouldn't have said anything if I knew," I said. "I wouldn't have even let myself think it. I'm not that person."

"I know. I mean, I don't know, but I'm glad to hear it." She sighed. "Truth is, there's nothing going on between us either. I just feel like there could be, you know?" He eyes were bright.

"I've seen it. The way you act with each other. But when you said there was nothing—"

"I said it wasn't allowed."

"Right," I said softly. "I guess I wasn't listening very well."

"I wasn't clear," she said. "On purpose. We weren't talking like this then."

"If you both feel like this, why aren't you together? Is it because of Roxanne and the other guy?"

"It is for me. I don't know what Nathan thinks. He gets out of here in January. Guess we'll see if he calls."

She was thinking about her so-called friend. The one she'd killed for.

"I'll call," I said. "I promise you that."

The sunshine was back. We were going to be okay.

CHAPTER TWENTY-THREE

Despite the good-natured ribbing I'd seen between him and his brother earlier, Jimmy was not having a good day.

"Sometimes I start thinking that no matter what we do, we are doomed or something, that no matter what, we're going to have the same lives as our parents."

Rick looked like he was clamping his lips together to keep from talking. The brothers shared that characteristic, allowing each to have his say. Not an easy thing.

"What does that look like to you?" Heather asked.

"A pile of shit, that's what."

Heather didn't blink. "Can you expand on that?"

Jimmy rolled his eyes, kicked out his legs. "I gotta wonder why our mother and Pa ever got together. Long as I remember they hated each other."

Rick clamped his mouth harder until his lips all but disappeared, looked at his feet.

"It got real bad after they split."

"Can you tell the others how old you were?"

"I was seven. Ricky was five, which is why he doesn't remember it like I do. She kicked Pa out hard and he went screaming, shouting and cursing too. Kept coming round and shouting more even though he was outside on the porch. Our mother changed the locks 'cause she was scared." He glared at his brother like it was his fault. "She told me that, said I was the oldest and needed to know." He turned back to Heather. "That stopped for a while when she called the police and got a restraining order, even though he was just yelling because she was the love of his life and we were his kids. He loved her. He loved us." His voice broke and we all stayed so still you could hear your heart beat.

"Jimmy?" Heather prompted.

Jimmy hung his head. "Yeah, I know," he said. "That's not how you show someone you love them. I guess it still hurts and I don't know why."

"That was a lot to take on as a small child."

"I guess."

"Have you talked to either one of them about that?"

"No."

"How is their relationship now?"

"They talk sometimes. I guess I started acting like my pa, at least she thought so, which is why she said it was okay for me to go live with him." He looked at Rick. "You didn't have to come with me, Ricky. You always got on good with her."

"You're my brother," Rick said, like it was everything. Maybe it was.

"Jimmy," Heather said. "It sounds like you're angry with your mother."

"I know it's not right. Don't you think I know? I just feel … I don't know. All jammed up inside."

"Have you talked to your mother about this?"

He shrugged. Shook his head. My heart hurt for him. "You can't just talk to people. It's not like it is here, in Group or one-on-one. They're gonna get mad before you get two words out, no matter what you're trying to say."

"Sometimes we don't even know what we're trying to say until someone slams a door and it's too late," Rick added. The brothers exchanged a look.

"Let's try something," Heather said. We all groaned. "What?"

she asked lightly, a teasing grin. "I thought you liked my exercises."

She handed out notebooks and pens. I held mine with a measure of guilt. I hadn't done any of that journaling she'd told me to. Nor did I plan to. The last thing I needed was a pen and ink reminder of my miserable life.

"You guys like movies?"

A few uncertain nods.

"Well, do you?" she asked with exaggerated animation.

General laughter, a few shouts of affirmation.

"You ever see a movie scene where two friends are sitting in a coffee shop?"

"Sure," Frankie said.

"Okay, I want you to imagine a coffee shop—any coffee shop—could be real, or one from your imagination. Imagine you're sitting there with someone from back home. Not a family member," she said, looking at Rick and Jimmy. Rick punched Jimmy in the arm and they both laughed. "Not *yet*. Just two friends, talking, or maybe someone at the grocery counter, or a busker on the street. Doesn't matter. Talk about anything. Maybe it's about a show you saw, or what you had for breakfast. Write that conversation down, just dialogue. It's not supposed to be a story."

"Just what we say to each other?" Jimmy asked.

Rick punched him again.

"Yes. No description. No action. Go ahead. I'll wait."

No one moved.

Heather tutted. "I get it. Maybe you feel a little uncertain. A little silly?" She looked around the room. Sheepish grins. "You are all practically grownups. If you don't want to do this, I won't make you."

Nathan pumped his fist. "Yeah!"

"I understand the septic system is due for maintenance. Noah will be very pleased to see you volunteer."

Crickets.

"No, this is good," Rick said. Jimmy nodded.

"Can't wait to have a chat with my friend Ronnie James," Nathan said, licking the tip of his pen.

One by one we opened our notebooks.

"That's what I thought," Heather said.

"Are you gonna check our work?" I asked.

"I will not. The value is in the journey, not the result." She looked around the room. "That said, if anyone wants to talk about anything that comes up, you can bring it to Group, or find me after."

Interesting. Okay. I'd give it a go.

Hey, Luda.

> *Hey. Long time no see.*

Hasn't been that long.

> *Thirteen days.*

I like it that you're counting.

> *Yeah, well, you're my best bud. No fun getting drunk without you.*

I paused. What *was* Luda doing with me not there? Who were they hanging with? We didn't really have any other friends. Just each other.

At least you can get drunk. I'd kill for a beer right now.

> *Seriously? Kill? Like that girl Frankie who's suddenly your new best friend?*

I didn't tell you about that.

Yeah, but you would have. Because that's what best friends do.

Why are you mad at me, Luda?

Why do you think?

My hand cramped and I realized I'd been writing furiously, pressing down so hard that if there were really such thing as Dr. Seuss's Whoville people they would have fallen into the canyons of my words.

Nathan laughed out loud. "Can we read these out loud?"

"If you like."

Nathan's Ronnie was also from Glace Bay, and Nathan stuffed in every bit of Cape Breton slang he could work into the conversation, as if he'd been a balloon waiting to let the air out. Even though more than half of what he said made no sense and the other half was so thick with accent he might have been listing off groceries and we wouldn't have known, we were literally rolling on the floor laughing as he finished. Heather laughed so hard she was crying and grabbed a handful of paper napkins from the dining table to mop her face before she could talk again.

"Thank you, Nathan. I think it's fair to say we all laughed our … arses off."

More howling.

"Anyone else?"

Frankie put her hand up. "Sure. Me. Except I decided to talk to myself. Is that okay?"

Heather smiled. "Of course."

"Hi, Frankie."

"Hi, Frankie."

A few chuckles from the group

"You're late."

"That's nothing new."

"Actually, it is, if you think about it. In some ways you have been early for everything. Early to leave home, to have a boyfriend, to get a job, to get fired, all that stuff."

"Other stuff too."

"Yeah, but this is supposed to be fun. We don't need to talk about that."

"Okay let's talk about when you got fired. That was fun."

"They needed a bartender so I used fake ID and said I could bartend. If Google was faster I would have lasted longer."

"I'm getting confused. Which Frankie was fired, me or me?"

More laughter.

"I'm the Frankie who has always been early. Maybe you're the Frankie of our future. Maybe you're the Frankie who says we don't have to be first for everything, like it's some sort of race."

"You know what's at the end of that race, Frankie?"

Death. She's going to say Death.

"No, and neither do you, because it's different for all of us, and what's important is that we're not going so fast that we miss a lot of good stuff along the way."

She finished and looked at me, wide grin. I'd never known anyone so damn open. It was near impossible to reconcile the Frankie here and now with the dark picture from her past.

"That was lovely, Frankie," Heather said.

"Me too?" Jimmy asked. His hand was up. He looked serious, and I realized he hadn't laughed along with the others. Not even when Nathan read his.

"Go ahead."

Jimmy gripped the edges of the notebook as if it were the helm of a ship and he was sailing through a storm, or maybe reins on a horse, to put it back in cowboyland, though I'd only ever seen him ride light and easy.

"You never cared when he went to jail."

His mother. He was talking to his mother. We weren't supposed to do that, but no one seemed to mind. Heather was listening intently.

> "Maybe I did care. You were a kid. You didn't need to know."

"I was a kid when you told me that he scared you."

> "You were the man of the house. That, you needed to know."

"I was a kid when you told me he was crazy, and that I better not turn out like that. I was still a kid when you kicked me out."

> "I didn't kick you out."

"You never said it like that, but I knew."

> "I was a single mother and you got big. I was afraid you would hurt me."

"Like him. Except he never hurt you, did he?"

> "Not physically. But fear is fear."

"He's a good man now. He's better."

> "He's better for you than me."

"You can't know that. You only mean you don't want me back."

Jimmy tore out the page, crumpled it in a ball.

"Talk to us, Jimmy," Heather said.

He looked to the ceiling, continued the conversation with his mother.

"What you don't know is that ranch work is good. I like it. I like Pa, and I like that Ricky was there too. Pa laughs about stuff. He looks funny when he laughs cause his bottom teeth are gone. Said they got bad when he was on the street. Yeah, I know he got a lucky break that Grandpa didn't leave no will and no, I don't think that money should have gone to us boys. What he got was a new life and what we got was a pa." He clenched his jaw, forced himself to continue, his voice choked. "I'm sorry I let you down." He took a breath. "It wasn't Ricky's idea to start stealing, and it wasn't Pa's neither. I just didn't want him to lose the place. Not after everything."

He deflated, like the words that held him up had gone, and there was nothing left. Rick just looked at him, expressionless. He knew the story, would have his own thoughts. Whether he would say them was his own thing to work on. Right now all that mattered was Jimmy.

Was he still thinking he might end up like his parents? Because that was wrong. It had to be. Screw the DNA and the way life ground into us, we still had *choice*. No way in hell I was like my parents. Eugenia Grimm had *stick*.

Frankie moved to the seat next to him, put her hand on his knee. Nathan moved behind him, hand on shoulder. Then Rick was there too, and so was I. We hugged him. No one said anything. We hugged him for a full eight seconds, as long as a rodeo cowboy rides a bull. Then we let go.

"Thanks," he said. "Thanks." That was all.

Heather sat in her same spot, but her eyes were glistening. "That's it for today."

We all got up to leave, except Jimmy. He kept his eyes on his feet, put his hand on his brother's as Rick patted his shoulder, then left.

CHAPTER TWENTY-FOUR

I knocked at the door, opened it. “Here I am,” I said to Melvin, and offered a mock salute. “Reporting for office duty.”

Melvin was by the file cabinet with a stack of papers, waved me to sit opposite him at the desk. “Just so we’re clear, I don’t like this, you up here messing with my stuff. I have a system.”

“Not my idea of fun either.”

Melvin narrowed his eyes. “You’re not here for fun.”

“I know that. I didn’t mean nothing by it.” I trailed off. What did I mean? “I’ll do whatever you need done, and I won’t mess up your stuff. I’m grateful to be here.”

He softened. “You said you were good at math.”

“I guess. I like formulas and stuff.”

“You don’t need formulas. That’ll be my work.” He sucked on his teeth. “Unless I say so. Can you file?”

“Not rocket science.”

He pulled a box of loose papers from below the desk. “Good. These are supply invoices. Find the company file and put them where they belong.” He stood, scooped up a set of keys. “Cabinet’s unlocked. I’ll be back to check on you, so don’t get any ideas.”

He left the door open, and I knew he meant it to stay that way. He didn’t trust me. Maybe he was thinking about what was in my file. I had stolen stuff in the past, even though that wasn’t what landed me here. Maybe he was thinking of that other kid who stole stuff from the office. What had Frankie called him?

Steven. That was it. *Steven, rhymes with thievin'*. I looked around, wondering what there was to take, other than pens and maybe a stapler.

Must have been hard on Noah, big as he was on trust. That was his own damn fault. It was his idea to bring a bunch of criminals into this place. What did he expect?

I looked at the box of paper, leafed through. The dates went back months. Darcy, who was always fastidious about his own paperwork, would be appalled. Maybe Melvin didn't have the same kind of training as Darcy did.

An image of my brother came to me, sitting at the kitchen table with his laptop open, recording receipts. Driving truck was his business, and so he kept up his records. What he did not keep was a shoe box. As soon as he returned from a trip, he recorded his expenses and saved receipts in neat, paperclipped files. Guess that education came in handy after all, just not how he'd imagined it.

Melvin must have the same education, otherwise Noah wouldn't have hired him. If you're gonna run any kind of business you need the right people for the right jobs, and you don't do anything that could mess up your books.

Like letting a punk-assed kid loose with your receipts. Thus Melvin's warning. But I had no intention of messing anything up.

Might as well get to it.

An hour in I was going cross-eyed. Melvin's filing had no discernible pattern. Folders were separated by company name but not by letter of the alphabet. It was like they landed where they did and that was that. I couldn't find any kind of logic, no matter how hard I looked.

He'd been doing this for a while. He probably had the place of things memorized.

An idea came to me, maybe even a chance to earn a few

brownie points. I would clean things up for Melvin. If nothing else, it'd make my task easier.

"What're you doing?"

I looked up at Melvin from the stacks of files I had piled around me on the floor.

"Putting them alphabetical," I said. "I was having some trouble, thought this would be easier." Here came the lecture. In hindsight I should have checked first, but this was the opposite of messing things up. "Sorry?"

He knelt, poked through the files. "Probably a good idea. I've been doing it so long I know where everything is even with the lights out."

"That's what I was thinking." I smiled, trying to feel as sunny as Frankie always looked. Mostly always. "So it's okay?"

"Sure. Good work. Nice to see the initiative."

I felt a little glow as he left again, then rolled my eyes. *Good puppy.* Whatever. This was what I had to do to stay here. I might as well take some pride in it.

Another half hour the folders were back in place and I filed the remaining invoices where they belonged. They went back to February. Looked like Melvin had begun the year with good intentions, then let things slide. That's how it was for most of us, but it shouldn't be that way in business.

I glanced at the computer. Maybe he did keep better records. Maybe he entered them online, and this was just a backup. That was probably it. I looked at the door, padded softly over to it. Couldn't hear any voices. I took a step out, looked over the rail into the great room below. No sign of anyone.

It was a no-brainer that Melvin didn't want me on the computer, but curiosity was getting the better of me. Would Melvin use a tax program like Darcy did, or a simple spreadsheet? I'd guess a spreadsheet. Nothing too complex.

I'd just take a look. If he didn't use anything, maybe I could help him with that. Set up a spreadsheet, make his life easier. Show some more of that initiative.

Bloop. Power on.

Who bothered to turn off computers?

It was an older looking desktop with green background, a *My Computer* icon in the top left corner, and a *My Documents* yellow folder. There were also icons for the recycle bin and a network connection. Did they even have internet up here? I hovered the mouse over the network icon, then away. That might be fun, but it would also be a sure way to get in trouble. Maybe Melvin was savvier that he looked. I knew how to erase internet browsing history, but if he walked in and caught me red-handed the jig would be up. I'd stick to business.

I clicked on the *Folders* icon. The screen filled with more yellow folders, this time against a white background. Some of them had dates. I clicked on the current year. The individual documents inside each had a series of numbers with lock icons. No names. Was one of these about me? Frankie and the others? No way to tell. I didn't see any spreadsheets, so I backed out of the folder, looked once more at the empty doorframe, and turned back to the computer.

There was a recipe folder, and one for photos. I clicked. Those were cool. Interesting to see what this place looked like in each season. None with people in them. Maybe they needed special permission for that, privacy laws and all. Or maybe the people pictures were in another locked folder. There was one marked *Horses* and another marked *Private*. Maybe that was where the tax stuff was.

I could just ask him. I should. I would.

I jogged through the doorway into the hall, leaned over the rail. "Melvin?" No answer. I heard humming in the kitchen, trailed my hand on the carved wooden railing as I made my way down.

"How're you doing?" Merry asked. She was seated at the kitchen island, writing in a notebook.

"Okay, I guess. I miss being outside. Melvin around?"

"He and Noah had some septic system maintenance to get to. If you need the bathroom, use the outhouse. Shouldn't take long."

Huh. Guess Heather hadn't been joking yesterday after all.

"No, I'm good. Just finished what he asked me to and had an idea for something else."

"He won't be long. Want a snack?" She nodded toward cut celery stalks next to a peanut butter jar. "My guilty pleasure," she said.

"Vegetables are a guilty pleasure?"

She laughed. "Just my current favourite, I suppose. You have a favourite snack?"

"Not really. I miss potato chips."

"We try and keep things healthier up here."

"I noticed. It's good though." What she and Heather gave us was always plentiful and tasty. I hadn't even thought about chips until she mentioned snacks. Thinking about chips made me think about other things back home. And people. Seemed so far away. "Everything you make is good. Were you a chef before you came here?"

She laughed. "Hardly. You know how stressful the hospitality industry is?" She lifted her eyebrows high. "Not for me. Always enjoyed it though, even when I was a little kid. Learned from my mom. Not that she cooked fancy or anything, but she did get me interested."

"Where did you work before here?"

"Manitoba," she said lightly. "It was an alternative program for kids who didn't do well in a regular school setting."

"You run into Noah when he was starting up this place, like Tammy and Hayden?"

She smiled. "Noah's my cousin. He called me up, asked if I felt like an adventure. Said I'd try it for six months."

"How long's it been?"

"Three years next month." She winked at me. "This place grows on you. The people too."

"Even us? The inmates I mean. Wards or whatever."

"People are people. We all got something, but kids like you who come through are mostly okay. Just need some clean air and good food. Besides, we don't get the kids that need more than we can give them. What do you think all that testing was for right up front?"

I swiped another stick of celery and peanut butter. "If you see Melvin, tell him I'm working on something, okay?"

Back upstairs, I got to work on setting up an Excel sheet. I thought back to small business class from school and decided it needed columns with category headers along the top. When Melvin got back we could work out something better. But what categories? Small businesses usually set things up so that tax filing was easier, and the government had specific tax categories, like vehicle expenses and office supplies. Okay, I would start with those. What else?

My imagination failed me.

I needed an example from good old Google. A very good reason to get on the internet!

Did I dare?

It was probably password protected.

Yup.

But this was Melvin. Any guy who stored receipts in a box probably kept it simple. Something easy to remember, so no weird letter-number combos.

Back at the grocery store, we logged on with a simple "1-2-3-4."

And there it was. Had it crossed his mind even once that given the clientele coming through this place he might want to put a little effort in?

That's when I noticed branches on the network. There was the internet proper, but there were also extensions with names of staff members. I guessed that was to keep their personal interests from cluttering up the main work of the ranch.

Whoa! I shouldn't even be close to this.

"What in the hell do you think you're doing?"

Shit.

"Hi, Melvin."

CHAPTER TWENTY-FIVE

I punched my pillow, had a bad feeling about all this. Like, really bad. Melvin so was steamed to see me at the computer he had no words. He wouldn't even let me explain. If he'd yelled, it would have been easier to yell back about how I was only making things better. Instead, I'd fumbled and stuttered until even I didn't believe me.

"We'll talk later," he'd said. "Time for lunch."

I hadn't felt much like eating and used my ribs as an excuse to get out of Group right after. "Paperwork is more tiring than you'd think," I'd said, which was pretty feeble, but I'd been excused with a hot cup of tea and electric heating pad from Merry.

Still had dinner to get through, though Noah and Melvin would probably talk before then, and I'd be called on the carpet to explain. That would be okay. I mean, I hadn't meant any harm. Noah would see that, no matter how mad Melvin was at me.

Beside my bed the notebook sat exactly where I'd tossed it after Heather gave it to me. I reached for it. I'd tucked a pencil inside the spiral binding. I pulled it out, tried sitting cross-legged, but it hurt too much so I moved to the small table, scraped out a chair from underneath. Sat.

Like Nathan had done, I licked the tip.

Except this was a pencil. I wiped my tongue with my sleeve. Didn't want lead poisoning, though I wasn't likely to be poisoned from one lick. How many licks would it take? Should have Googled when I had the chance.

I tapped the pencil on the closed book. Opened it. I didn't feel much like writing about spoons. Said all I had to say on that.

I pushed a checker on the checkerboard, looked around the room, wished it were evening already, and Tammy and Frankie and I were sitting around playing checkers or cards.

This had the feel of being stuck. What was it I'd said to Rick?

Not having a choice is like being stuck in a box and having it taped up tight. Maybe you like the box and maybe you don't, but you can't know if it's not your own choice to stay in or get out.

I'd had a choice about coming here. It was a no-brainer, but it was still there. This, or what might be coming, wasn't up to me. I was completely at Noah's mercy. That sucked.

I needed a friend: Luda.

I put pencil to page.

Hey Luda.

Hey. So you got yourself in trouble.

Maybe. Something I'm good at.

You need a drink.

You know I do.

You got a bottle stashed around there?

Maybe.

Maybe I stuck one in your bag.

Of course you did. Thanks.

But you're right. I don't know anything about that place, or what you're going through.

You could call sometime.

Yeah, about that.

What?

I been kinda busy.

I sighed, closed the notebook. I wished there was some way I could make the exercise fun, like Nathan had, or thoughtful, like Frankie versus Frankie. Maybe I was just too serious. Too plain. Probably more like Darcy that I'd ever admit out loud. Maybe things would have been different if Jackson had taken me in instead of him.

I barked a laugh. Different, maybe, but same result. Maybe worse. It was like Jimmy said, we are who we are destined to be.

He'd said parents, but I couldn't really draw on mine as an example.

Stashing the notebook on the bedside table, I lay back on my bed. Nothing to do but wait.

Frankie popped her head in. "You okay?"

I looked at the clock beside my bed. Group was over, and it was Nathan's day for a one-one-one. He was supposed to have it yesterday, but because Jimmy needed that time Nathan was switched to today.

"Yeah, good."

"Okay. Just wanted to make sure."

I looked at her. "It's not my ribs."

She sat on her bed. "Yeah, I didn't think so. You hardly moaned at all last night in your sleep. Not like the first night."

This begged for a comeback quip, but nothing came to mind, and I wasn't feeling playful.

"I screwed up," I said, told her what I'd done in the office.

"Shit."

"You think I'll get booted?"

She shrugged. "There's no boot rule saying you can't go on the computer."

"That's because the office is always locked." I looked at her. "Did you know there's an actual rule for pilots that says they can't let anyone walk on airplane wings when they're flying unless they're wearing a parachute?"

"Random."

"I did a project on aviation for school. Point is, as obvious as it sounds, they probably only have a rule because someone tried it."

"So, no rule because no one's done it."

"Right."

"Maybe you'll be let off on a technicality."

"We'll see."

The door swung open. "Noah wants to see you," Tammy said. She didn't ask about my ribs. I probably hadn't fooled anyone.

"I don't much like the look of this," I said. Melvin and Merry were with Noah in the office. Tammy was behind me.

"Have a seat, Eugenia." He motioned to the couch. Tammy sat beside me while Merry took Heather's usual spot. Noah and Melvin dragged chairs over from the desk.

"I didn't do anything wrong," I said.

"You'll have a chance to speak," Tammy said. "Just hold tight."

The disappointment in Noah's face was misplaced. I wasn't his sister. I wasn't his kid. I was a *ward*. What right did he have to make me feel guilty, especially when I'd only been trying to do good?

"Melvin said he left you to do some filing, that he checked on you once and was satisfied that you were doing good work. Merry said you came down once looking for Melvin, then went back to work. Melvin said when he came back to check on you again you were at the computer."

"Say it like that it doesn't sound so bad. What's the big deal?"

Noah and Melvin exchanged a look. "You were not given permission to be on the computer. You're smart enough to know we'd likely have sensitive material on there."

"Yeah but those files are locked. I mean, I am guessing they'd be locked." *Shit*. More looks. "I was just making a spreadsheet."

"There's no sign of that."

"That's because I pulled the plug when Melvin came in."

No one said anything. It was like they were letting the weight of what I'd just said sink in.

"Yeah, I know how that looks. It's just that he made me jump."

"Do you always pull plugs when you jump?"

I was sunk. They knew it and so did I. I wasn't one to beg for mercy. What will be will be. "I'll say it plain and ask that you believe me. It's more in my nature to get mad and stuff. I know you know that, but maybe because we're sitting here where I've been talking with Heather, there's a bit of spillover calm and feeling like it's okay to talk. I know you have no reason to trust me more than anyone else who comes through here. But I really was trying to do some good. I found a better way to do Melvin's files. Did he tell you that?"

"He did," Noah said.

I resisted the urge to ask if that was hard for Melvin, knowing how he felt about my being in the office. Looked like it wouldn't much matter now anyway.

"And Merry already told you I came looking for him. I finished the filing and wanted to ask him if I could make a spreadsheet. Actually, I wanted to ask him if he already had one, and if he didn't, I was gonna offer to make one."

"You said you had an idea for something," Merry said.

"Exactly."

"Did you get on the network?" Melvin asked.

This was the point where I could lie. He had no way of knowing, seeing as I'd pulled the plug. "I did," I admitted.

"How'd you get past the password?"

"You need a better one. 1-2-3-4 is as bad as a-b-c-d."

Noah stifled a smile. "As you rightly noticed, our important files are electronically locked. I don't like that you know that. It means you had a look around. But you told the truth about getting the network booted up, and that makes me inclined to believe your intentions."

"We knew you got on," Melvin said. "Pulling the plug doesn't erase the record of your log-in. It just meant your spreadsheet didn't save."

"We're going to put a note on your file," Noah said. "You didn't technically break a rule, but you bent Melvin's good intentions beyond where you should have. If this is going to work, you need to do exactly as you're told."

I heaved a sigh of relief. "I will. Thank you. Thanks." After saying thanks three more times I stumbled out, down the stairs and into the great hall.

My stomach growled.

On cue, everyone began filing in for dinner.

CHAPTER TWENTY-SIX

Everything should have been okay. A note on my file, fine. So why did everything feel weird this morning? The air was perfectly still, like in the eye of a storm, except it wasn't even cloudy.

While I was washing the breakfast dishes, Noah walked in with a look like I'd stepped in it again. I hadn't. How could I? After dinner the night before I'd played crazy eights with Tammy and Frankie and gone to bed.

"Melvin won't need you in the office this morning. Why don't you help Rick and Jimmy clean tack?"

He said he had to make some calls and left before I could ask any questions. "You know what's going on?" I asked Merry and Heather. They shooed me out of the kitchen. They seemed quieter too.

Frankie and Nathan were in the pens brushing horses, getting ready to ride. They were going with Tammy to Turtle Lake to prep our campsites.

"You were pretty quiet over breakfast," Frankie said.

"Lots to think about. Did the staff seem weird this morning?

"No more'n usual," Nathan said. "What's going on?

I filled him in on what had happened.

"But you cleared all that up yesterday," Frankie said. "Maybe they're just being weird to make sure you don't feel like you got away with anything."

"But I didn't. I told the truth. And anyway, I didn't break any rules, so even if I did lie about it and get caught, I don't think I would have got booted."

"Noah's big on truth," Nathan said.

"And trust and no pressure and all of that stuff. I know. So why does this feel like the opposite?"

"Come wash these saddles, Eugenia!" Jimmy called. He had everything prepped for me so I wouldn't have to bend or strain too much. Nice of him.

I started walking and stopped. "I just can't figure Melvin out, you know? One minute it's like he has it in for me, and the second he's all, 'good work, Eugenia.' He's not so great a bookkeeper. I could help him do better."

Frankie added, "Noah likes you, and he believes in you. We all do. You even made Tammy like you, which is crazy. All you did was look at something you shouldn't have. If anything, it will be Melvin who's in trouble because he shouldn't have left you alone with anything he didn't want you to see."

"I cracked the staff network password."

Nathan raised his eyebrows, whistled.

"You never mentioned that part," Frankie said.

"I'm no hacker. It was simple."

"Don't worry about it," Nathan said. "It's not a boot-rule."

"Was it worth it? Anything interesting on there?" Frankie asked.

The sound of the lodge door banging shut got my gut going again. It was Hayden and Tammy. I met them at the gate.

"What is it?"

"Just wait," Tammy said. She looked pissed. "Noah will be here in a minute."

"What's going on?" Nathan asked.

The lodge door banged again and out came Noah carrying my bag. I heard the sound of the Navajo start up.

"Shit."

"Hang on!" Frankie cried. "You can't boot her for what she did. She apologized. And she didn't break any rules!"

The Navajo taxied into the field.

"Noah, I don't understand."

"We'll talk during the flight," he said, and turned to Frankie and Nathan. "Meeting inside. Now." He called to Rick and Jimmy, who were standing and watching. "You too, boys!"

I grabbed hold of Frankie, one hand on each shoulder. "I never had a friend like you."

She held me in the same way, eyes glistening. "You'll be back," she said. "We'll figure this out!"

"Go!" Noah ordered the others.

My head whirled, but then I was on board the Navajo and we were bumping across the field for take-off. Noah sat across from me. The way he looked at me felt like a kick in the gut. "What happened?"

He didn't answer. I looked out the window as we circled up and away. I hadn't even said goodbye to Red.

"Those must have been some interesting calls you made."

"Protocol is to move quick. Anything you want to tell me?"

This made no damn sense. "I know I screwed up, but … it wasn't a boot-rule!" His face told me he didn't get it. "Boot-rule. The rules that if you break them, you get the boot. Noah, I told you, I was trying to do something good!"

A flash of uncertainty. "When you were in Fort St. Luke with Hayden, did you see anyone? An old friend?"

"No. We saw the doctor. That was it."

"At no time were you left on your own?"

"No! I mean, the bathroom at the airport."

Noah frowned.

"Why? What is this about?"

"Vodka. Tammy found it under your mattress after reading your notebook."

"That was private!"

"Nothing's private." His voice was firm. "We can search your belongings and your space at any time. That is also in the rules."

I thought about what I wrote. "There was nothing in there. Just an exercise from Group. Ask Heather!"

But it was clear he was done. "We'll talk more in town. Get your thoughts in order. We'll meet with your lawyer first."

"Boyer?"

He opened up a file, started writing. I couldn't see what it was.

If we were meeting with Boyer, that meant the judge was next. This was more than trouble. It was a one-way ticket to jail.

If I'd snuck in a bottle of vodka, I would definitely have broken a boot-rule, but I hadn't. That meant it belonged to Tammy, or ...

Frankie?

No. She hadn't been off the ranch, and there'd been no one to visit her. Unless she'd gotten it before I'd even arrived, maybe hid it in an unused bed so that Tammy wouldn't find it if she'd searched her stuff.

Stop it, Eugenia. Don't shift blame to someone just because it's easy.

It hurt to see Noah look at me like that. It hurt that he wasn't listening, that he didn't believe me.

I'd told him I didn't want special treatment. Guess he listened.

So now what? Frankie said she'd figure this out. She didn't even know about the vodka. Or did she?

I smacked my forehead with my palm. It was so easy to turn on the people who cared about you. But how well did I know her, really? We'd only been friends about five minutes.

She wouldn't do that, Eugenia.

I groaned, put my head in my hands. When I looked up, Noah was frowning at me. "Not a hangover," I sniped.

This wouldn't have happened if I'd never picked up that dumb journal. I closed my eyes. Imagined myself back at Luda's place.

You're in trouble again.

Yep. And just like last time, I shouldn't be.

You're saying that a lot lately. Ever think it's because you started making changes that you shouldn't have?

I don't know what you mean.

Yes you do. You're forgetting about me. You said you'd never do that.

Like you said, you've known Frankie five minutes and she's already taken my place.

No one could do that, Luda.

Good.

I miss you.

Good.

I opened my eyes. This was my imaginary conversation. Why couldn't I make Luda say they missed me too? I closed my eyes again.

Nothing.

Because they weren't like that, that's all. They didn't talk about their feelings, they showed them. One good thing about being back in town, it would be easier for them to call.

But would they?

Ole flicked a radio switch. "Base, this is Captain America. You there?"

While Ole called the ranch, Noah explained how things would go. We would meet with Boyer and talk things through. After that we'd get back up in front of the judge, soon as Boyer could arrange a hearing.

"I'm pulling for you, Eugenia, I really am. But we can't have you breaking the rules and getting away with it. I can't let you slide on this. Even if I wanted to, how would that look? What if we get shut down? Where would that leave Frankie and the others?"

I wanted to tell him again that it wasn't me. But he wasn't listening, so I kept my mouth shut.

"No one's answering, boss," Ole said.

"Don't worry about it. We'll call from the ground."

My stomach swirled with the motion of Ole tilting the aircraft to bring it around, line up with the runway. A woman's voice on the radio told him he was cleared to land. A gentle thud indicated the opening of the landing gear doors, and I readied for the bump on landing. Flying wasn't bad, but I preferred the in-air part over landing and takeoff.

A horn blasted.

Ole shouted something in Norwegian.

Panic exploded from the centre of my stomach. "What happened?"

"Landing gear didn't lock," Ole said. He tapped at red lights on the control panel and we climbed back up into blue sky as a voice on the radio said she checked the missed approach and asked if there was a problem.

Before he moved up front to assist Ole, Noah put a hand on my shoulder. "Air traffic control will get out their binocs and tell us what they see."

"What will they see?" My belly was full of hornets.

"The landing gear fully extended, is my hope. Just a hiccup."

I looked again at the red lights. "Why are those still on?"

Ole and Noah exchanged a look. "Could just be an indicator problem," Ole said. "Or the landing gear hasn't extended."

Noah called the ranch. "Base, come in." Still no response.

"Don't worry," Noah assured me. "Everything will be fine."

Fire trucks pulled up to the runway, lights flashing.

Ole circled around again, and the controller cleared him for a "fly-by."

"We're going to buzz the control tower," Noah explained.

There was a figure in the glass tower cab, binoculars glued to their face. The controller's voice crackled through the radio. "We can confirm your gear is only partially extended," she said. "Repeat, only partial."

Ole's voice was calm. "Roger, Tower. We'll try a manual extension."

The controller cleared him into a holding position south of the airport.

It felt like we were circling forever. Time felt distorted. I wanted to believe this wasn't really happening, that it was a dream or something.

Noah peeled back a piece of grey felt between the pilot and co-pilot seat. He pumped the exposed lever. After about fifty he stopped, rubbed his shoulder then pumped again.

The lights remained red. "Those should be green, right?" I asked.

"Right," Ole said, his voice raised above Noah's grunting effort. They exchanged another look and Ole nodded as if Noah had spoken. He radioed the control tower and took the aircraft out of the holding pattern.

Noah looked grave. "You know crash position?"

I'd seen enough movies and showed him I did, adjusting for the pain in my torso.

"We're going to do one more low-and-over so the controller can see what's what, then we are going to go slow as we can and land with the gear as it is."

"Is that bad?"

"Ole is an excellent pilot. We'll prepare for the worst, but I want you to know I expect we'll be fine."

I wanted so badly to believe him.

"Crash position when I tell you, okay?"

"Okay."

Lights flashed along the runway as Noah told me it was time. I reached for my ankles, held tight, felt a slight tip to one side, then bump, bump and we were spinning. And then stopped.

Quiet.

Sirens wailed, and then they were cut too.

Everything was confusion after that as arms pulled me out of the aircraft.

Ole and Noah were out too.

"How are your ribs?" Noah asked, his face creased with concern.

"Okay." My voice was coming from somewhere else, like I was back at the ranch and only imagining this. "I'm okay."

Someone clapped Ole on the back. "Nice landing!"

"Oh, you know," he said. "I save the good ones for when I really need them." He was joking, but he was pale.

Back in the airport, the conversations began, along with paperwork.

"This could take a while," Noah told me. "We need to get you checked out in hospital."

He rode in an ambulance with me, even though I said I was fine. No one ever listened. In emerg, they got me right into a room.

"The doctor will be right with you," the nurse said.

Noah's phone rang. He looked relieved. "Merry."

"Sir, you'll have to turn that off." She pointed to a sign. No cell phones.

"I'll be right back," he said.

I watched him disappear.

Just a matter of hours before it was forever.

"Where's the bathroom?" I asked the nurse.

CHAPTER TWENTY-SEVEN

My breath came fast and shallow as I walked slow along the hospital corridor past security, turned left and followed a yellow line. I didn't see Noah. I found another door.

Minding my ribs, I ran.

No going back. There might have been a minute that I could have, but by now or soon Noah would get off the phone and know I was gone. He would call the police.

Protocol is to move quick

I hadn't given him much choice. He'd done all he could for me. I was just another Grimm gone bad, like my brother after all.

Three blocks away, I knelt behind a garbage dumpster to steady myself. Catching my breath would have been infinitely nicer almost anywhere else, but I needed to stay hidden, and I needed to keep moving. But where could I go? I needed help.

Darcy? If he was home, he would be pissed.

Luda! I would find them and we'd blow this town, just like we always talked about.

One foot in front of the other, from street to alley to bicycle path and park. There were a few cars in the lot. No one official looking. A couple of kids playing Frisbee. Joggers.

I ran, slowing to a fast walk when there was someone else on the path. Jogging in jeans and boots didn't look right. Didn't want to draw attention. The clay path split, and split again, but I knew it like the back of my hand.

Because it was my neighbourhood.

Puffing, I paused. My path to Luda had taken me right past Darcy and Jen's.

My body refused to move on. Too many people had disappeared from my life without saying goodbye. Darcy could shove it, but I couldn't just walk away from Jennifer and the boys. Especially not the boys.

You have time, Eugenia

No I don't. The police will check here first.

Yes. You. Do. You have to.

I'd be quick. Just a hug and goodbye.

As I jogged toward the house I exhaled. No sign of Noah, or the police, and Darcy's truck was not in the driveway.

Relief brought on guilt.

You're such a shit, Eugenia. I shouldn't be happy Darcy wasn't home. My brother was a part of me, had taken me in when I was in need, and even though I hated his constant lectures, I always knew it was because he cared.

He'd only tell you to turn yourself in.

He also had a stick up his ass. Do the right thing, do the right thing, where in the hell had that ever gotten anyone? And who in my life had followed that creed?

The right thing would be Pops still living.

The right thing would be Ma still here.

The right thing would be Darcy staying home with his family instead of running off like a chickenshit every chance he got.

The right thing would be Jackson being in our lives. Okay, maybe not Jackson. Every family had a lost cause, and he was ours.

And me.

Shut up, Eugenia.

I had to stop talking to myself like I was an insane person. But if I thought myself crazy that meant I wasn't. That's how it worked. Except I was. In this instance, I was.

Maybe we were all nuts in different ways. I understood that Pops was sick, not crazy, but still. In that moment, he couldn't have been thinking right. He couldn't have been thinking at all. At least my crazy was only gonna take me out of town.

Jennifer was on the front lawn, hand to her mouth. She woulda been watching out the window as she worked in the kitchen, always on the lookout for strangers who might snatch her boys. She was paranoid but loved her kids to the ends of the Earth. My eyes misted as I threw myself into her arms.

"Why, Eugenia Grimm!" She hugged me back, then pushed me away, alarmed. "What have you done?"

"Nothing. Here on ranch business." I wiped my eyes with my sleeve. "Thought I'd come by and say hello."

"Shouldn't you have a chaperone?"

"Time off for good behaviour."

She didn't believe me. She'd always had an extra sense about when I wasn't completely truthful. A hasty look each way up the street, and: "Come in."

Conner and Tip barrelled around the corner and wrapped their four-year-old selves around my neck and knees. Hurt like hell but I didn't care. After hugs and tickles they were away.

Jennifer set out two mugs of steaming black coffee and joined me at the table. "Noah called." My blood turned ice. "Day before yesterday," she added, and I exhaled. "Your ribs okay?"

I took the coffee but didn't drink. "Fine. I was at the hospital today to get them checked." Wasn't a lie.

"They wouldn't let you call when it happened? I mean, you must have been in town for a few hours."

"Sorry, Jen. I didn't think of it. Shock, I guess."

She nodded and took a long look at me. "Outdoor work agrees with you. You look good."

I gave her what I hoped was an apologetic smile, got up from the table and moved toward the door. "I can't stay. Just wanted to say hello. You give those boys an extra squeeze for me."

"Wait." Her voice was firm. I stopped. "It's a shame you'll miss Darcy."

"Maybe if he wasn't gone so much."

Her eyes clouded. "You used to be so close. All of you."

What was she going on about? "That was a long time ago, Jen. You know that."

A memory came, sudden. Bright sunlight, squinting through younger eyes. I was hiding behind the fence, but I remembered like I was still there: what the heat smelled like as it rose from the sidewalk, the asphalt, the hood of the car. The real joy of childhood was that you only thought about what was right in front of you. Most of us don't even notice when that changes. Maybe we weren't supposed to.

I'd hid from the sunlight and more that day, but my brother found me.

"There was this one time Darcy took me to a movie," I said. "Ma and Pops were bickering, and Darcy and I were sitting there, trying to pretend we were somewhere else. Jackson was already moved out. Then Ma followed Pops out of the room and Darcy said, 'Come on, chum.'" I smiled. "I remember thinking that was a funny word. Chum. Anyhow, it's not the movie I remember. It was after. We got ice cream, and the ice cream melted faster than I could eat it, running all down my wrist no matter how fast I licked. We both thought that was pretty funny."

As if on cue, the kitchen door rattled opened. Darcy froze in place when he saw me.

I glanced at Jen. She'd delayed me on purpose. Her face was stone.

"Daddy, Daddy!" The boys dashed into the kitchen and were all over him.

Jennifer peeled them away. "Boys, settle down."

Darcy hadn't taken his eyes off me. "You boys go wash up. You're sticky."

"I like sticky," Tip said, giggling.

"I'm sure you do. Go wash up anyhow."

Jennifer followed them out while Darcy held a chair for me, then sat opposite. "What are you doing here, Genie?"

I cleared my throat. "Time off for good behaviour." Darcy didn't buy it any more than Jennifer had.

He narrowed his eyes. "Your sentence was to last the summer and more. Seems odd"—his lips curled around the word—"that you're on your own."

"What, you think I just flapped my arms and flew out of the mountains?" Annoyance prickled up my back like ant bites. "Like I told Jen, I'm here getting my ribs checked."

"Don't get like that. You know what I mean."

"Maybe I do, maybe I don't. The truth of the matter is you don't want me around. You never wanted me here to begin with." Just like that we were back in the middle of our last argument. My face flushed.

"What in the hell are you getting at?"

"You know exactly what. When Ma left, you were the only stable legal guardian I coulda had. Jackson being Jackson was no option. You were forced into it, and you hated me for that."

He looked stunned. Anger edged into his voice. "Again, what in the hell are you talking about?"

"Settle down, Darcy," I said silkily. "Don't let the boys hear." I was pushing buttons, didn't care.

"Don't you tell me how to talk in my own damn house, Eugenia!"

"There it is. *Your* house. I've only ever been here temporarily in your eyes. Not really part of your family, not this one, though it does seem you try your best to stay away from this one too."

He pushed his chair back so sudden it fell back with a clatter, stood and leaned on the table, palms flat. An ugly red crawled up his neck and he spoke slow. "What line of crap have they been feeding you up at that ranch, Eugenia?"

"Nothing. It's just the truth of things, and you know it."

"Not my truth!" He paced back and forth about to spit fire. He pointed a finger at me like he had something to say, paced, then stopped, opened his mouth, and paced some more.

"Hey, settle down."

"Now you're telling me to …?" He threw his hands in the air, picked up his chair and settled back at the table. He folded his hands in front of him and stared hard at them.

This was taking too long. I stood. "Darcy, I—"

He threw a hush-finger my way, pointed me back to sitting.

"But I—"

He shushed me again, pursed his lips. "Eugenia, I hardly know where to start."

A sixth sense told me it was time to get gone, but I was uncertain now. Curious about where his head was at. "Wherever you want."

"All right, though this seems more your issue than mine."

"You deny that you don't want me here?"

"Damn right I deny it!" He winced and swiped a hand over his face. "Okay, that isn't quite true."

A stab to the heart, even though I knew it.

"But it's not what you think," he added. "Putting aside the fact that you should be in custody right now"—His look told me it wouldn't be put aside for long—"I always thought you could do better, Genie."

I leaned back. "That's what you wanted to say? Join the

club. You know how many times I've heard words like that? I'm such a disappointment. Well, so what? I'm getting by just fine. I accept my—"

Darcy slammed his fist down on the table. "That is NOT what I mean!"

The house was shocked silent. No noise. Not from the boys, the refrigerator, nothing, only my heartbeat, right in my ears. And Darcy's breathing.

He wiped his forehead, looked around the room before settling back on me. "Did it ever occur to you that some people have a certain kind of life because it's the only kind of life we can have? Sure, we find ways to make it work, find ways to be happy and everything is perfectly fine."

"You talking about you and Jennifer?"

He looked tired. "You're still not listening. Think about it. From the time you were a little kid, the way your mind worked. We all thought it was amazing. Remember that time at Mr. Wuzik's ranch? With the bucket? You remember what you did?"

"What bucket?"

"Oh, no, don't give me that. You remember. We played some sort of prank on you and you retaliated in a big way."

The memory took shape and I grinned. "Bucket of pee. My pee. I filled the bucket."

"Not only that, but you rigged the door so that it dropped on us when we opened it. What seven-year-old does that?"

"Hey, you had it coming. Pretty sure it was more than a prank what you guys did to me."

"Maybe it was and maybe it wasn't, but that's not the point, Eugenia." He sighed. "After we got over being mad, we were pretty impressed. You were so young, it was incredible. Maybe even scary. We all knew you were special and that one day we'd lose you, but it would be a good kind of losing. You were supposed to go to university, study something, whatever. I always thought you'd go somewhere, maybe end up doing something important."

"Like what?"

"I don't know. Cure cancer or something, how the hell should I know? But instead you stuck yourself in the same life as all of us. You'll stay in this town, get a job at a gas station, maybe, or stocking shelves at the grocery, and you'll be lucky to get that, way you're headed." He shook his head. "Maybe that's just how it goes."

I spoke softly. "There's nothing wrong with this life, Darcy."

He blinked like it hurt to look at me. "No there isn't. But you had choices, Genie. Choices some of us never get close to. Ma knew it too, she always said—"

"Ma left."

"But she knew, Genie, and she did her best to—"

"Her best?" I choked, stood again. "Ma! Left!"

I was done. I let my last look at him, this image of his face red, flushed, angry, burn into my memory. The door slammed behind me and I ran and ran and didn't stop until I reached the park.

In the distance, the *yow* of sirens.

It was the beginning of the end. Unless I kept moving.

CHAPTER TWENTY-EIGHT

Where the hell was Luda?

I'd stuck to back alleys much as I could, ducking, hiding, keeping my face turned away from traffic cameras, but when I finally got to Luda's they weren't there. Chest heaving, I stared blank at their apartment door. No one home and my key, all my personal stuff, was probably on the plane.

Slapping the concrete wall in frustration I silently screamed, *where are you? I need you!*

My one forever friend.

After Pops's suicide, after weeks of not speaking, I found my voice, but it felt like I was sleepwalking. I stayed that way, moved through the world without really being in it, until I met Luda. They helped me find my true voice and it was like nothing I'd imagined. They told me to forget what I'd been told, that I could flip the bird at society's expectations and be and do whatever the hell I wanted, whatever *we* wanted. And so we did. They made me feel alive.

This was getting me nowhere. Coming here had been just as dumb as going back home. Noah didn't know where Luda lived, but the police would figure it out.

I had to think, move smart, check our usual hangs.

In case they came back, I dropped my hat at their door. So they'd know, and find me.

Outside, in the late morning calm that always preceded what passed for lunch rush traffic in this cowboy town—a stream of pickups and motorcycles headed to Rosie's, known for its beef soup—I hunched my shoulders, shoved hands in pockets, and strode down the sidewalk. Just another high school dropout, folks. Nothing to see.

The pool hall, the Cheese Toast, Seeby Gees, Central Park. Luda might be any one of those places or none. I kept my chin down, eyes up, watched for the Nova, Noah and the cops. Too early for drinking, even for Luda, and they wouldn't hang in the park alone. The Cheese Toast was closer than the pool hall so I made a sharp right where 8th Ave met Midway, nearly tripped over a sidewalk barrier. Construction.

"Heyyy, Sis!"

I froze, then the ice fell away. "Jackson!" There was only one voice in the world like that. Singsong and sweet in beautiful defiance, tats and scars bedazzling his arms and torso, and a face that said, *don't mess with me.* He was a renaissance man, interesting and charming, instantly likeable to most, once they got past his surface. His voice thrummed a vibration as deep as the universe.

My brother leaned on his shovel, lifted his right hand for a high five, which morphed into a hug as he dropped the shovel and wrapped his arms around me. The giant-sized bulk of him was warmth and love and everything I hadn't even known I'd missed.

"Good to see you, Jackson." And it was. There was no one in the world like him. For all his vices and woes and lack of contact, he loved his family. You could see it in every part of him.

"It's been a while." He called over his shoulder to a man in a white hard hat who'd shouted his name like he'd just shit on the carpet. "Give me a minute, man, I'm talking with my sister."

"I heard you got parole, that you're in a halfway house."

"Sweet freedom!" His eyes crinkled and he cackled with unrestrained joy. "Don't worry about me. I'm a workin' man now, earning some cash, breathing in all this wholesome air." Which made him laugh even more, as the fresh tar his crew was putting down was acrid.

"How's the family?" he asked, then frowned. "Why were you at court that day?"

He had no idea what happened.

Jackson looked over his shoulder again, saw his supervisor glowering at him. He flipped him the bird, then grinned and held up a palm. "I'm just kidding with you!" He turned back to me and whispered. "Guy was born with a spade up his ass."

"I can't really talk now, Jackson."

"Give me an hour to finish up here, and we'll grab something to eat, okay, Genie-cake?" His childhood nickname for me brought a lump to my throat.

"I gotta go, Jackson. I'm leaving town."

Eyebrows up, then a smile. "Good for you! Better things on the horizon. Bus?"

"No"

Eyebrows higher and a head wobble, implying I was suddenly hoity-toity. "Flying?"

"No."

"Then what's the rush?"

I didn't answer. And then I didn't have to. His eyes narrowed and he nodded once with a flash of knowing. My nervous looks up and down the street probably gave me away. He lowered his voice. "All the more reason to meet, Genie. I can help you."

My eyes watered, and I sniffed. "Where?"

"Seeby Gees."

Seeby Gees was one of me and Luda's favourite underground drinking pits, always good tunes on the stereo and a steady supply of cold beer. Most folks had no idea what went on in some people's basements and garages. For a fee, you were in,

24-7 and no questions asked. It was also safe. If the police knew about Seeby Gees, they woulda shut it down already. "Okay."

"Go, Genie. And don't worry, I never saw ya." He squeezed my shoulder, turned back toward the street with arms spread wide like a preacher. "The lilacs are out, people! Can you smell them?"

"Get back to work, asshole," his supervisor growled.

Don't think, just go, I told myself. But not thinking was impossible. A minute ago I was in the mountains working with Red, now I was back on the streets I'd lived my whole rotten life, remembering the things I'd got up to and the people I'd got up to things with. Just in time to say goodbye.

Seeby Gees wasn't far, and I didn't see a single cop car on the way. Behind a green and white war-era bungalow that had seen better days, there was an aged and paint-chipped single garage. Or so it appeared. What was that saying about looking beyond the surface? Between the house and garage there were steps tucked between two overgrown hedges leading down to a bunker. A previous owner had thought it prudent to build it during the Cold War when everyone lived in fear of falling nukes. As far as I could tell nukes were still a danger, but no one built bunkers. Guess we just got used to it.

I rapped my knuckles on the door, waited, then rapped again. Door opened a crack. "Eugenia?" The door opened wider to reveal a slight man, his face an interstate of ropey creases as faded as the property and long hair the colour of oat grass in autumn. He peered at me through chunky eyeglasses that made his eyeballs look googly.

"Hey, Paul."

"Why didn't you text?"

"Lost my phone." Again, not a lie. He swung the door wide and I followed him into a network of hallways and rooms. The bunker was much larger than the garage above, taking the whole space of the backyard and butting up to the basement of Paul's house. Somewhere there was a connecting door, but no one had ever been able to find it.

I grabbed a beer, told him Jackson would pay, and settled myself into an empty room, not that there were many customers this time of day. In one space Old Donald was snoring softly on a couch, probably hadn't left from the night before. There was a neatly stacked deck of cards and a crib board on a coffee table next to him. Paul had likely tidied up after Old Donald's friends left. He kept a cleaner place than many of the legal establishments around town. Even had a toilet, and if you paid extra you could use the shower room, which he otherwise kept locked.

At twenty minutes past two, Jackson arrived. I didn't call him out on being late. For Jackson there was right now time, and time somewhere "out there" which could be 15 minutes away or five hours. If you tried to get on him about it, you only tied yourself in knots.

"Hey, Genie," he said softly. His inner Tigger had lost its bounce. "What's going on?"

"I'm in trouble."

"I know. I called Darcy."

"He narc on me to the cops?"

"Why would he?"

"Did you ask him?"

"Family don't do that to each other."

"Maybe not some families. You haven't been around, Jackson. Things change."

He took a long draw on his beer, nodded toward my full glass. "How many you had?"

"None. Ordered it outta habit, but I gotta keep my head clear." I wanted it. Holy crap, did I ever. Condensation clung to

Jackson's glass and made slow drips downward. My tongue felt dry, and I craved the beer's cool, bitter bite. I reached for my glass. Held it. It was warm now, no teasing drips. I put it down.

"Darcy said you've been in a program."

"That all he said?"

"Said you got in trouble beating on some girl, and they sent you to a ranch instead of locking you up. Good deal."

"Noah Danby's place." No reaction. Like ice, my brother. Used to make a few bucks playing cards at Seeby Gees. Maybe he still does.

"That's real interesting." He took another long draw on his beer.

"He told me you worked there."

"I did." If he wondered how much I knew, he kept that close.

"It's different now. He changed it into a supervised program for reprobates." I didn't mention that Jackson was the one that gave Noah the idea.

He drained the rest of his beer, reached for mine, winked. "Since you're not gonna drink it." He didn't seem to care that it was warm. "So what kind of things he got you doing?"

"Typical ranch chores. Same stuff you did." I leaned forward. "I ditched, Jackson. I gotta get outta town."

His face lit up like he wasn't even listening. "Hey, you remember the old days, Genie? When you, me and Darc used to work at old Mr. Wuzik's?"

"You and Darc worked. I hung out."

"Me and my brother," Jackson mused. "Good times."

"Jackson, I didn't come here to shoot the shit—"

"How're Jen and the boys?"

I sighed. "Good."

"I should stop by, lend a hand."

"Jackson, you said you could help me," I growled.

"Relax, Genie. You're safe here. Paul's got cameras. If he sees a cop coming, and you know that won't happen, he'll get us out."

"I don't know how you can be so calm."

"Been through it a time or two."

"Should you even be drinking?"

"Mind your business." He was getting testy. So was I.

"You're breaking parole by drinking."

Jackson's eyes darkened. "Pot. Kettle. Black."

"You're the one drinking my beer."

He drank down the rest, then set the empty glass upside down, like some sort of statement. His eyes turned gentle again. "It's tough for an old dog to change his ways, sis. If I was out of line, I apologize. I didn't mean nothing by it."

It was a cool cloth. I needed my brother, and for more than just help out of town. "I'm sorry too. I guess we all have our own ways of dealing."

Jackson tipped an ear like he didn't quite hear.

"There's a lot of talking in the Program, makes me think about stuff I don't want to, but I guess it's good. You and me the way we are, it started when Pops died. And maybe it's why Darcy drives truck so much."

Jackson folded his arms on the table, pulled them in tight. "We never really talked about that night."

The veins in Jackson's neck and forehead popped, and there was something else. Tears. "You were just eight years old," he whispered, his face contorting.

I remembered. I didn't want to, but I did: running to my room to get my hunting gear, then a loud bang, and the smell of burnt gunpowder. Seeing my tough, rebellious, often criminal brother come apart was almost worse. I touched his arm. "Hey, Jackson. No." This wasn't right. *My* strong brother.

"Maybe if I'd stuck around, been there for you, things mighta' turned out different. Maybe for both of us."

Pain flooded through me. "Jennifer said that she and Darcy talked it all through."

"You weren't talking at all."

"I couldn't."

"Doc said there was nothing stopping you."

"I was stopping me." My throat felt squeezed and I could barely get the words out.

"I shoulda been there for you, Genie. If I'd been there before, maybe none of this—"

"No Jackson."

"No, I mean it. I can't shake that it was my fault. Pops was sick, I knew that, and he musta got tired. If I'd been there—"

"Jackson, you gotta stop."

"No, Genie." His eyes were wet, his breaking voice cracked my heart. "I am such a screwup. You think I don't know that? But if I'd been there—"

"Jackson!" My heart ached. "Jackson, please stop. There's something I need to tell you."

The thing I'd never said, never thought I would. But I had to, if only to ease a guilt Jackson was not responsible for.

"What's wrong, Genie-cake? You're all white."

"I'm sorry," I whispered. "I'm so sorry."

He wiped his face. "For what? What are you talking about?"

Bile rose in my throat. I swallowed it. "I didn't say anything back then, I couldn't, I just couldn't, it was too awful, Jackson." I forced the words to keep coming. The room, all of Seeby Gees disappeared until all I could see was Jackson's face. "I brought him his gun." The thing I'd never told.

He was like marble, turned to stone. Then his mouth opened, but no words came out. His eyes lost focus.

"It was me, brother," I wept. "It was my fault. I good as killed him."

As he came back to me, he looked haunted, his eyes all aching and pain. I wanted to reach for him, but everything about him screamed *Don't touch me!* A vein in his neck pulsed.

I saw it clear. He hated me.

Kapow.

Talking was not good thing. The Program was a lie, a dream I'd had for a while, but this was reality. My miserable life.

"I'll leave," I choked.

He didn't stop me.

My legs moved, but slow, like pushing through quicksand, then *snap!* I went fast, too fast, and stumbled on my way to the door. A last look back showed Jackson sitting with his chin dropped to his chest, Paul behind him, watching me go.

CHAPTER TWENTY-NINE

My brothers. Life was hard and we weren't close, but we were family, and I always believed that was a cord that would hold. How arrogant could I be? How stupid? All cords could be cut if the knife was sharp.

Darcy's rejection, Jackson's hate, this was on me. My fault. I deserved all of it, long overdue. I did this.

A fog came over me so thick it snuffed breath. I leaned against a stop sign, sank to my knees under its weight as that terrible night of my eighth birthday took over, memories like claws.

I'm standing in the hallway. I can't see them, but Ma and Pops are in the kitchen, talking, and not about my birthday. It's the kind of talk that puts flutters in my tummy. Ma sounds sad, and I can't decide if should go to her, or stay put. I stay. The flutters are a magic that won't let me move.

"I'm sorry I'm like this, Theresa. It's not about you."

Ma sighs, but it's an impatient sigh, like when I'm taking too long to get ready for school.

I hear a chair scrape.

"Of course it's about me, Carl. And the kids. You're supposed to be a husband and a father." The chair scrapes again, and bangs against the wall. Ma must have moved, because when she speaks again, her voice comes from a different place. "But you're not. You're not any kind of a man. Not anymore."

"You can't mean that."

"I do. The kids and I can't live like this, Carl. What kind of an example are you setting for them?" Ma's voice catches in her throat,

and I think she might cry. "You're hurting them, Carl. You're hurting all of us, and it has to stop."

"Theresa—" Pops's voice sounds funny, like he might start crying too.

"I'm going to Barb's."

I wonder if Ma means to take me with her, but then the outside door opens and closes, and I don't hear her anymore. Instead I hear the kitchen chair scrape, and Pops sort of moans, same as he does when he gets up from his armchair after he falls asleep for a while.

He begins to weep.

The weeping turns to sobs, and flutters in my belly turn to bee buzzes that fly up into my head. I never heard Pops cry. It makes me want to run.

And so I do. Back to my room where I duck down beside my bed, flatten myself and slide underneath. I'm being like a cat, like the Johnson's cat from next door. Whenever Snick gets scared, he ducks under his front porch.

I'm not scared. Not exactly. I just want to be someplace else. Maybe Pops will feel better if we go hunting.

"Eugenia?"

I looked up. "Luda."

"Holy shit. Genie!" Then a clap on my back and they don't see my pain. They laugh. "What are you doing here?" They picked me up from where I'd let myself fall. "Why didn't you tell me you were out?" They were joy personified.

Breathe in, breathe out. *Get yourself straight.*

"No I …" Blink. Blink again. Shake off memories. I wasn't eight. I wasn't hiding. I was sixteen and in trouble. The sound of my foot scraping against sidewalk helped it all fall away. After I slapped the numbness from my arms I hugged Luda like they hadn't just done so.

"Are you okay?" another voice asked.

It was bougie-girl from the pool hall. Justine. She tilted her head.

The hell?

I turned back to my best friend. "Luda, what are you doing?" *Hanging with this dough-head* was the part I didn't say. But they knew. I looked the question at them, but they didn't notice or chose not to.

"Holy shit I'm glad to see you, Genie! I thought you were gone until winter."

I gripped Luda's arm, spoke into their ear so Justine couldn't hear. "I'm in trouble, Luda."

Their eyes widened.

"I took off."

Their eyes widened more. "No shit?"

"I need your help. They catch me, I'm going to jail, and for a lot longer than a few months. We need to leave. Just like we always talked about."

"Hang on," they said.

"Come on, Luda! I got no time. Just ... grab your stuff and we'll figure it out."

"Wait!"

"Why?"

They stepped back and clasped Justine's hand.

I looked from Luda to Justine, and back to Luda. "So that's how it is?"

Luda shrugged.

I leaned against the stop sign. "I don't get it."

"We're together now," Justine said, and stroked Luda's cheek with her finger. It was like that first time at the pool hall, but tender. They looked into each other's eyes with trust and care and I thought I might puke.

"I went and saw Justine after you got sent away," Luda said. "Thought I'd make amends for you. Thought it might make things easier for you if I could talk Jussie into letting it go."

"Jussie."

Luda grinned, almost shy. "We ended up talking about a whole lot, so much I didn't even get around to talking about you."

Justine's eyes shone. "And so they came back the next day."

"And the next."

"And I forgive you by the way. If it hadn't been for you, there would be no"—she and Luda shared a look—"us."

"Us," I repeated. They swung back to me, faces like moons. Shiny, happy moons. "What about me, Luda? What about us-us?"

"It was never like that with you and me."

"It was better." How many gut-punches could a person take before they broke? "I'm real happy for you guys"—No I wasn't—"but Luda, you're my best friend, and I need you." I got stern. "Right. Now."

Luda frowned. "To be honest, I'm surprised you didn't lead with something else."

This reunion was losing its charm. "Like what?"

"An apology? To Jussie?"

"Serious?"

Their eyes darkened.

"How could this, the two of you, mean more than our friendship?"

They said nothing.

"You're not coming with me." It wasn't a question.

"I'm different now, Genie. Better."

I took that in. Let it settle. "That's good." I wanted to mean it, but what gave them the right to sail off to some better place? If they hadn't had it in for *Jussie* in the first place, none of this would have happened.

"Not even drinking so much."

My laugh was bitter. "Yeah, me neither."

"Be happy for me?"

"I am." My voice was flat.

They were out of words. So was I.

My gut turned sour, but there was truth in this, much as I hated it. It was like this glowing thing in a steaming pile of shit. I saw it, even though I didn't want to. *Damn Group.*

To Justine I mumbled, "For what it's worth, I am sorry."

"You don't mean it," Luda said.

I looked Justine full in her awful, hateful, but kind of sweet face, and understood. I closed my eyes, dug deeper, found the ball of hurt inside of me I'd clenched so tight, imagined yanking it from where it rooted, let it go. Fluff on the wind. When I looked at her again, I was sincere. "I do mean it. I wish I could take back what I did. I'm glad you're okay." I lifted my hand to Luda's cheek and felt an echo of all our years. "You had my back."

Their eyes shone love and grief. "And you had mine."

We stood there, awkward, then they dug in their pocket, handed me some bills.

"No."

"Take it. It's not much, but it'll help." When I didn't move, they stuffed it in my pocket.

I walked away.

CHAPTER THIRTY

I leaned back against the dumpster behind the Inky Mart. Laughed. What was it that Heather had said? I was always exactly where I was meant to be. I pulled a longneck from the case beside me.

Luda's voice rang out in my head: *That's what I'm talking about.* I clinked bottles with their ghost.

They'd known Justine five minutes and just like that, love. My best friend forever, not so forever. Five damn minutes and I'd been replaced. How? That's what I wanted to know. Crazy.

Who's crazy?

"Shut up, Luda."

I needed to kill that something inside that was hard and hurting, or fuzz it up a little. I needed to not care. Not feel. I tipped the bottle, drank down half in one swallow, then another swallow and another.

That's what I'm talking about.

After the first bottle, a second. I'd finished four before I had to pee. Giggled out loud, remembered the story Darcy told about the bucket.

Then I was sad again.

But still sober enough to use the can in Jumbo Joe's Hot-Dogs next to the Inky Mart.

Back outside I leaned into painted concrete, willed the wall to straighten my frame enough so I could move on. The sun-heat against my cheek soothed almost as much as the beer, so I stayed that way until a woman walked by, handed me five bucks, which made me laugh, which made it hard to stay upright. It was like the building moved and moved again every time I tried to find it.

"What're you lookin' at?" I snapped at another woman who screwed up her face like I smelled bad. Then I saw her kid, a little girl all in pink clasping her mother's hand. "Sorry," I mumbled, and glued my shoulder back against the wall.

Then I lost the wall and hit the ground, which I knew had to be funny so I laughed. Arms helped me up, but I pushed them away, staggered around the back of Jumbo Joes and then I was in the street and in the park and the ground passed beneath me fast like I was moon-jumping and then it was dark and I was at the tracks.

"Luda?" they didn't answer. I cupped my hands around my mouth. "Luda!"

We used to come here to drink and shoot the shit, watch freight trains back up, connect, pull, whatever. I liked the noise and the colours, always wondered who tagged those cars, and from what cities. I thought about the old days when people would hop on and head out anywhere to another life. Good times. We'd drink and watch the trains and drink some more then look for trouble, any kind of trouble, and then we'd drink again. We'd put crap on the tracks to flatten, nickels and shit, and we'd talk about stuff, like their mom beating on them and how they boomeranged in and out of foster care, but we'd also talk about planets and TV shows and a woman who always walked by at the same time every day who wore so much makeup it looked like you could peel it away.

Now I was alone.

But I had beer. Felt the weight at the end of my arm, saw my hand hooked into the small case and wondered how it got there. Must've finished the last one or lost it and got more. Vague memory of a long-haired dude pulling for me after I got kicked out of the liquor store.

The tongue was hanging out of my blue jeans pocket. Must've given him the rest of Luda's dough.

I sat and fell then sat again. "Hello, my only friends," I slurred. I cracked open a bottle. Drank it all.

Everything and nothing changes. Time doesn't march it has no feet all there is is now and now and now and now and it doesn't matter nothing does.

No more Jackson. No more Darcy. No Luda no Frankie and no-no-Noah. No one. Just me.

I tipped and swallowed.

"Jackson, my brother, how I loved you. You hate me now and didn't want me around when I was little. You thought roughing me up was toughing me up and it was funny. I knew you loved me, at least back then. You had your own set of rules, but if you ever heard even a whisper of someone being cruel to me, you were all over that, even if I never asked you."

Swig.

"Darcy my brother, you were the one that stuck. Took me in hook line and *stinker* even though you were hardly more'n a kid yourself. You were as good as you wanted to be and you wanted a lot. You took me in, and that got in the way. Expectation killed you, my brother, and so it killed us. P.s. I loved you too."

Swig.

"Luda, my sibling from anotha mutha. You got it and you got me. My past was shit and so was yours but we didn't get all boo-hoo. We took life as it came and when it didn't come fast enough we found our own rockets. I don't get how all that changed. In the end you were someone I never knew."

Swig

"Ma, how could you walk out on me? Was I that unlovable?"

Swig, swig.

"Pops. What can I say? Nothing. Wish I could."

It was dark, so very dark, but trains still came and left like people and days and good things back and forth in and out come and go like life.

Skreek, clack, bam. Skreek, clack, bam. Skreek, clack, bam. Chugga chug.

I threw the empty bottle on the track. *Smash, tinkle. Gone.*

This world was full of empty spaces where grief steps in, haunts shadows, hides from light and lessons learned, regret in darkness grows in sorrow. I am salt with tears unshed, a pillar to shatter in wind.

Why can't I see the wind?

Because it was behind me.

An idea, so small, seeded and grew from shoot to vine then all the way through and into my mind like great neon tags spray-painted on the night. Jimmy thought we were doomed to live the same lives as our parents. What about their deaths?

I was a dirt smudge on humanity lower than algae scum in a slough. If I disappeared, no one would notice. No one would care. I was born here, and here I would die.

Snap.

Something broke.

The stars loosed their hold and fell into me and I was face pressed in dirt. My breathing slowed, too tired for even that.

Chugga chug.

Far away and deep in my core: *chugga chug, chug, chug.* My ear to the ground I heard it. There were many tracks before me but only one that lead to the yard and I needed it I needed this train and so I breathed and found my feet and put them under me and jolted toward the line and kept going until I saw it. The light.

I stepped onto the track.

Don't think.
Don't think.
Think.
There was someone on the tracks.
Pops?

Good to see you, Genie.

It's been a while, Pops.

I love you, baby

Then why did you leave?

I was sad.

I loved you.

You don't know how it was for me, baby. You don't know how I couldn't get away. I know you've talked to people and learned in school that depression is an illness and what I did was not my fault and it wasn't about you. I know you know that.

That doesn't make it okay.

You're angry.

Yes, I'm angry! I am so fucking pissed that you gave up and I don't care that it wasn't your fault because when you left you killed me too.

Baby—

You killed our family and yes, I'm angry that I'm not supposed to be and I know it wasn't your fault but I'm still angry and I hate you and I love you and I hate you and I hate me and you taught me that girls could do whatever boys could and I'm just like dear old Dad and the train and the light and the light and—

"*NO!*"

I stepped back and fell away. The train passed and I wept.

I whispered, "I love you, Pops."

I always would.

And I loved my brothers. In that one moment of choosing I saw everything like I was zooming out and looking from the stars. I understood. I could see what my leaving would do. It would hurt them and harden them and weaken them all at the same time; it would rip them to shreds, like paper in a storm. They'd already been beaten enough. I loved them, no matter what. I would not shatter them.

Nausea overtook me and I puked until there was nothing left except my soul.

A scuff in the dirt meant someone was near, but with eyes closed and lashes sticky with tear-salt, I was too empty to even look.

"I screwed up, Genie."

I rubbed my eyes. "Jackson?" I was still in the dirt, still on my knees, beside the track. His darkened face blotted out the stars.

"Back there, at Seeby-Gees? I was wrong. I didn't mean to make you think that." His voice choked. "I thought I could forget." He sat beside me and I wanted to cry. I never used to be a baby, not even when I was little. I'd suck it up buttercup, show I was just as strong and tough as anyone, but especially my brothers.

I rocked back next to him, put my hand on his back, rubbed his rigid shoulders.

"I don't understand."

"I didn't mean to make you think what you thought. It wasn't your fault he died," Jackson cried. "It was mine."

He heaved himself into my arms and sobbed while I held

him tight, willing what was left of the beer to leave me so I could understand. I needed to understand.

"I was such a screwup," he sobbed. "Always causing them grief. I stole from them, Genie." His eyes were red, and from more than just tears. The sour smell of bourbon was strong on his breath. "I used to play cards back then, and mostly did pretty good, but I got into trouble and Pops wouldn't give me the money so I stole it. From them. They needed that money. They were gonna lose the house, and I didn't care. That was why he did it."

At first I was too stunned to respond. But I saw the pain in his eyes, the hope and the shame, and realized I was doing the same thing he'd done to me. He needed me to speak. "No." I gripped his shoulders and looked him straight in the eyes. "It wasn't your fault. He didn't do what he did because of you, any more than me. He was sick, Jackson." I started crying again too. "It was all him, and we'll never know why." I gulped a big breath and hugged him again. "There is no why." We rocked together as the tears went away, and the stars shone brighter in the deepening night sky. "But it wasn't because of us," I whispered.

When I stopped talking at age eight they called it selective mutism, thought it was the shock, but it wasn't. It was guilt and fear. Maybe I needed all these years in between to understand, really and truly all the way inside of me, that it *wasn't my fault*. Nor was it Jackson's.

Yes, I brought him his gun and Jackson stole his money. Those things would never go away. But he was the one who left, and he wasn't thinking about paying his bills or who gave him the gun. He wasn't thinking at all because if he was, he would've known he was sending us to hell. He wouldn't have wanted that. He loved us. I know he did.

My father's voice in my head: *Let it go now, Genie. I'm sorry. I love you.*

That's what he would say if he were here. Maybe he'd also say we gotta fix what he broke, find the shards of what might have been, put them back together like Ma's chipped china cup.

Jackson sat straight, wiped his face roughly with both hands. "I blamed myself, Genie. That was why I stayed away. I was running. But you can't never run hard enough to get away from something like that."

"I'm sorry you thought what you did. I'm sorry we didn't talk."

"Talking don't change anything."

"Maybe not the past. But it can help us live with it, see it different. Keep us from making more mistakes."

He nodded over and over like he couldn't stop, like a bobblehead doll, lips curved down like a freakish upside-down smile. Then he stiffened, flexed his hands flat in front of him. "You gotta help me, Genie."

Alarm shot through me. "What is it? What's wrong?"

"I'm gonna kill someone. I know I am." He looked at me, eyes desperate. "I been close before. I start beating on someone, and I can't stop. Most of the time I'm too stupid and too drunk, but I got this moment, this one clear second. Take me back to jail." His voice cracked. "I don't think I can do it on my own. I need you, Genie-cake."

I understood something else then, about what Boyer the Lawyer and Noah and Hayden and probably Heather too said about doing good when you get the chance. I mean, it was a no-brainer—he was my brother—but I had a glow in me that my brother needed me. For so long it had been the other way. I ached for him that he was hurting so, but I was here for him. I would help.

"What happened?"

"After you left, I went kinda went crazy. Went to The Hornet where I used to go, drank some more, played some pool. Got into it with a guy out back. Started beating on him."

He showed me his reddened knuckles. Not so different from my own when I'd used them on Justine.

"I stopped, but I didn't want to. Thought of you." Jackson's eyes burned like he was sick, like there was a fever eating him inside out. "It was the craziest thing. It was like you were right there in front of me. I felt like if I hit him one more time, I would really be hitting you." He cupped my hands in his. "I would never hurt you."

"I know it."

"But if I don't change things up, I will end up killing someone." He swallowed and croaked, "I'm scared, Genie."

"What can I do?"

"Take me to jail. I'll turn myself in for breaking my parole, for drinking and beating on that guy. It's what's right." He blinked heavy lids. "I don't know the last time I did right. Plus there are programs inside. I can't do this on my own. I'll change my mind at the last minute, I know I will. Help me do this, Genie."

Jackson cried the whole way, leaning on me to help him walk. As we drew near a bar across from the cop shop called the Tipsy Cow, I saw a truck parked on the street out front. When we got closer, I saw it was Darcy. He wasn't alone. Noah was there too.

Darcy sprinted to meet us and the three of us hung together in a hug. "He wants to go to jail," I said.

"That right?" Darcy asked. By this time Noah had caught up.

Jackson nodded.

"You okay?" Noah asked me, his voice anxious, not angry.

"Taking Jackson to the cop shop," I said. There was more to say, so much, but not now. I glanced across the street. "They looking for me?"

"No," Noah said. "I was. Darcy too."

"I need to help my brother," I said.

"I'll come too," Darcy said.

"I'll wait," Noah said.

We three Grimms walked together arms and elbows locked, Jackson in the middle. Outside the cop shop, Jackson turned to me and solemnly, drunkenly, shook my hand. "You do better. You hear me?"

"I guess."

"I mean it, Genie-cake." He wrapped me in a hug, then Darcy, then walked the rest of the way on his own, pounded on the front door of the cop shop, demanding to be let in.

The door opened, then closed and I smiled, as it likely hadn't been locked. Always the showman.

"He did the right thing," Darcy said.

Jackson's tears were still wet on my cheek. "Yes he did."

"We better get going," Darcy said.

I turned to him. "Thanks, Darcy. I don't think I ever said that, but I mean it."

"For what?"

"For being my brother. For being a pain in the ass when you needed to be. For not leaving, even though you probably wanted to."

"I didn't. But I did make mistakes, Genie."

"We all do. Some are just messier than others." The air was suddenly crisp, with a shine that had nothing to do with the streetlamp overhead. My head was clear too, more than it had been in a long time. "Better get Noah. I'm gonna need you both inside."

It was my turn to walk to the front door.

I didn't look back. Didn't need to. I knew Darcy was there, watching out for me, like he always had been. So was Noah. So were a lot of other people who cared about me. It was time I cared for me too.

CHAPTER THIRTY-ONE

Before ink of night gave way to first glow and endless stars began to fade, a bird called, like it knew the earth was about to tilt, like it held time under its wing, like it had waited for this all night. And then that bird was joined by another and then a few more. I suppose I'd been waiting too, for answers, illumination and ideas, while cocooned in a wool blanket, breathing, listening, thinking. I'd not slept. I'd been asleep too long. This night, our solo camping, had been for wide awake dreaming of owls and pussycats and cabbages and kings.

I only remembered the end part of that nonsense poem from my youth.

> *And hand in hand, on the edge of the sand,*
> *They danced by the light of the moon,*
> *The moon,*
> *The moon,*
> *They danced by the light of the moon.*

After Tammy dropped me on the beach the night before, those lines came to me like an ice cream headache and stayed in my head until I'd danced too, on the stony beach as light gave way to the gloaming, careful swaying, as it would be another few weeks before my ribs fully healed. I waved my hands in the air, bowed and swooped, soundless, the music inside of me.

Also, we were only spaced about five football fields apart from each other, and sound carried.

There was an occasional soft note, a vibration in the air, maybe Jimmy playing his guitar, but no one had called out, which made me believe we'd each embraced the experience for what it was meant to be, what *we* were expected to be: alone with ourselves. And our ghosts.

I thought about how Jackson said he saw me, like I was there, right when he'd reached a point of no turning back. I thought about how I'd seen Pops at the very same point, maybe that same moment, and I wondered if there was something bigger at play.

Life was a gift, one with joy but also pain. All part of the package, might as well get used to it. But maybe the pain helped us understand other people better, especially when they were hurting. Our pain, our dark times, helped us to reach out, ease someone else. And that felt good. Another gift. Same package.

There were rocks to skip along with dinner as I chose to fast and turn back time, slap, slap, the rocks sank, rippled reflections of northern lights. Softly, I whistled them down.

"Hello, Pops."

He shimmered big and bright and clear in the middle of the lake, with others behind him, a shoulder-to-shoulder wall, but indistinct, like looking through oiled paper, and I knew they were our ancestors, our kin, those who came before. I knew them even though I never met them, and they knew me, connected through time and this man who filled my heart with warmth. The pain that had lingered so long would always be there, but so would the love.

"Pops, I'm sorry I yelled, back at the tracks. I'm not angry anymore." Or not as much. I knew he hadn't meant to hurt me, nor Darcy nor Jackson.

Nor Ma.

"Don't make me think about her, Pops."

He shimmered, said nothing.

"I don't want to."

He shimmered, silent.

"I get it," I whispered. "Maybe she left because she lost herself too. Maybe she thinks it's her fault you did what you did. Darcy said I should ask her. He knows where she is, how to reach her. Can you believe it? Even talked to her. I'm not ready to do the same."

He listened until I said all that was in me, then faded into those others, up and away into the shimmering light where he and they would always be.

That night back in Fort St. Luke, before Jackson got sent back to jail, we three Grimms, me, Jackson and Darcy, talked, just like Jennifer always wanted. We said stuff that we'd kept shut up in our heads and hearts for so long it was hard to get out. But it got easier. Darcy even talked about Luda and our argument last winter, said he'd come to understand that gender wasn't the same as gender identity and how neither was the same as gender expression. On gender expression he admitted he was still confused, but he was trying. We shared fears and laughter and everything in between. There were lots of tears. We held hands and gave a squeeze when one of us needed it. We were gonna be okay.

I'd got lucky—again. I told Judge Marg Gordon everything. Would've been easy to lie, say I was shook by the crash and got lost for a bit, but that didn't sit right with me. Not the me I am now, the me I want to be.

Didn't matter. She said she expected I was shook up from the crash and got lost for a bit. Noah agreed to take me back into the Program. He didn't mention the vodka. Turned out there was another truth there, one Frankie and Nathan found after we flew away.

Melvin had been doing little things to sabotage the Program

ever since Noah got it started. Turned out he'd been drawing a little off the top for his own bank account before Noah tied himself in with the Corrections system. Melvin cut out his thievery at first, not wanting to get caught if an official took a close look at his books, but then he started missing that something extra lining his pockets. He thought if he could make the Program more trouble than it was worth, Noah would turn things back to the way they used to be.

He only told because he was a chickenshit and Tammy threatened him. She only threatened him because Frankie and Nathan made her believe what in her heart she already knew to be true. That's what she said when I got back—the Frankie and Nathan convincing her part, anyway. Then she said something about *golfurnaking hugger-muggers* and stomped off to the pens. She wouldn't want me to think she was gonna go any easier on me. I didn't, and she wasn't, but it was like Noah said. She was fair, and she cared. I knew that now.

"You look like twelve miles of bad highway," Tammy said as she paddled up.

I grinned. "Stayed up all night."

On rejoining the others back at the main camp, I saw we were all bleary. And something else. I don't think I was the only one conversing with ghosts.

After a hot breakfast, Jimmy picked up his guitar, strummed, and spoke over a soft melody. "*A fool sees not the same tree that a wise man sees. He whose face gives no light, shall never become a star.*"

"Whoa, brother, where did that come from?" asked Rick, punching him in his arm.

"Not very cowboy," Frankie said. "But I like it."

"Me too," I said. Jimmy's eyes fell on me like I'd said something smart, and I felt my cheeks flush. Frankie winked at me and I reminded myself that anything I might be thinking in that moment would be *against the rules.* Even if it wasn't one written down.

"It's from a poem by William Blake," Jimmy said. He pulled out a folded paper from his back pocket. "It's hard to understand if you read it all at once, but I like to pull out a line or two sometimes. Think on them. Music helps me with that."

"So what's it mean?" Frankie asked.

Jimmy shrugged. "Damned if I know." We all laughed. "I think it's different for everyone. Maybe even depends on when you read it."

"I'm not much into poetry," Rick said, handing it back.

"That's what songs are, brother. When I played these words last night, I let them get into me. I thought about how I don't need to see things the way I used to. I need to give myself permission to let go of what happened with Ma."

"You haven't called her that in a long time," Rick said softly. He looked like a weight lifted off of him. I could see it, like a shadow coming out and losing itself in the light.

"I know. That poem also means that if I stay stuck in the hell of my past my future isn't never gonna get bright. Like a star, sort of thing."

"I thought about stars last night," Nathan said. "I mean, did you see them suckers?"

Then Jimmy punched Rick in the shoulder and it was time to pack.

As we gathered up camp dishes to wash and go, I said to Noah, "Sorry about Melvin." Noah nodded his thanks. "Guess you're gonna need a new bookkeeper."

He raised an eyebrow. "You angling for a job after you're done here?"

I laughed. "No, I gotta go to school. Sounds strange even to me, but I'm looking forward to it." It would be weird, because

I'd be with kids who had always been a year behind me—not to mention they'd know I'd been in trouble. But so what? My tree looked different now, to paraphrase Jimmy's poem-song. I wouldn't worry too much about being a star, but it was time to step out of the dark.

That wasn't quite how the poem went. Maybe I would ask Jimmy about it. Maybe he would sing the words so I would better understand. I flushed again.

Against the rules.

But I did know someone for Melvin's job. Noah had always had an interest in my family. Maybe Darcy could finally put his business certificate to use.

I clamped my mouth shut before I got stupid. Darcy liked driving truck—he'd told me often enough. One way or another, we all found our own paths. Maybe there were lots of paths, each just right for different times in our lives.

As I washed and dried the cutlery, a horse wandered out of the bush and was met with gentle cheers. It was the last one lost, no more. I looked to the sky. The northern lights were hidden, but I knew Pops was there. He'd stay with me, different than before. Better. What had been damaged for so long had changed and begun to heal. It would take some time, but that was okay. That was why I was here, me and these other reprobates I was beginning to know as friends. We had each other's backs.

A movement caught my eye. It was my reflection in a spoon. I held it straight out, spun, looked at the me that was upside down and I knew: in this here, and this now, I was exactly the me I was meant to be.

Fin

EPILOGUE

I drummed my fingertips on the tabletop, made myself stop, opened the menu, closed it again, stared at the door.

Was I ready for this?

Before I'd finished my time at the ranch, Heather and I had talked a lot more about forgiveness. Rather, I talked, and she listened. I came to understand that forgiving someone was more about you. It was about freeing yourself.

But what about when you couldn't forgive no matter how hard you tried or wanted to?

That night at the rail yard, I imagined Pops saying: *Let it go.* Or maybe it was his ghost, or spirit, or whatever talking to me, telling me what I needed to hear all the way into my heart.

I'd felt abandoned by everyone I ever cared about, but the one person I'd been unable to forgive was my mother. She'd left me. She wasn't sick like Pops. She made a choice.

But then I thought, it was okay to be angry. Maybe the real reason I didn't want to forgive her, was unable to *let go*, was because then she would be all the way gone. Staying mad was a way to keep her close. But then it came to me, like a window opening and flooding me with bright understanding: the only part of her that I was keeping close was the worst of her. She was also so much good, other memories that I'd shut out.

When you forgive someone, you let go of the hurt.

Let go.

Live.

Dance by the light of the moon.

All my ancestors gathered close. I felt a gentle weight like a shadow hand on my shoulder, and knew it was Pops. He wanted me to know it was time. *Let it go.*

The jingle of the bell above the door.

It was her.

Her eyes were haunted, her face pinched with nerves. Her hair had strands of grey and she wore it swept up in a bun. That never used to be her style. Maybe it was her way of feeling more proper. More responsible. If it made her feel okay, then that was fine. Whatever she felt, it was right for her.

I smiled.

Slowly, tentatively, she smiled too.

We had a long way to go, she and I, and it wouldn't be easy, but every journey began with a first step.

A Note from the Author

As I age and grow, I am drawn to deeper and more difficult questions with a hope to be courageous enough to truly "bleed" on the page. In *You Don't Have to Die in the End*, I wanted to allow my character opportunity to show how even though she understands that depression is an illness and that her father is not to be blamed for his suicide, it is okay to feel angry. Our emotions are honest. We can't hate ourselves for what we feel. It is in acknowledging and addressing our truths that we can begin to process and move forward.

Acknowledgements

This novel took ten years to write. Correction: to *get right.* In 2009, inspired in part by a program in the US where convicts are sent to work with wild mustangs, I set out to write about a young offender accepted into an Intensive Support and Supervision program, which is an alternative to incarceration under Canada's Youth Criminal Justice Act offered under specific conditions. I used elements from existing programs to create my fictional one.

To flesh out this imagined program and world, I wrote to western horse trainer Glenn Stewart who, with his wife, Dixie Stewart, invited me join his natural horsemanship students for a week in the Rocky Mountains of northern British Columbia. My photos and memories of this time are many. Unfortunately, my journals were lost when a pipe burst earlier this year and our home underwent extensive repair and renovation. I checked Facebook archives to see if I'd shared details and discovered my 2009 updates were primarily concerned with the H1N1 scare, joining Twitter, two novel launches, and a party at the home of former *Winnipeg Free Press* Books editor, Morley Walker. There was only vague mention of my time in the mountains.

Irene and Lawrence Lemoine to the rescue! From their journals, my memories and a few scraps of transferred notes, these are the wonderful people I thank for this life-changing experience: Glenn Stewart, Dixie Stewart, their daughters, Carson and Keily; Irene and Lawrence Lemoine; Bob Boyer; Roland Sawatsky; Nicky and Ryon Hemingson; British Nicky; Dillon;

Cody; Vicky; Gwen; and Shyanne. They gave me the heart of the mountains, which I kept close these many years of writing. Thanks also to Barry Tompkins, owner/operator of North Nine Outfitters Camp for sharing your beautiful lodge home, the inspiration for Reason's Wait.

For technical and procedural elements of this story, I would have been lost without the input of several first readers who are exceptional in their professional fields: Heather Gobbett, Judge Margaret Gordon, Bradley West (Bradley, you still make my face happy!), and Kalyn Bomback, Esq. Thanks also to Keith Murdock; Marta Nelson; Elana Sokolov, Area Director of Winnipeg's Female Offender Unit; and Marg Synyshyn, Chief Executive Officer of the Manitoba Adolescent Treatment Centre.

Any inconsistencies or persisting errors relating to natural horsemanship, court procedure, Youth Criminal Justice, aeronautical mechanics, gender identity, gender expression and all other researched details are mine alone. Any blame rests on my oft befuddled brain.

Deepest gratitude to my now retired agent, Marie Campbell, who was with me through early drafts, bumps and roadblocks. I'd not have found my way through this story without her unflagging support and love. Kris Rothstein and Carolyn Swayze of the Carolyn Swayze Literary Agency, your belief in me during a low time gave me courage to finish the novel that was in my heart. Thank you!

To the team at Great Plains/Yellow Dog, you rock! It was a great pleasure to work once more with my insightful editor, Catharina de Bakker; impassioned publisher, Mel Marginet and ever creative publicist, Sam MacKinnon. Thanks also to Sam for their sensitivity reading, deeply appreciated.

Writers are forever trying to balance the drive to create, with the need to pay bills. Financial support through granting programs is not easily gained and is a boon beyond keeping the heat on when received. It means a project has been examined and debated and deemed worthy of pursuit, which can add booster rockets to seeing it through. My thanks to The Winnipeg Arts Council for a Creation Grant, and the Manitoba Arts Council, which made possible my research travel into the mountains.

My thanks to Eric Walters, Canada's most prolific and giving children's book author, for reading and offering comment. To readers who don't know about Hope Story, a charity created by Eric and his wife Anita to send kids to school in Africa, learn more at hopestory.ca.

I often borrow names as tribute. To those I didn't warn, surprise! These names comforted, inspired, and kept me company through the many months of conjuring characters entirely made up: Noah Danby, Canadian actor and son of renowned Canadian artist, Ken Danby; Darcy Fehr, Canadian actor, friend, and coach; gentle giant "Chris Kazu"; Irene Lemoine; Bob Boyer; Judge Marg Gordon; Canada's funniest poet, Ron James; The Stampe Collection; pilot Ole Knut Kvalvik; Copper, our beloved and dearly departed hound; Wendy Robinson, horse trainer; my sisters, Merry Franz and Heather Gobbett; my husband Jim Daher and his long time buddy, Rick Stewart.

Auntie Terry and cousins Gerry, Rob and Greg. I hope you will recognize your added inspiration and smile.

To my husband and daughters, you are everything. You kept me grounded and sane during the weeks, months, and years it took to write Eugenia's story. My loves, I am nothing without you.

One addendum. The "punch game" did exist once upon a time, much to the chagrin of the wives of the (then younger) men who played it.

p.s. Sorry for the swears.